# LANDSLIDE

KATHRYN NOLAN

That's What She Said Publishing, Inc.

Editing by Faith N. Erline
Cover by Kari March
Photo: ©Regina Wamba

ISBN: 978-1-945631-22-1 (ebook)
ISBN: 978-1-945631-23-8 (paperback)

*041921*

# PROLOGUE

## JOSIE

*Two years earlier*

My best friend was trying to get me drunk the night before my wedding. Technically, the night of my *bachelorette party*, although it was just the two of us.

And there was a shocking dearth of penis straws.

"How much do you want again?" Lucia asked, as she poured half the bottle of champagne into a plastic cup that said *Married AF*.

"Are we discussing the pros and cons of being horrifically hung over on the most beautiful day of my entire life?" I asked, knocking my cup against hers in grim celebration. But Lucia only shrugged, tossed her long blonde hair, and leaned back on the hood of her car.

I'd had three requests for this night: For it to be just the two of us. For it to be quiet. And to not get drunk.

So far, she was only fulfilling two of the three.

Lucia had parked her car off Mulholland Drive, a famous road with an equally famous view of the entire city of Los Angeles, rising smoggy and sultry beneath us. The sun was slowly dropping behind the countless skyscrapers and palm trees, painting the canyon in hues of orange and pink. The soft, continual roar of traffic was everywhere—L.A.'s version of birdsong.

"I won't let you get drunk," she said, nudging me with her foot. I was sitting next to her, spine straight. I could feel my muscles rigid with anxiety. "But I *will* suggest you have a little, you know..." she paused. "Fun. At your own bachelorette party."

"I'm having fun," I said defensively, glancing at my new pearl-colored nails. I'd been painting my fingernails black since I was thirteen years old, but Clarke had said it was unbecoming for a bride to have black nails on her wedding day. He'd said the same thing about my many piercings until I'd dutifully removed them.

I couldn't do anything about the tattoos decorating my body. Clarke had been disappointed about that.

But he was probably right. I wanted to look like a *bride* tomorrow.

Not a punk.

Another nudge from Lucia. I turned to look at her.

My best friend was a glowing goddess. She was white, with long blonde hair, dark blue eyes and a dazzling smile that turned mischievous when she was joking. *She* looked like a bride—at ease in her own skin. Comfortably relaxing on the hood of her car, sipping champagne.

Lucia had been my best friend for seven years. I was a makeup artist, and we'd first met when she was fifteen (and I was twenty-one) on her very first high-profile photo shoot. Lucia had been hesitant and trembling, half-naked in a chilly room filled with strangers, told to look "sexy" by a man with a camera. So I'd stepped in, came up with a silly idea to teach her Spanish on the spot.

It had worked. Gotten her out of her head as I lavished her lips with crimson, lined her blue eyes with smoky gray liner. Lucia had requested me at her next shoot. And the next and the next, and as we both grew increasingly more famous, our friendship became one of the most important things in my life.

People always asked if it was hard to be best friends with a famous supermodel. But it really wasn't. Sure, sometimes when she stopped by my apartment and I was wearing stained sweatpants and my old Clash tee-shirt—and she was *just coming from yoga*, dewy with sweat and looking like she'd just stepped off of a *Maxim* cover—yeah, sometimes it was hard.

Except I had found that true friendship could exist without jealousy. And that described my friendship with Lucia.

"Hey," she said. "How ya doin'? What do you need? Are you nervous? Excited?"

A longer pause.

"Do you need me to break you out of this situation and drive us across the border? Because I will. *Thelma and Louise-style* but without us dying in the end."

I laughed, taking a tiny sip of champagne. The bubbles made me sneeze.

"I feel fine. Happy," I said, running my fingers over the giant diamond ring Clarke had slipped on my finger barely three months ago. "I just want it to get here, you know?" I said, and Lucia nodded as she listened. "I want to be married to

Clarke. To leave the reception and float away on our magical honeymoon."

I trailed my fingers through the balmy summer air. Everyone was here in the city—my entire family from both Los Angeles *and* Mexico. All four of my older brothers plus their wives and partners and children.

It was happening. This time tomorrow night, Clarke and I would be married.

I glanced at Lucia again, smiling. "I'm really ready. *Lo prometo.*"

I watched as she suppressed a look I couldn't quite understand. But it was gone just as quickly, so I had probably imagined it.

"Good," she said, reaching forward to squeeze my hand. "And I'm really happy *for* you." Another squeeze. "Although, if I was being honest, I'm a little surprised you wanted such a *tame* bachelorette party."

"Really?"

Lucia laughed nervously. "Yeah, I guess. I thought it'd be like one of our usual nights in the city. Sushi at Katsuya. Cocktails at The Varnish. Burlesque and dancing at The Edison. Tip off the paparazzi early so we're in all the gossip rags. Go to bed at dawn." She poured a little more champagne into her glass, offering me more, but I shook my head. "That kind of night. But you'd be wearing a cute white sash that said *Last Night of Freedom* or something."

My chest hurt, just a little. I took a deep breath, and it eased.

"I know," I said. "And I know you would have planned a wild night filled with scandal that we would have talked about until we were ninety."

"We can *still go*, you know," she said, starting to slide off the hood. "I keep an emergency stash of high heels and see-through shirts in my trunk. I'll call my agent and get us on the list at—"

"No, no," I said laughing, pulling her back up. "You're nuts, *mija*. I just want to sit here with my best friend and drink a responsible amount of champagne. Talk about my wedding day. Look at the lights."

Lucia was smiling, but it looked strained. She was usually vivacious and funny and down for *anything*. But she looked... weighed down in some way.

"Clarke likes to stay in," she said simply.

I nodded. Shrugged.

"He's definitely a homebody. He didn't even have a bachelor party," I admitted, which I did think was odd at the time. But his friends had busy work schedules, and it just didn't pan out. *The only thing that matters is we'll be married. Together forever,* he'd said.

"And I like that. It's... different. I'm not twenty-two anymore, Lu." I clinked my glass against hers again. "You'll know what I'm talking about soon. When you get older."

"But I'm never getting older so..." she said dryly, tapping her finger against her lips.

I rolled my eyes. Super models were on a tight time limit, age-wise. Something she obsessed about every day. I watched her face go from joking to serious again.

"I never want you to lose yourself," she said softly. "With Clarke. I never want... Marriage doesn't mean you're not an individual anymore," she said, then chugged a mouthful of champagne.

"I wouldn't worry about that, *mija*," I said, laughing fully now.

Her face softened a little, and she laughed with me.

"Okay," she started. "Not to bring the night down, but I wouldn't be your best friend if I didn't tell you the truth. I'm Team Josie, always. Also—"

I glanced at her, slightly worried.

"Also, I know I was joking about the *Thelma and Louise* thing. But if you need..." she looked around suddenly. "If you actually didn't want to get married to Clarke. If you... I don't know, if you wanted me to just drive us away from here. From your parents and your brothers and the venue and the cake and the bouquets of roses... I would. In a heartbeat. No questions asked. No judgment."

She was gripping her plastic cup so tightly I thought she'd crack it.

And then the strangest feeling washed over me—a sudden desire to jump in the car and whisper "*go,*" because she would.

Lucia would do anything for me.

But then I shook my head fiercely, effectively tossing that wayward thought back out into the hot California sky. I wasn't sure where it had come from, and I was deeply uncomfortable that I'd even entertained it for a second.

This was *Clarke*. My soul mate. The love of my entire life. Sure, things between us had moved fast—I'd always thought I'd *never* be married. Never be tied down to another person, never have to *rely* on another person. I'd been relying on myself successfully for years—proudly, even. I put myself through cosmetology school while working two jobs. Pulled myself, tooth and nail, up the ladder, finding and securing the best celebrity clients as the years went by. Routinely worked twelve-hour days and *still* found time to go dancing with Lucia, both of us addicted to the pulsing thrill of L.A. nights.

But then... well. Then Clarke happened, like a tornado I couldn't help but be sucked into. Most people in my life, including Lucia, were shocked when I told them we were engaged.

*Too soon*, I heard them whisper.

They didn't get *us*, and really, they didn't have to.

"I appreciate that," I finally said, pulling her in for a sloppy hug on the hood of her car. Kissed her cheek. "Really, I do. *Tu amistad significa el mundo para mi.*"

"*Si*," she said softly. "Your friendship means the world to me too. *Siempre*." Lucia pulled back, wiping her eyes quickly, although it didn't hide the small tear that slid down her cheek.

"Lu?" I asked, concerned. I held up the champagne. "It's *my night*, remember? I haven't been a Bridezilla *once*, but heaven help me, I will turn into one if you don't finish the fuck out of that champagne."

She laughed with me and obliged, knocking her cup back. She reached into her pocket and turned on the speakers in her car. An old Mary J. Blige song came on, her smoky voice lilting through the open windows. I grinned, leaning back on the car, laying my head next to Lucia's.

"You know champagne makes me weepy," she finally said. "Now let's talk about all the things you're excited about for tomorrow."

"The dress," I said, watching a few stars twinkle above us. They were particularly resolute, shining their light through the layers of smog that coated the L.A. sky. I loved that sky. I was a child of smoggy sunsets and hot asphalt summers; mariachi horns coming from my neighbor's house on a Saturday night; abandoned cars parked in front of vibrant graffiti; break-dancers in front of crisp white mansions.

I would never live anywhere else.

"Your dress is perfect," Lucia said softly. "What else?"

"The first dance. When I get to say *I do*. The first moment that Clarke will see me, walking down the aisle."

My throat tightened with a sudden spike of emotion as Lucia held my hand, both of us gazing up toward the stars. The music continued as we finished the champagne, our voices blending together.

Tomorrow, everything would change.

Tomorrow, my dreams would come true.

# 1

# JOSIE

*Two years later*

"I think I got it," I said, sketching out ideas on a white sheet of paper. "Shay Miller wants 'wild child' meets Haight-Ashbury with a dash of wood-nymph sprinkled in."

I pictured the texture of leaves woven through blonde hair, peace signs, and suede fringe.

"Gold eye shadow. Bold lips." I glanced up at Lucia, who stuck her tongue out at me. I laughed. "I'm thinking... deep magenta. Maybe some body paint."

Ray, the creative director for this shoot, nodded vigorously. "As usual, Josie, you're a goddamn genius."

"Why, thank you," I said, pressing my hand against my chest. "Although Lucia *is* the best canvas."

Lucia responded by contorting her face into a terrifying grimace.

"See what I'm working with? Pure poetry."

Lucia burst out laughing.

Ray rolled his eyes. "Remind me to never book the two of you for a potentially career-changing project ever again."

Lucia and I exchanged a look. Both of us had worked with Ray Freeman often throughout our respective careers, and he was never *not* overwhelmed and anxious. He was in his early forties, white with salt-and-pepper hair. Brilliant creatively, but at least half a dozen times over the past day, Ray had gripped my shoulders, shaken me, and said *this is a career-changing project, Josie.*

The chance to work with Shay Miller, L.A.'s current fashion obsession, *was* a big fucking deal. He'd recently launched a new fashion line called *Boho* and wanted Lucia, and our friend Taylor Brooks, in a provocative photo shoot that would display his bohemian, funky clothing.

And out of every single celebrity makeup artist in the city —and there were many—Shay Miller had chosen *me*.

I picked out colors and palettes from my giant black bag. I loved the *texture* of gold, and it would shimmer on Lucia, but I also wanted to test out something charcoal-colored.

"Sit," I said to Lucia who complied dutifully. She immediately took out her phone and began scrolling through her many social media platforms.

"Eyes closed."

"But then I can't Snapchat," she whined.

I tilted my head at her. "At this point, can't you just do it from memory?"

She grinned cheekily, then fluttered her eyes closed. I leaned forward, gliding on a blend of colors. Testing and seeking, my endless quest for artistic perfection.

"I'll keep working on it," I said softly to Ray. "Send Shay some mock-ups and my initial ideas. Prove to him I can do it. When do we leave?"

"In a week. And he already thinks you can do it. That's

why he hired you. And you're going to do great," Ray said before sighing loudly again and sinking into a chair. "And, just so you know, we'll be on location for three days. Up in Big Sur."

"That far?" I asked, tilting Lucia's head to the left and right. Even with her eyes closed, her fingers were flying over her cell. "I've never been there before."

"Shay liked the idea of it. It's kind of a bohemian place, and the main location is this old bookstore called The Mad Ones. Which used to be famous. The town is right along the coast, very rural. Just a bunch of hippies and artists living along the cliffs."

"Huh," I said, writing something down. "Sounds like I'd hate it."

Ray flashed me a grin as Lucia snorted. All three of us were born-and-raised in Los Angeles, and would never even *consider* living elsewhere.

Especially not someplace described as *rural.*

"Also there's no cell service up there and very little internet," Ray said calmly.

Lucia's shoulders stiffened.

"It'll be all right," I soothed. "It's just three days."

My best friend could barely go a minute without checking her thousands of fan notifications—let alone 72 straight hours.

"I think there's an internet cafe?" Ray said, and Lucia literally growled.

"Somehow we'll find the will to survive, Lu," I said sardonically. "And eyes open."

Her blue eyes looked annoyed. But also gorgeous with the eye shadow. Gorgeous and very... *bohemian.*

"What do you think?" I asked, turning to Ray. Lucia struck a pose.

Ray shook his head, muttering beneath his breath. "A goddamn *genius*."

Lucia and I high-fived.

---

AN HOUR later and we were sipping kale smoothies on a patio, watching the hustle and bustle of Los Angeles on a Monday morning. Punks on skateboards and a man dressed as Santa Claus hula-hooping. Men and women in high-end business suits, barking into cell phones. A few celebrities in giant glasses, ducking their heads down to avoid the flash of the paparazzi (Lucia and I had already posed sweetly for a few of them).

The morning was sticky with heat, the sun rising up between the palm trees and the bright pink jacaranda.

"When do you leave for Paris?" I asked, biting my straw.

"Two more days," Lucia sighed then slapped on what looked like a fake smile. "That's when I meet with Sabine to go over the *Dazzle* contract. And then off to Big Sur."

I shook my head in disbelief. "I still can't believe you fucking scored *Dazzle,* Lu."

It was one of the largest cosmetic lines in the world. And they wanted Lucia to be their cover girl for two years. The only down-side was they were moving her to Paris. A reality that made me alternately thrilled and nauseous.

Because Lu and I were inseparable.

"You'll love it there. Right?" I said, kicking her leg beneath the table.

She was gazing into the distance with a strange expression. "Oh, of course," she said and then took a giant gulp of smoothie. "I mean...it's *Paris*. What's not to love?"

"Your best friend won't be there, *mija,*" I said. "*But* you'll get a lot of French cock."

Lucia spit out her smoothie, laughing into a napkin. "Nothing gets me more turned on than the idea of a disembodied penis with a French accent."

My cell phone buzzed. A text from Jason. *Had a great time last night. When can we do it again?*

I ran my hand over my bare left finger—an old reflex—then turned the text toward Lucia.

She leaned in, read it. Arched an eyebrow at me. "What are you going to text back?"

I grinned. Composed a message: *Never. We can never do it again.*

Lucia shook her head. "Fucking *maneater*."

"Hey," I said, palms up, "I tell them from the beginning. It's one night, and that's *all*. I can't help it if I'm absolutely extraordinary in bed."

"Josefine Torres," Lucia laughed. "The Maneater of Los Angeles."

Briefly my throat tightened, a hoard of memories clamoring to be let out. But I swallowed against it.

"That's me," I sighed, turning back toward the hot, burning sunlight.

## 2

## GABE

When I was just a gawky fourteen-year-old, my dad shoved a backpack into my hands and informed me I was not to come back to the house until the sun had set.

"Where am I supposed to *go*?" I had asked.

"Out there," he'd said. "The woods. Where we live."

"By myself?" I'd asked in the endlessly petulant tone of teenagers. "And do what?"

"Walk," he shrugged. "Find a trail and follow it. You know your way around this forest."

Which was true. You couldn't really live in Big Sur and *not* be familiar with the wilderness. I'd spent the majority of my formative years under a canopy of redwoods, leaping over logs and climbing branches and running through creeks. I knew, because of television, that a lot of kids played on things called *jungle gyms*. Or on street corners or small, orderly patches of grass called *backyards*.

But in Big Sur, the Ventana Wilderness *was* your backyard, and there wasn't anything small or orderly about it.

So I was familiar with the forest. I *wasn't* familiar with what I was being asked to do.

High school had started a few months earlier, and so far the experience had been atrociously awkward. My friends had grown a foot overnight, were going on dates and sneaking out to party.

Meanwhile, I was a late bloomer: still at five-and-a-half feet tall with no facial hair, and every social interaction felt like it was happening in a foreign language.

Things that had once come easily (like *talking*) now felt like a giant mystery. A mystery that everyone *else* seemed to have the answers to while I was left stubbornly in the dark.

I'd been listless and sulky. Even my siblings, Austin and Isabelle, didn't want to be around me.

My parents definitely noticed.

"Learning to embrace nature, to search for stillness. It changed a lot of things for me," my dad had said, indicating the great big world outside our window. "And I learned to embrace it at a very important time in my life."

He glanced at my mother, eyes softening. She winked at him.

"This is going to sound like complete and utter nonsense to you right now. But focus on your surroundings. The grandness of it, the sheer *size*." He placed his hand over my heart. "The stillness."

"What the *fuck*?" I asked. Puberty had made me aggressively defiant.

But my parents were nonplussed by my teenaged antics. "The woods," he repeated. "Go. And don't come back until you've learned something. I packed you lunch *and* dinner."

I shrugged on the backpack, wincing at the weight on my shoulders. "Fine," I said miserably, slouching off to the door.

"Also, don't die!" my mom called back sweetly.

I had ignored her. My feet crunched along the worn trail that extended past our house. The landscape continually changed, making it even more beautiful. I kept walking, staring at the trees. The way the sun lilted through the branches. The call of birds all around me.

I hiked some more, for over an hour, and found I was thinking less about what was going to happen in school tomorrow. Thinking less about the upcoming dance and if the girl I liked was going to go with me.

I was really only focused on my feet. The trail. The sounds. The slight ache in my back from the pack. The burn of my muscles as I climbed a hill. An exhilaration, an *aliveness* that I hadn't felt slouched in front of the television and endlessly ruminating on the perils of being a teenager.

When I finally trudged back, triumphantly, my parents were waiting with amused expressions.

"Well?" My dad said. "What did you think?"

I rolled my eyes and shrugged, having prepared a dozen sarcastic remarks. But I finally settled on a casual: "It was cool. I guess."

They exchanged a smile, and that night, they sat on our deck beneath the stars for a long time, holding hands.

Things began to slowly change. I was still fourteen, and the realizations I'd come to that day didn't entirely obliterate the challenges of puberty. I was still awkward and weird and worried night and day that I'd never be normal. Or attractive. Or kiss someone.

But... when those thoughts threatened to overwhelm me, I went for a walk in the woods. And something about it calmed the core of my anxiety.

Gave me tranquility.

I'd been coming to the woods to make sense of my

thoughts for almost twenty years now, the hiking trails as familiar as an old friend.

And this morning, I'd woken with that same thirst for absolute stillness. For rushing streams and birdsong. To be completely alone. As I hiked, the rocky, jagged coast of California stretched out before me. It was still early, the sun rising behind the forest, turning the Pacific Ocean a rosy pink color. Fog caressed the beach, curled against the waves.

I hadn't seen a single soul in more than two hours. Had breathed deeply and noticed the complex beauty of my surroundings. Tried to let my thoughts move and sway like the wind.

But it wasn't fucking working this time.

Last night I'd taken a woman home—a tourist. A complete stranger. The sex had been fine, and she'd left immediately afterward, but we had zero connection. We'd barely spoken, just exchanged the basics. She was nice, about my age, and cute. That was about it. No passion or fire. No possibility of seeing her again—she was just passing through on a road trip down to Mexico.

And when I woke this morning, I'd felt... unsettled, like my skin no longer fit right.

Maybe it was because my natural inclination was *romance*. Love. Neither of which had a place in the throes of a one-night stand. And when I was younger, it was easier to quiet that urge. But Sasha and I had been broken up for almost ten years now, and life was rushing full speed ahead.

Yet I was stubbornly stuck searching for the one thing that continued to elude me.

A branch broke beneath my feet, startling the quiet. I was hiking past the tree that still held our old tire swing and the tree next to it where my parents had built a fort for us, high in the branches. Which meant I was close to The Bar.

I checked my watch, sighing. I needed to clean and prep to open by noon when the boozier locals came by for a lunchtime beer. Maybe a quiet forest wasn't what I needed. Maybe I needed the comforting hum of bartending, of gossip and conversation.

Except I knew the fact that Gabe Shaw had taken a stranger home last night would be all over the Big Sur Channel—the locals' affectionate nickname for what was essentially a network of endless gossip.

*Goddammit.*

That thought propelled my feet, and The Bar appeared in the distance. I'd inherited ownership of Big Sur's only dive bar from my father, who'd inherited it from his grandfather. The only true sanctuary for local residents looking to escape tourists. Looking for a place that was truly *theirs*.

From the outside, The Bar looked drab and shabby. A gray, two-story building set back into the forest with a small parking lot out front. The sign was worn and illegible—my grandfather *had* given this establishment a name, but no one remembered it, and The Bar it remained.

Intrepid hippies had taken paint to the side wall in the early seventies, designing a psychedelic mural that bothered the eyes if you stared at it for too long. And in the middle, a quote from Thoreau: *All good things are wild and free*.

The very essence of Big Sur and people who made this place their home. The very essence of this isolated town, perched on deadly cliffs. Of the ocean and the trees and the heavy fog that greeted us every morning.

Wild. Free.

There was no other place like it in the whole world.

I'd never live anywhere else.

## 3

## JOSIE

Big Sur was magic.

We'd arrived for the photo shoot only an hour ago. I was standing with Lucia on rocky cliffs, hair whipped by the wind, and staring at an angry ocean. Dark storm clouds hovered on the horizon, and rows of lavender-colored lupine spread down the rocks toward the sand.

I inhaled the colors and textures of this outcropping and turned around to look at the tiny cabin I'd be living in for the next three days.

"I fucking love it," I told Lucia who stood huddled and annoyed next to me. "And you know I'm not nature's biggest fan. But this... *this* is inspiration."

I looked at Lu, picturing the colors of Big Sur painted on her porcelain skin. All that wildness come to life.

Lucia glanced behind us toward Calvin Ellis, our host for the next three days. He was talking with Ray or rather being talked *at* by Ray. Cal couldn't seem to maintain eye contact, continually blushing as Ray's hands waved through the air. Calvin was tall, white and wore huge glasses. He had thick, dark brown hair and a five o'clock shadow.

"He's cute," I said to Lu, nudging her with my shoulder. "And his bookstore is cool."

Her lips tugged up, but she didn't say anything at first. Before modeling took over her life, Lucia had been a total bookworm. I knew she'd fallen in love with The Mad Ones—our funky location for the next few days—but hadn't said anything yet. The cabins we were staying in were an extension of the bookstore, previously owned by his grandfather who had passed away five months ago. Calvin had told us that The Mad Ones used to be a bohemian hideaway for famous writers and poets, and they'd often stay in the cabins as a sort of retreat, gaining inspiration from the dramatic scenery around them.

I understood that desire. I wasn't a writer, but I *was* an artist even though people often rolled their eyes when I told them what I did. Makeup wasn't considered an art form, but I sure as hell believed it was.

And standing here, overlooking this view?

*Inspiration.*

"When was the last time you traveled to some place so far off the grid?" Lucia finally asked, tucking her arm through mine. We started to walk along the edge, the wind growing stronger.

"Maybe... never?" I said, thinking back. When my parents and I returned to Mexico, we always stayed in the urban hub of Guadalajara. And for work, it was always London, Milan, Paris: bright, bustling cities. "It's not my usual scene," I admitted. "Although maybe the change will do us some good. See... trees. Or... shit I don't know, birds? Do birds live up here?"

Lucia laughed again.

I tugged her closer. "Plus, you'll be moving to Paris soon. Think of this as a three-day best friend retreat. There's no cell service, so we can actually talk to *each other*. Take a break from the nightlife. Actually sleep."

"And the internet?" Lucia asked with an edge to her voice.

As a celebrity makeup artist, I had to sell an image of myself just as much as Lucia, but I'd decided early on to keep it in check. To not let it run my entire life. But Lucia was online every waking moment and had been antsy since we'd pulled up to The Mad Ones.

Antsy and irritated. Except when she was talking to Calvin.

"It's three days; you can make it," I reminded her. "Plus, when you're done talking to *me*, you can talk to Calvin."

"Why would I do that?" she said dryly, but she peeked over her shoulder toward where he stood.

"Because he's cute, and he wears glasses, and he loves books."

Lucia stiffened. "Not *my* scene anymore," she said firmly.

I dropped the subject. "The photo shoot's going to go great, *mija. Te vas a ver hermosa,*" I reminded her.

She nodded but didn't respond. We stood in silence for a while, and I let Big Sur soak into my skin, my thoughts.

And then I heard Clarke's voice. *Do you think Shay Miller would have chosen you if Lucia hadn't persuaded him*?

On instinct, I reached for my phone, needing a distraction.

And then I remembered. No internet. No service.

I grit my teeth, willing his voice to go away. Angry that after two years he could still crowd my brain with barbed words.

"What are you thinking about?" Lucia asked me, eyes searching my face.

"Oh, nothing," I said breezily, turning away.

She squeezed my fingers in silent understanding. Lucia understood most of all.

Maybe this time in Big Sur without distractions would be *good* for the healing process. After what Clarke did, I filled my life with light and sound. Anything to drown him out. In fact, standing here, overlooking the ocean, was the first time I'd heard him in months. He seemed to sense when I was getting stronger, even though he was no longer in my life.

But maybe if I stopped distracting myself, he'd finally go away.

These past two years, I learned that my rational thoughts were a goddamn joke against the manipulations of my irrational mind. An outsider would say: don't listen.

But it was like trying to concentrate on a challenging math problem while a radio blared in your ear.

A radio you could never *ever* turn off.

"We should head back," Lucia said. "You and I need to meet with hair and wardrobe to go over tomorrow's first looks."

"Of course." I smiled weakly then held out my arms dramatically. "Let's do the damn thing. Josie and Lucia Take Big Sur. Experience Mother Nature For the First Time."

"Learn to live without Instagram," Lucia said.

"See a real-life bird."

"Go to sleep at a *reasonable* hour."

I was laughing now. "Maybe even... see the sun come up from *bed*. Not walking home from a club."

Lucia stopped in her tracks, looking appalled. "Let's not get ahead of ourselves."

I laughed louder, the sound loosening the tightness in my chest. "You're right. I'm sure we'll be murdering each other by sundown."

## 4

## GABE

"They're penises," I said to Gladys with an arched eyebrow, but she only rolled her eyes and sighed. Next to her, her twin sister, Gloria, did the same.

"And what is this, Puritan England?" Gladys asked. "I like them. And I think they'd look great hanging on the walls here. Give it a real *hey fuck you* vibe."

"With... dicks," I said, fighting to keep a smile off of my face.

At least once a month, the sisters came by with new art they'd either discovered or done themselves. The art was always strange and eclectic.

And always *very* sexual.

"Mrs. Manahan likes them," Gloria said. "Don't you, hon?"

All three of us turned to the woman who'd been my fifth grade math teacher, who'd been slowly downing whiskey and watching the football game on the television over the bar.

"What do I like?" she called back, eyes trained on the screen.

"The uh... the paintings of erections," I said.

Mrs. Manahan mumbled something nonsensical to which Gloria and Gladys both said "*See?*" in response.

"The crowd's really going wild," I drawled.

Gloria and Gladys graduated from high school with my parents on a Friday, got engaged to their high school sweethearts that Saturday, and started work at the Post Office on that Monday. The pair were die-hard Harlequin fans, routinely reading the romance novels under their respective desks at work. They were damn near identical too, with the same curly red hair, pale skin and obsession with brightly colored reading glasses.

"I mean, how can I say no?" I said, holding up a painting of a dick completing a crossword puzzle. "They're classics."

"Ex*actly*," Gloria said. "And you're welcome."

They headed back to their bar stools, and I chuckled softly to myself.

Every night at The Bar was like this.

Like most of Big Sur, The Bar was one-half eclectic bohemian and one-half leave-me-the-fuck-alone. A place for locals, although we saw more tourists now than we used too. Ten years ago, we had started appearing online as a "must see" attraction, a place where you could get the "real" Big Sur experience, which mostly consisted of endless, nonsensical gossip through the Big Sur Channel.

And silence.

I clapped Kevin on the back as I walked past, opening up another beer and sliding it to him.

"We have penises on the wall now," I said.

Kevin dropped his head to his hands. Kevin was Gladys and Gloria's long-suffering supervisor at the Post Office. "At least they're not hanging it at work," he said grimly, lifting his head. "And you and I need to talk."

"About what?" I asked innocently, submerging wine

glasses in the sink in soapy water. I glanced up and nodded as Geoff, Fritz and John ambled in.

"I heard you had quite a night on Wednesday."

I looked down at my hands in the water, pretending to ignore his question. It had been two days since I'd slept with a stranger, and I'd been shocked that no one had mentioned it last night—although I'd gotten some looks.

As the bartender, I held a coveted role in the Big Sur Channel and gossiped as much as anyone else. But Kevin had gone to high school with my parents as well. And had an annoying tendency to funnel all gossip related to me directly into their ears.

It made family dinners awkward.

"A woman came here a couple nights ago," I said cautiously. "Just passing through. We talked a little, we were both looking for some fun, and she spent the night." My stomach clenched at my admission—not from embarrassment but as a sudden feeling of *loss*.

"Any other questions?" I asked Kevin, who was grinning like a loon. If you got trapped in the Channel, it was best to lay it all out there.

Or it got laid out there for you.

"Nope," Kevin said, whipping out his phone.

"Just don't tell my parents," I laughed.

Kevin's fingers flew. "Just texted them," he said, triumphant, slamming his phone on the table.

"Oh, goddammit," I said, head back and sighing. Ruth, my second grade teacher, and Mrs. Manahan were pinning me with the same inquiring look.

So I ducked under the bar like a coward, grabbing the first bottle of wine I could see. And stood up to find myself face-to-face with my sister Isabelle and her wife Maya.

"When did you two get here?" I exclaimed, coming quickly around the bar to wrap them both in a bear hug.

Isabelle squealed in my ear. "Did you somehow get *more* massive? Also I'm going to need my bones after this, so try not to crush 'em."

I laughed, giving Maya a kiss on the cheek. "Hey gorgeous," I said to my sister-in-law.

"Hey you," she said back. "You going to open that wine?"

"Absolutely," I said, grabbing an opener and two glasses. "And to what do I owe this surprise visit?"

"Date night," Maya grinned. "Even though we're both fucking exhausted. Your sister here hasn't taken me on a date since Lola came."

I looked at Isabelle in mock horror, but she only grabbed the wine glass from me with a cheeky grin.

"That's because most nights we're in bed by seven," she teased.

Isabelle and Maya were brand-new parents to a six-month-old baby named Lola. The adoption process had been long and brutal, but I was there when they placed Lola in Isabelle's arms. I'd been overwhelmed with the sheer amount of tangible love in that room.

Maya squeezed Isabelle's shoulders, causing her to laugh. They'd met in college and had been inseparable ever since. Isabelle looked like me—tan skin, dark blonde hair, brown eyes. Maya was Black and had long braids piled high on her head.

Lola had darker skin like Maya and big, luminous eyes—the first moment she'd reached towards me, wrapping her little fingers around my thumb, I was a goner.

"Speaking of, where is the light of my life tonight?" I asked.

"Left her at home by herself," Isabelle said. "She just lays there, so what's the harm?"

I laughed, and Maya shook her head. But the look she gave Isabelle spoke volumes.

It spoke of a love so deep you'd never get to the bottom of it.

I swallowed roughly, pouring two more glasses of wine for the twins who I knew would be calling for more any minute.

"Actually, we're staying with your parents for the next few days," Maya said. "Just to get a little... break, you know?" Another look passed between them.

"Mom and Dad must love that," I grinned. "Can I come see you tomorrow? Help out a little?"

"Yes, please," Isabelle said softly. She reached forward to squeeze my hand.

"It's not a problem, you know that. And if you need more help, I'm there. The next time you want to do Date Night in Monterey, let me know. I can always close early, drive down to watch Lola."

Relief washed over Isabelle's face. "We'd appreciate that. I think we're both feeling a little isolated."

I nodded. "Of course. Give me a few dates, and I'll make it work, Iz."

"The world needs more people like you, Gabriel," Maya said.

"I'm all in on this Uncle stuff," I said, grabbing the wine glasses.

I was halfway to Gladys and Gloria—who were trying to convince Kevin the new wall art was a political statement on the role of the government in our lives—when the shrill ring of the phone sliced through the hazy air.

I jogged back behind the bar, grabbing the phone.

"What's good?" I said and heard Calvin's telltale nervous stutter.

"Gabe? Um... would you want to come to a party with, um... well with some models?"

I laughed. Calvin and I had developed a close friendship since he'd moved here five months earlier, but he still seemed nervous every time we talked.

"Calvin, my man," I boomed. "Are you inviting me to a party with the *Hollywood People?*" I said the last part loudly, and a strong contingent of locals looked my way.

They, like everyone else in Big Sur, were particularly intrigued by the arrival of big-time, fancy Hollywood super models to our tiny hamlet. I didn't entirely understand why they wanted to do a photo shoot for a fashion magazine at Calvin's bookstore, The Mad Ones, but then again... I wasn't the kind of person who understood fashion. Or Hollywood. Or, for that matter, how to use most cameras.

But the supermodels had arrived in full force not forty-eight hours earlier, and the Big Sur Channel was *abuzz* like it hadn't been in a while. On their first day of shooting, the bakery had saved the day, carting up coffee and breakfast items when their food service people had been stuck in traffic. And the bakery folks had come back with *mountains* of information (which I'd gleaned when I'd stopped in for coffee—only took me a full hour to hear the minute-by-minute breakdown). There was an entire crew—hair, makeup, wardrobe. Two models, the kind you see on magazine covers and on television. A woman and a man, both stunning, and several of the hornier elderly people had already been banned from spying on them through the windows.

"I am indeed," Cal said. "Or... um, I guess it's not really a party? But a gathering on the patio. I'm not sure if you want to close up early or bring liquor or... whatever," he finished and I could hear the sounds of people in the background. I glanced outside. A massive storm had been predicted, but so far, the night was still warm. And about half the people here at The Bar would come with me if I left.

"When will I ever get a chance like this again?" I grabbed a large bucket and started to stock up on beer. "Count me in. I'll grab a few of our more... discerning residents," I said, grinning as the twins shot me a dirty look.

"Okay, um... okay, good," Cal stuttered and promptly hung up.

I liked Calvin, a *lot*. His grandfather, Robert, had died six months ago—a Big Sur legend. An institution. His grandfather, along with my father and a few other members, were the foundation of Big Sur's bohemian, counterculture history. The Mad Ones had been open since the late 1950s and until recently had been the home of late-night poetry readings, famous authors-in-residence, and parties that lasted until dawn. In the sixties and seventies, Beat poets would travel up from the North Bay, bringing pot and jazz and their air of artistic defiance. After a reading, they'd grab a burger at Fenix or a glass of whiskey at The Bar, and slowly Big Sur's wild, artistic reputation took hold.

And now our little bohemian hamlet was being invaded by Hollywood People, and as usual, it was alcohol to the rescue.

"Listen up, everyone," I called out, and immediately the room silenced. "We've all been invited to The Mad Ones for an impromptu party with some Los Angeles models. If you're in, come with me. If you're not, try not to trash the place and leave money on the table." I tossed a wink at Isabelle. "I'll know if you stiff me."

She rolled her eyes then dutifully slapped a twenty on the table. Which I would only return later—I never took money from family. But both my siblings *and* my parents always paid their bill when they came by for a visit. And I'd always take the cash and slip it back into their coat pockets or under their coffee pots.

"Do you want to come see some hot models?" I asked Isabelle, who only wrinkled her nose.

Maya agreed. "We just want to drink quietly then immediately go to sleep."

I laughed. "Sounds like a magical Date Night."

I kept grabbing liquor, and Ruth and Kevin stood up to join. I glanced at the ranchers. "Takers?" But they only turned their eyes back to the television. Gladys and Gloria sidled over, but I shook my head.

"No," I said firmly. "You'll scare them away."

"Then we'll just get our binoculars and spy on you from the bushes," Gloria sniffed.

"I'll allow it," I said. "But *no* pictures." Which was a crock of bullshit—they'd document the entire event, put up a fucking slide show in the post office for the customers.

I kissed Maya and Isabelle on the cheek. "See you soon?" I asked, and Isabelle gave me a shove.

"Go, go," she said. "Maybe you'll meet a famous model and fall in love."

"Sure," I said dryly. "Those are the kinds of things that *always* happen to me."

It was time to meet the Hollywood People.

## 5

## GABE

Turns out the Hollywood People were just regular people—not that I'd spoken to any of them yet. Calvin and I were leaning against the railing on the patio just outside the bookstore. Big Sur's usually starry sky was blanketed with thick, heavy clouds.

I handed him a beer. "So what's it like having the bookstore overrun with supermodels?"

Cal snuck a glance toward Lucia Bell, who was talking to a dark-haired woman at the other end of the patio. Lucia was a famous supermodel, as opposite from Calvin as you could be, yet it was obvious to me they already shared some kind of strange connection.

"Oh... you know," Cal shrugged. "Definitely not something I ever thought I'd experience, this kind of... fame... To be honest, it's definitely not the kind of thing I ever thought my grandfather would participate in. He was so *against* all of that. Being obsessed with image, American culture." A wry smile. "Capitalism in general."

"Which I always found ironic since he owned his own business," I said. Robert had been like a second grandfather to me growing up. His death six months ago had rocked the community.

"Exactly," Cal smiled, shaking his head. "And I can't tell... well, I can't tell if he, um, was that desperate for money? To help the debt? I have absolutely no idea."

Cal and I had been friends for months now, drinking together a few times a week, and he'd been open about his concerns with the legacy that had been laid at his feet: whether or not to sell his grandfather's store. After Robert had died, ownership of The Mad Ones had passed to Calvin.

Ownership... and a mountain of debt. But The Mad Ones was a Big Sur institution, as important to our town as The Bar. He was currently in talks to sell it to investors that planned on building a spa there. The Mad Ones had once been a place where countless authors and poets had read their historic works. The thought of it being sold was painful for me, and I could *feel* Cal hesitating.

But I hadn't wanted to push him, even though I had the full weight of the Big Sur Channel behind me, begging me to make him change his mind.

I knew Cal needed to make this decision himself.

"Or maybe Robert knew that having the Hollywood People would be some necessary excitement for the locals," I replied, grinning at the scene around me. Ruth was fawning all over a male model named Taylor. Kevin was animatedly talking to a man named Ray, who'd introduced himself as the 'creative director.'

"We're going to be entertaining bar patrons with stories from this night for weeks. It's like this... extra gift from your grandfather, even though he's gone."

"Sure," Cal laughed. "He *was* concerned that Gladys and Gloria didn't have enough people to spy on."

I snorted but cast a wary glance into the trees, eyes

narrowing. It was likely they were eavesdropping on this conversation.

"You can tell these people aren't from here because they're glued to their phones," I pointed out.

Cal shook his head. "I did the same thing when I first moved to Big Sur, trying to get a signal. I've been with them for two days now, and every free moment, they all whip them out as if the situation has suddenly changed."

Knocking my beer against Calvin's, I hoisted myself up onto the railing. "I want to tell them to *slow down*. You're in Big Sur now. What could be more important?"

I turned to Calvin, but he was not-so-subtly staring at Lucia. I hid a smile, scanning the crowd. Watched the Hollywood People check their phones as the Big Sur locals lit joints and prattled on about their experimental art. The Grateful Dead crooned from the stereo, the fire pits were lit, and the air was heavy with that just-about-to-rain feeling.

I inhaled.

Big Sur curled against my heart.

I exhaled and caught the eye of the dark-haired woman talking to Lucia.

It lasted barely a moment, and then she looked away. I did too, not wanting to stare, but I'd gotten a brief-but-compelling impression of her: dark eyes, tattoos flowing over her light brown skin, ripped dress.

I chanced a second glance, and luckily the woman was talking animatedly to Lucia, laughing at something she said. There was something... *distinct* about her: the proud tilt of her head. And she wasn't checking her damn phone every second.

"How was your... um, date, the other night?" Cal asked, and I turned to him with a disapproving look.

"Even you, Cal?" I said

Cal shrugged. "I went to the post office, and the place was

*abuzz* with the news that Gabriel Shaw, Town Lothario, had engaged in a romantic encounter."

I picked at the label on my beer bottle. "I haven't had a serious relationship in almost ten years. I'm not sure a random hook-up qualifies me as *Town Lothario.*"

"In the eyes of the Big Sur Channel, it does," Cal said. "And... you didn't answer my question."

"It was okay," I finally said, waving as two patrons from The Bar walked onto the patio. "It wasn't bad. It just wasn't anything special, like the whole night existed in some kind of vacuum. No connection. No feelings. But also no consequences. Just sex."

"Sex is good."

I caught the eye of the dark-haired woman again. This time she gave me a sly grin before looking away.

"Sex is good," I replied slowly. Her wavy hair was tipped in lavender. Every time she moved, the purple strands brushed across her bare shoulders. I turned back to Calvin. "Sex is great. But that *kind* of sex..." I trailed off, uncertain of how to continue.

My sexual fantasies—and sexual reality—had never met. At night, my mind filled with a sea of images I couldn't make sense of, of sharp commands, the sting of pain, the way the floor would bite into my knees. And yet the fantasy also pulsed with *emotion*—strong and urgent like high tide sweeping away the sand. The emotion didn't exist without consequences.

And it wasn't what I'd felt the other night.

No. The commanding tone, the ringing *slap* of palm against flesh: these desires were woven through with a fiery, bright intensity.

"Gabe?" Cal asked, and when I turned, his eyebrows were knit together with concern. "Are you okay?"

"Oh, yeah," I said. "Just... you ever wake up and realize time is moving more quickly than you'd like it to?"

He nodded in understanding. "Yes, I have." He squeezed my shoulder. "And there aren't a lot of opportunities to meet your soul mate up here in Big Sur, huh?"

I cleared my throat and swigged my beer. "No," I admitted. "No, there aren't."

# 6

# JOSIE

It was his man bun that did it.

That and the fact that he looked like an honest-to-god Viking. He was white with dark blond hair, a full beard and a barrel chest covered in a plaid shirt.

He was easily a head taller than the tallest person in the room.

A ferocious Viking, newly arrived from another world, sent to seduce milk-maids and princesses, leaving them sighing and heartbroken.

We'd just wrapped the second day of shooting, and Lucia had convinced Calvin to throw a party on the patio outside The Mad Ones. We only had one full day left in this bohemian paradise, and I was soaking it all in. The weird hippies intermingling with the crew, the majestic redwoods surrounding us, the electricity sparking through the air.

"You look happy," Lucia said, nudging my shoulder. "And stop being so *obvious*."

I laughed, sipped my beer. "I am happy," I admitted, acknowledging the light, joyful feeling in my chest. No Clarke tonight. No bad memories. And I'd just spent two days on an artistic photo shoot with my best friend, creating experimental makeup looks inspired by the gorgeous scenery that surrounded us.

"Blissed out, even," I continued. I turned to her, wrapped my arm around her shoulders. "This has been a really good best-friend trip, don't you think?"

Lu smiled easily and kissed my cheek. "The best."

There was a burst of masculine laughter, and our heads whipped toward the sound. Calvin and his friend, Viking Man Bun, were laughing broadly. He crossed his arms in front of his chest, exposing his thick, veined forearms.

"Oh wait," Lucia said, bending down dramatically. She stood up. "Here's your jaw. Picked it up off the floor."

"First, shut the fuck up," I teased. "Secondly, *you* should talk. You've been eye-fucking sweet Calvin all night long."

"Eye-*flirting*," she corrected. "Calvin's too polite for eye-fucking."

I arched an eyebrow at her.

She blushed a little. That was new. Lucia Bell, *Maxim Magazine's* "Sexiest Woman Alive," did *not* blush.

"And you've got *maneater* written all over you tonight. You're on the prowl," she said.

I shrugged. It was true. "I haven't had sex with anyone in months, and I'm horny as fuck," I said as Lu snorted into her drink. A few of the male techs gave me the side eye, but I ignored them. "I'm assessing my options."

"You literally slept with someone the day before we left for Big Sur," Lucia pointed out.

"Right," I admitted. "But what I really mean is... I haven't had *good* sex in months."

And I wanted more than just *good* sex. "Good" was a word too paltry to describe what I thought fucking *should* be.

An art form. A religious experience. Bite marks and clothing torn in half and broken headboards.

Since Clarke, I'd been on a tear across Los Angeles, desperate to drown my sorrows in life-altering sex.

But one-night stands so rarely provided that. My stranger-lovers were just that... *strangers*. They hadn't spent months learning the sensitive areas of my body. What gave me goose-bumps. What made me scream.

Viking Man Bun met my gaze for a second before pulling Calvin into a side hug, laughing uproariously. He should have had an ax slung around his back, a shield across his broad frame.

"Well, assess away, *chica*. Calvin told me he's single," Lucia said.

My heart sped up at the news, the rush of excitement as heady as any drug. Just call me the Black Widow. Viking Man Bun was my next victim.

"Interesting," I said. "He looks like a challenge."

"Oh, please," Lucia drawled. "He'll take one look at you and fold in a second."

I grinned in response. There was nothing more affirming than working every day with your best friend.

"You're too kind, *mija*," I said, wiggling a little and making her laugh.

"Plus, he looks nice."

I shook my head, taking a real drag on my beer. "I don't care much about nice."

Nice didn't get you far in my book anymore.

"What *do* you care about?" she asked.

"Big dick," I said, holding out my palms to indicate size and laughing. Lucia threw her head back in a laugh. Those same techs just about drew a scarlet 'A' on my chest.

"What?" I said to them, hands on my hips. "You guys talk

about tits all damn day long, and as soon as I mention dicks, I'm the pervert?"

They moved along, properly chastised, leaving Lucia and I alone by the table of drinks. Viking Man Bun was getting low on his beer, which meant he'd probably come over here. Soon.

"You staking out this territory?" Lucia asked.

"*Si.* How do I look?" I asked, striking a pose.

"Fucking divine. This dress is killer. As in could *literally* give a man a heart attack and kill him," she said, tugging it down a bit.

I swatted her hand away playfully. "Hands off the threads, *Mom*. Also, you know Calvin has been staring at you longingly this entire time, right?"

I was mostly joking, but she perked up a little, tossing her hair over her shoulder.

"You should go talk to him," I said. "He actually *does* seem nice. Nerdy, but nice."

"Not nice. Kind. He seems kind," she said, automatically.

"Well, get over there, *mija.* At this rate, he'll blush himself to death every time he accidentally locks eyes with you across the room."

"How do *I* look?" she asked genuinely, which was an odd thing about supermodels. Even they worried about looking good.

"You're giving every man in this room a massive boner," I said, "Now go." I gave her a little push, and she made a goofy face, sticking her tongue out. But she went, dutifully, and I watched her light up for Cal like I'd never seen her do for anyone else before.

The alcohol was finally making me feel a little loose. A little wanton. I mean, I *always* felt wanton, but there was something... something *about* this place. It was so beautiful, so free from the distractions of modern life. I'd felt my heart physically respond to it the moment we'd arrived.

It made me feel wild.

It made me feel reckless.

I caught the gaze of Viking Man Bun again, and this time, I held it. Calvin had left. Lucia had left. The Viking and I were separated by a throng of people, yet I could have sworn it was just the two of us.

When he began slowly walking across the patio, empty beer in hand, my breath caught in my throat. I was standing by the table, leaning against the wall, legs crossed in front of me showcasing the platform heels with leather laces that wound past my knees. And I actually *felt* when Viking Man Bun's eyes locked on those heels, felt his eyes glide up my ankles, my calves, the sensitive skin near my knees.

He stopped just short of my thighs (what a gentleman), but now he was looking right at me—staring actually—and a warning sign the size of Texas unfurled behind him.

When he grinned at me—a little crookedly—that warning sign lit up with fervor, attempting to get my attention. But I would have bet real money that my Viking didn't heed warnings—no, he'd charge ahead, first into battle, alive with adrenaline and bloodlust.

And tonight, I wouldn't heed warnings either.

## 7

## GABE

*Compulsion.*

Before tonight, I'd never truly understood the word. But staring at her across that patio, I was *compelled* to talk to this mysterious tattooed vixen.

I flashed her a small smile as I got closer. She merely tilted her head, eyes tracking up and down my body. A lioness, bemused at the antics of an antelope, seconds before sinking her teeth into its neck.

A dozen cool lines flitted through my head, but she didn't look the type to fall for them. So instead I went with a classic.

"I'm Gabriel, but you can call me Gabe," I said, holding out my hand. "Can I make you a drink?"

"Josefine," she replied, sliding her hand into mine. "But you can call me Josie. And I'm a beer-with-a-shot girl, which I'm pretty sure I can make myself."

She had a voice like midnight with a slight hint of an accent.

"A woman after my own heart," I replied, reaching into the cooler for two PBRs and a bottle of Jameson. I held them up and she nodded, smiling now.

"That'll do *just* fine." Josie sank onto the bench in the corner, directly in front of the fire, and beckoned me to join. She crossed her legs toward me, flashing smooth skin and bright ink. "And I just have to say… I like your bun."

I ran my hand over my hair self-consciously, shrugged. "It's been like this for years."

"I'm not teasing," she smiled. "It fits you."

"I like your tattoos," I said, indicating her bare arms and legs. "They fit you."

"Thank you," she said. She paused then, looking me up and down. "*Me gusta tu barba. Vikingo.*"

"I *am* incredibly handsome."

"Big ego," she said, laughing. "And all I said was that I *also* liked your beard."

"I'm like this all over my body, I'm afraid," I said, loving the way her laughter lit her up from the inside like a lamp being turned on in a darkened room.

"Ah, a hirsute hunk?" She asked.

Who *was* this woman?

"Fancy word for hairy. I like it," I said. Behind me, I heard Calvin's laughter. I turned to see Lucia leaning in, clearly flirting with him.

"Are you as intrigued by them as I am?" Josie asked, and I nodded.

"Absolutely. I've known Calvin ever since he moved here, and he's one of a kind. Definitely deserving of love."

"You think that's what's happening there?" she asked softly.

I ran my hand down my jaw. "Who knows? But I'm already rooting for them." I watched them again for a minute. There was a comfort there, like two lovers meeting after years apart.

"How do you know Lucia?"

"She's my best friend. And I'm also her makeup artist. We

met when she was fifteen, on her first set and fucking terrified. I chatted her ear off, attempted to teach her Spanish. Took her mind off of what was happening." She smiled at the memory. "The rest was history. As often as she can, Lucia asks for me to be on set with her."

I looked at Josie, at the tattoos and piercings and beautifully orchestrated *color* that wandered along her skin. "You're an artist," I said, and her eyebrow arched.

"Yes. Makeup artists are indeed *artists*."

"Of course," I said, surprised at the passion in my voice. "Your canvas is just different than another artist's. But it's still a canvas, right?"

Her eyes widened a little. "That's... well, that's how I feel about it. Because I love it. And it makes me... feel alive."

Golden tendrils of light sparked from the fire.

"I get it, I totally get it," I said. "I'm a bartender here in Big Sur. At The Bar."

"Is that its name?"

"Well, yes... my grandfather first owned and named it. But no one remembers the name anymore, and it's really the only dive bar in town, so the name stuck. It's a place for locals, not a tourist attraction. So I own it, run it. Work the bar most nights. There's an apartment on the second floor, which is where I live. In fact, my family and I lived there until I turned ten."

"That's some dedication," Josie said seriously, and I nodded my head. Shifted an inch closer to her on the bench.

"I got my business degree in Monterey, and the other students were constantly dismissing my profession."

"Why?"

I shrugged. "From their limited perspective, bartenders are uneducated and lack ambition. Except, for better or worse, this is my family *legacy*. It's an institution in our community, same as this bookstore. I feel proud to work there. Does that make sense?"

Josie laughed a little. "Yes… I mean, fuck *yes*. It's infuriating when people put down your profession. I used to…" she trailed off. "I was close to this person in my life once, and they thought what I did was *low class*. I'll never forget that feeling. Of them dismissing something I'd worked my entire life to build."

There was a long pause while Josie and I stared at each other, and *fuck* those eyes were going to be my undoing. I could feel it. Taste it in the air.

"I think we should take a shot," I said slowly, turning to grab two shot glasses from behind me. "What do you think?"

"We seem to be on the same page about a lot of things," she said.

My hands tightened on the bottle as I poured it, suddenly nervous to complete a task I'd done at least five thousand times in my life. When I handed her the glass, the tips of our fingers brushed together.

"To Big Sur," she said, knocking her glass against mine before taking her shot like a frat boy on spring break.

"You know, some people *savor* whiskey," I teased, taking a pointed sip.

"I think you'll discover that I'm not that kind of girl, Gabriel."

"What kind of girl are you?" I asked as firelight danced between us. That cool gaze assessed me once more, and I shivered beneath it.

"The kind of girl that takes it all at once."

# 8

# JOSIE

Up close, Viking Man Bun—Gabriel—was all *warmth.* Warmth and ease: easy grins, constant laughter, and a total comfort in his skin. He belonged in Big Sur, he belonged with these people: it all but radiated from his skin.

The whiskey was still sliding down my throat when Gabe's eyes landed back on mine.

"Tell me more about what you do. About what you love."

I opened my mouth to say something snarky. But then closed it. Thought for a moment. This was the strangest conversation-before-a-one-night-stand I'd ever had. Typically, these moments were one-dimensional for me. *Where do you work? Do you have siblings? How about pets*?

Gabe was different.

"Everything," I finally said honestly. "The color, the texture, the constant excitement. There's nothing like the rush of doing makeup for a runway show in Milan—the speed, the adrenaline, the sense of working together to create art on the human body."

"And you've always done this?" he asked.

"Always," I replied, finger stroking my shot glass. "I remember the day I graduated from high school so clearly: my gown, how hot the stage was, sitting with my friends and wondering what in the ever-loving-fuck I was going to do next. They were going off to college to study something general like business or psychology." I bit my lip. "I knew it wasn't for me. Not at *all*. So I worked during the day at the Clinique makeup counter at the mall in downtown Los Angeles. And at night, I took cosmetology classes."

I shrugged, laughing a little. "Obviously there are long days. Hard-to-please clients who I want to stab in the face with an eyebrow pencil. Depending on the set, the job can be absolutely thrilling—or incredibly tedious. But really, even dream jobs have a fair amount of bullshit, don't you think?"

"Of course," Gabe nodded. "I love being a bartender with every fiber of my being. And some days, I want to punch every customer in their goddamn stupid face."

"See?" I grinned. "You get it."

"I get it," he admitted. "And I wouldn't change it for all the money in the world."

"All the magnificent things outweigh the bad. I had a..." I paused for a second, took a sip of beer. "I had kind of a shit couple of years recently and found that makeup was very meditative. Whatever terrible things were awaiting me after the job—loneliness, sadness, anxiety—in the moment, all I needed to do was carefully apply mascara to every single eyelash on a woman's face. Do you know what I mean?"

Gabe's eyes searched mine for a moment, but he didn't press. "For me? Hand-drying glasses."

"Really?"

"Absolutely," he said, lips quirking up. They looked full and soft beneath his beard. "Towards the end of the night, when I'm starting to get tired and customers are fading fast, the simple act of drying a glass with a towel is oddly calming."

"Yes," I said, laying my hand on his arm before I could stop myself. I felt a burst of electricity when our skin touched, but I quickly removed it. "That's it exactly." I noticed a few people were starting to leave the patio, but I felt glued to this spot. This moment. "Tell me more about Big Sur."

Gabe sighed, leaned back against the low wall and turned to me with a good-natured smile. "I've lived here my entire life. Born and raised. The Shaw family were some of the original homesteaders here. In fact, The Bar used to be an old school for the children of lumber workers at the turn of the century. Living in Big Sur was even harder then. It was even more isolated, even more removed from society. Your relationship to the wilderness was one of *partnership*." He stroked his thumb across his lip, thinking. "That pioneering spirit is alive and well here, just mixed in with a bunch of artists and farmers and poets and people who live off the land. Some kids still ride donkeys to school, down from the mountain."

"I thought donkeys only existed on television," I smirked. "I'm a city girl. The only way I've *ever* gotten to school was on a crowded bus stuck in smoggy traffic."

"I think you're the antithesis of Big Sur, Josie," Gabe said, eyes trailing up and down my body. I looked down at my ripped dress, my vibrant tattoos.

"You're probably right," I laughed. "And *you're* the antithesis of Los Angeles."

He winked at me, and my heart tripped over itself. "I think that's awfully true."

I leaned a little closer to his body heat, still not touching but almost. Almost.

"You're so passionate," I said.

Gabe arched an eyebrow at me. "Not a lot of people want

to listen to me talk about lumber workers from the early 1900s. It's not exactly..." He trailed off, looking down.

"Not exactly what?" I nudged his leg.

"Romantic," he finally said, eyes on my mouth.

That word cut right through me.

"Well that's where you're wrong, Gabriel," I said, reaching past him to grab the Jameson. "I could talk about lumber workers for *days*."

He laughed, and the moment lightened. I topped off his shot glass and my own.

"I could do that for you," he said, reaching for the bottle. "It's technically my job."

"*Puedo verter esto por mi cuenta,*" I shrugged. "I'm an independent woman. I can pour this on my own."

I knocked my glass against his but sipped it instead. Savoring.

There was the hint of a grin on Gabe's face before he took his shot like a champ. He coughed a little.

"Amateur."

"Please," Gabe said, taking the bottle back from me. Another brush of fingers. "I grew up in a fucking *bar*."

I laughed at that, head thrown back, and when our eyes met again, his were bright with amusement.

"Enough of this getting-to-know-you," I said, waving my hand through the air. "Let's get down to brass tacks. The good stuff." I leaned in, giving him a suggestive glance. The amusement darkened, and for the first time, I saw real *lust*.

The warning sign was back, but I shoved it aside, even though the last time I'd ignored an instinct, Clarke had happened. But the lust in Gabe's expression was so *ardent*... ardent and hungry... at odds with the friendly, easy-going Viking sitting in front of me.

He had his lust under control. Leashed.

And the sudden thought of Gabe Shaw *unleashed*... out of control and savage with need, was enough to steal the breath right from my lungs.

*Holy shit.*

"Josie?" He asked, his rough palm landing on my bare knee. "Were you going to ask me something?"

My words faltered. "How do you... um, how do you take your coffee?"

## 9

## GABE

I could have sworn Josie was going to kiss me.

No, not kiss me. Josie was the kind of woman who'd knock our drinks to the floor, step over the glittering shards of glass, and straddle me in front of everyone at this party.

But then she'd pulled back. "How do you... um, how do you take your coffee?"

"Coffee is my life," I said slowly. "Might as well put it directly into my vein."

She grinned at that, relaxing.

"Same." She narrowed her eyes at me, tossing her hair. She had piercings up the entire right side of her earlobe, tiny pieces of metal that twinkled like starlight. "But how you take it is important."

I paused, considering her. "Cream and sugar."

Josie reached forward, topping off my glass. "Take that shot."

"Why?"

"Because you have terrible taste in coffee," she said,

laughing and knocking hers back. I did too, almost choking on it again, which made me laugh more.

"And how do *you* take your coffee?"

"Black, like you're supposed to."

"Says who?" I asked.

"*Everyone.*"

I shook my head in disbelief. "Before you leave Big Sur, I'm making you a cup of coffee with cream and sugar. And you're going to love it."

"Fuck, no," she drawled, teasing tone back in her voice. "And I'm leaving soon."

That reminder slammed into me harder than I was expecting. "When, exactly?"

"I go back to Los Angeles the day after tomorrow. Two more nights, then you'll never see me again."

She seemed to warm to this thought, and I wondered about the kind of relationships she'd had. "You miss the city that much? It's only been a couple of days, right?" I asked.

"But I've lived there my entire life. Born and raised, same as you. All of this," she said, waving her hand at the dark forest surrounding us, "is totally *new* to me. And kind of scary."

"Scary?" I asked. "No way. There's nothing scary about this place."

"But it's so *secluded*. Where are the people? The 24-hour diners and rowdy nightclubs and street-lights? There's an endless... energy that thrums through Los Angeles."

"There's energy here; it's just different. You don't feel it?" I asked.

She tilted her head, thinking. "I do feel it. A little."

"What does it feel like?"

Josie thought for a second, fingers tapping on her lip. There was a small bumblebee inked onto her middle finger and a moon and sun on her index and ring finger. "Big Sur feels... reckless."

"Reckless?" I asked.

"Like... wild. Out of control."

I nodded, starting to understand. "Absolutely. It's not contained or polite. You either accept Big Sur for what it is or..."

"Or what?"

I smiled. "You get the fuck out."

Josie laughed at that. "Sounds like some neighborhoods in L.A."

We were suddenly interrupted by Kevin, who cleared his throat loudly until we looked his way.

"Hey, Kev," I sighed, already knowing what this would be about.

"Oh, hey Gabe, I didn't see you there," he lied.

Josie flashed me a bemused expression.

"You heading home?" I purposefully didn't introduce the two of them—not that it would change anything at all.

"Yep, yep," Kevin said, shifting back and forth on his feet. "Yep." He gawked openly at Josie, widening his eyes at me.

"Well... I'm stopping by the post office tomorrow to send out some packages. I'll see you then?" I turned my attention back to Josie, indicating it was time for him to leave. Another awkward thirty seconds stretched out before he shuffled away.

"Let me guess," Josie said. "Kevin is a scorned lover?"

I laughed so loudly every remaining person on the patio glared at me. But I didn't care. "God, I wish I could say yes. But no. He runs the post office and is a true foot soldier for the Big Sur Channel."

Josie arched an eyebrow. "What's that?"

"The very intricate network of busybodies that carry forth the town gossip."

"Ah," she smiled. "They're curious about—" she pointed at the space between us.

"Absolutely."

"Do you gossip too?"

I opened my mouth to lie but couldn't. "Unfortunately... yes."

Josie shoved me a little.

I laughed again. "Comes with the job, I'm afraid. It's basically inherited. My grandfather was *the* Town Gossip. Then my dad and Cal's grandfather, Robert. They knew every single *thing* that happened in this town."

"People always talk too much to the bartender," Josie mused. "You must hear a lot of secrets."

"I do," I said. "Will you tell me some of yours?"

Something dark and mysterious flashed through her eyes. "Maybe. I'm not sure yet."

"That's okay," I said, wanting this night to go on forever, "I'll tell you some of mine."

## 10

## JOSIE

"If you spill your secrets to a near-stranger, are they still secrets?" I asked, finally allowing my thigh to press against his. A steady hum of sensation pulsed where our bodies touched.

"What do you mean?" he asked.

"I don't know... if you feel comfortable enough to share them with someone you don't know, doesn't that take away the *secretive* part?"

He narrowed his eyes, thought for a second. "I don't know. Why don't we drink and not worry about it?"

I laughed and responded by knocking back the shot I'd been carefully sipping. Massive head-rush, warmth pooling between my legs, nerve endings sparking to life under his gaze.

Gabe wasn't eye-fucking me.

No. It was more *sensual* than that. Just a continual, lingering perusal of every inch of my body. Over and over again. And somehow during the course of the evening, I'd flown past general arousal, flown past mild attraction and a way to pass the time—the two criteria I usually looked for in a one-night-stand.

This was something else entirely.

"I didn't have my first kiss until I was eighteen, the summer after high school," he said, blushing just a little.

"Um... what?"

"My first kiss. When did you have yours?"

"Fourteen."

"Who was it?"

"Ricky Something," I said. "He was actually two years older than me. We were at the mall, probably Hot Topic, and he said I had pretty eyes. Then he kissed me."

"And it was?"

"Absolutely awful," I groaned.

Gabe laughed.

"Tell me about yours."

"The first girl I ever kissed, Sasha, was actually the girl I ended up dating for almost seven years. Our last year of high school. All through college. A couple years after, here in Big Sur."

"Why so late?" I asked. "I guess I pictured you having a ton of girlfriends. You're... you know, *massive*. And handsome. And the beard..." I clamped my mouth shut, suddenly very aware that I was dropping my cool exterior.

"Late bloomer," he smiled. "I shot up six inches right before I left for college. Had nothing to do with lack of interest on my part, that's for sure. Although I don't know what girls in high school thought about me until Sasha. I'd just get so *nervous*. You know, in Big Sur, the one good thing is you can always underage-drink in the woods. Plenty of frisky business happened beneath these redwoods. Couples would pair off to awkwardly smash their mouths together, and I'd just be sitting on a log with my braces, trying not to throw up on the girl next to me."

I tried not to smile, thinking of this bearded hunk in front of me, as a scared, awkward teenager. "What changed? Why was eighteen different?"

He thought for a second. "She kissed me, I guess."

"You liked that she took the lead?" I asked before I could stop myself. An idea flared in my mind.

"I did," he said simply, gaze open and searching. "I really did."

His thumb landed on the inside of my wrist, and he stroked gently along the delicate skin. Up and then down.

"I bet you were cute with braces," I finally said, a distinct shake in my voice.

"I bet *you* were cute with braces," he grinned.

"Braces," I said, pointing at my teeth. "Bowl cut. *Huge* glasses. And I had no control over my artistic impulses, so I just wore, like, *all* of the colors. All at once. Always. Like I'd wear this hot yellow sweater I had with daisies on it with this polka-dot skirt and purple rain boots."

Another swipe of his thumb.

"I bet you were magnificent," he murmured, and my heart did this odd *thump-thump* I hadn't felt in two years.

"Weird," I corrected. "I was weird. Still kind of am."

"I like weird," he smiled. "And tell me more, please."

"I just told you all about my bowl cut," I teased.

But he shook his head. "Make it... I don't know, the most embarrassing thing that's ever happened to you. Bare your soul, Josefine."

Gabe was grinning and joking, but Big Sur was making me feel *reckless*, and his kindness was pressing on all the delicate, tender spots of my life that I kept hidden. I wanted to slip up, to deliver the ultimate mood-killer:

*The most embarrassing thing to ever happen to me? Try being stood up at your own wedding. Not months before or even weeks before. No. At the fucking altar, in the dress, as your parents are about to walk you down the aisle.* The memory caused a swirl of nausea—it always did, even two years later—and I wanted to spill my secrets to this Viking. Cry against his barrel chest and let him sweep me to safety.

But I didn't. And I wouldn't.

"I hate macaroni and cheese," I finally said.

Gabe pointed his finger toward the woods. "Get out," he said.

I grinned, wiggling my shoulders. "You said *secrets*. And I never tell people that one."

"So you made fun of me for liking *cream* in my coffee? But you *fucking hate macaroni and cheese*?"

I sighed, looked away for a second. "Okay. If you asked me what my favorite music was, I'd tell you old-school hip-hop and punk rock. But *secretly*... I want to dance to Top 40 all night long."

"Pop music? You sell-out."

"Beyoncé just *gets me*," I said, placing a hand on my chest, and his laughter was like a drug. "Now you go. That's all of my secrets."

*Liar.*

"I don't have any social media pages," he said.

"Why not?"

A shrug. "The longer you go without the internet, especially social media, the more you realize you don't need them. The more you realize how *distracting* it is. Or for me, I was slowly shifting my decision-making to try and impress people online. People I didn't even really care about, like, old high school friends or acquaintances from college. But I don't want to live my life like that. Does that make sense?"

I thought about Lucia, whose followers sometimes dictated what color she dyed her hair or criticized every single flaw they found on her body. "It does. And I think you're right. Social media can contribute to this pressure to... conform. Do what everyone else is doing. I'm sure at least half of the decisions I make are automatic."

Gabe was nodding. "Exactly. And the longer I stayed away, the more liberating it became. And maybe part of it is living in Big Sur versus a big city like Los Angeles, but it *is* easier to avoid toxic shit up here. When I'm not at The Bar, I spend a lot of time hiking. And this place is so awe-inspiring; the scenery is so overpowering, it takes you out of your immediate anxieties or worries about 'measuring up' to other people. I've had a lot of sudden realizations on long hikes because my thoughts are free to roam without distraction."

He paused, suddenly looking embarrassed. "Again... not really *romantic* conversation." His thumb stroked my wrist in a wide circle but more deliberately.

I shook my head. "Nature as therapy. I'd like to try that, actually."

"Yeah?" he asked, looking hopeful.

"I mean... sometime. Not on this trip," I said lightly, directing us away from the future. We only had this night. This time. "Tell me one more secret."

Gabe looked down where his thumb kept circling my wrist. We watched the movement together, and then he slowly dragged his thumb up the inside of my arm and then back down again. My eyes briefly fluttered closed.

Such a *reverent* touch. Except every stroke, every drag, I felt between my legs. As if his thumb was on my clit, gently and slowly working me to climax.

There was no one else left on the patio. I had no concept of time. Only sensation.

"I've always wanted to be married. Always wanted to be a husband," Gabe finally said, looking up at me. I swallowed hard.

"A true romantic," I said, wondering how this was possible. Since Clarke, I avoided men like Gabe, men who wanted to sweep me off my feet, overwhelm me with romantic gestures. And yet here I was, desperately trying to fuck this man who loved romance.

"Do you believe in love at first sight?" I asked.

"I don't know," he said with a wry smile. "My parents were high school sweethearts, and I always loved the idea of growing old with someone you'd known for your entire life. Falling in love with someone and then watching them change and grow, discover themselves over the course of a lifetime." He paused. "I always thought a relationship like that would be beautiful."

"But?" I asked, sensing his hesitation.

"But... I thought that was Sasha. *Really* thought that was her. And then we broke up, and I despaired of ever finding..." he trailed off, looked away. "Of ever finding the person I'm supposed to be with."

Gabe replaced his thumb with two fingers, trailed them down my palm. Up and down my fingers. In a trance, I watched as my Viking lifted my hand to his lips and pressed a gentle kiss against the inside of my wrist.

"Do you believe in love at first sight?" He asked.

"No," I said. "I'm not sure I believe in love, at least not for me." A look of shock came over his face, but he recovered quickly. "I think love is for other people. I *want* love for other people. But I plan on living my life one amazing, earth-shattering one-night stand at a time. *Fucking* is what I believe in."

The tension between us shifted from flirtatious to urgent

need. I flipped my hand over, the one he'd been touching, and laid it high on his muscular thigh. His eyes darkened.

"Let's keep talking secrets then," he said, a new scrape to his voice. "Secret fantasies."

"You go first," I said, letting my fingers dance up his thigh. I could already see the hard outline of his cock, straining against his jeans.

"I want to fuck a woman in public."

I arched an eyebrow. "Because you want to get caught? Or you like the idea of people watching you as you fuck?"

"Both," he said but didn't elaborate.

My fingers danced higher. "I want two men to fuck me at once." I threw whatever remaining caution I had to the wind.

This night was happening.

"How?" he asked but didn't demand.

"At the same time. I want double penetration. A cock in my pussy. A cock in my ass."

"I'd like to watch that," he whispered, his hands tightening on the bench.

"Yeah?"

"Yes," he growled. "I want to watch your fantasy come true. See your pleasure." He swallowed. "Watch you take two cocks at once."

"I'd allow it," I teased. "Now you go."

"I want to fuck two women at once," he said, eyes tracking the movements of my fingers. His thigh was flexing beneath my touch.

"Can I be one of those women?"

"Fuck yes," he said, that tight leash unraveling right before my eyes. I was pushing him, and I loved it.

"What would you do?"

"Let you ride me while some sexy little tease sat on my face. I'd want you to watch her."

"Watch her what?" I taunted.

"Come."

We were both panting, leaning closer and closer. Not touching except for my wandering hands. His cock looked huge and *so fucking hard,* and I'd never wanted to grip something more in my entire life.

"I've always wanted to fuck a woman with nipple piercings," he said.

I grinned lazily. Tossed my hair. Because he noticed, and I fucking loved it.

"You've got a real eye for detail," I purred. "And you're in luck since I got my nipples pierced the day after I turned 18."

His eyes were back on mine, locked in a battle of wills. We were two predators, circling the other. Looking for weaknesses.

"What does it feel like? What does it feel like when they're sucked on?"

"Heaven on Earth," I said.

He groaned audibly, the sound hitting me in the gut. Christ, he was sexy. I was waiting for him to demand another secret from me, but I realized he wasn't going to.

He was waiting.

On me.

I thought about my ultimate fantasy. The one I'd never tried, never attempted, but that captivated my imagination, burning me up in my dreams.

I'd said it out loud to Clarke, only once, and he'd laughed at me. Cruelly. *You don't have what it takes*, he'd said, and that mean voice was lodged somewhere in my brain.

I wanted to crush it.

"I've always wanted to dominate a man," I said firmly, chin tilted, expecting Gabe to brush it off too. He was big and confident, and my gut instinct was that he was a total alpha in bed, dominating the women he fucked, yanking their hair back as he took them on their hands and knees.

Gabe stared at me for a long time.

"That's interesting," he finally said. "Because I've always wanted to be dominated."

## 11

## GABE

The images came back to me. Those middle-of-the-night-fantasies I'd never told anyone about. A bite of pain. My knees pressed to the floor. Sharp commands.

And now here was Josie, fingers an inch from my cock, expressing a secret desire for the *exact same thing.* My brain fought to catch up with my reality.

"How long have you... how long have you thought about this?" I asked.

"For as long as I can remember," she whispered. "Too long, Gabe."

Josie nudged the tip of her shoe up the side of my calf. Then flexed, her spike heel digging into my skin.

I didn't think it was possible. But my cock grew harder.

I hissed in a breath. Josie noticed. Her fingers slid higher, *just* brushing my cock.

"How about you?" she asked.

I nodded slowly, more aroused than I'd ever been. More fucking *alive.* "I think about it every day."

And suddenly Josie was on her knees, leaning toward me.

Hovering those gorgeous lips over mine. "Then I think we should explore this fantasy. Don't you?"

On pure instinct, I reached forward, curling my fingers around the base of her neck. Our eyes were locked intimately, breath synced. Tension about to snap.

I wanted to explore this fantasy. I fucking *needed* to.

But just as quickly, a memory slid harshly through my thoughts. Taking home that woman for lackluster, impersonal sex. The lingering loneliness of the next morning. Already, Josie felt like something *more* than that. Right now, we were a fire about to spark. A match about to be struck.

And the thought of losing that was more painful than delaying this pleasure.

"Wait," I said, removing my fingers.

She stopped. "What's wrong?"

"Nothing," I assured. "Absolutely nothing. But I… aren't you here for one more night?"

She looked startled at the abrupt change in tone. "Um… yeah. Tomorrow night, then we leave."

I nodded, a plan forming in my mind. "Then let's wait until tomorrow."

Josie sank further back, brow furrowed. "Why?"

My cock couldn't *believe* what I was saying, but it felt right.

"Let me chase you, Josie. Just for tomorrow. Just for one day."

"*Chase* me?" she asked, disbelieving.

"Yes. Chase you. Make it more like… a date."

Josie stood up, reaching for her purse. "I don't date, Gabe. I fuck, and that's it."

I reached for her wrist, stilling her. "Then, *shit*, okay, we won't call it a date. But… come hang out with me on your last night. At The Bar. We can spend all night acting out this fantasy we've both had for years."

Josie looked like she wanted to say something. Started to. Stopped. Bit her lip and looked away.

So I stood up, backing her against the nearest wall, both hands on either side of her head. Not touching but almost.

"I'm not blowing you off, Josie," I promised, ghosting my lips over her ear. She shuddered, arching toward me. "Not at all. Just the opposite, in fact. I don't want to rush this."

And then I pulled back. "Don't you think waiting makes it that much better? That much *sweeter*?"

I wanted her to see. Wanted her to see that she might just be a stranger passing through but she deserved more.

A myriad of expressions flooded her gaze. Disbelief. Annoyance. Worry, although I couldn't figure out *why*. Had something happened to put her guard up?

"Josie," I whispered, waiting for her answer. She swallowed, shifting from unsure to *decisive*. Gave me a long look, eyes trailing down my body. Landing on my cock. With deft skill, she reached down and palmed me through my jeans. Gripped tightly and slowly jerked her fingers up.

I almost broke the wall in half.

"Waiting," she repeated, giving me a half-stroke.

"Yes," I growled. "Please."

It was the *please* that did it. Josie stroked me again, and my eyes closed with pleasure.

"Look at me," she snapped, and they flew open.

"We can delay," she said slowly as she worked my aching cock. "We can *delay* all night, Gabriel. Because tomorrow?" Josie leaned closer, lips hovering over mine. "Tomorrow I'm going to put you on your knees for hours. Make you eat this pussy until I tell you to stop. And if you think I'm going to let *you* come..."

She pulled her fingers back from my cock, and I groaned in frustration, forehead landing on hers.

"Then what?" I whispered. "What next?"

She let me wait like that, drawing it out. And even though I wanted to fuck her through the wall, this was better.

So much better.

Her midnight eyes met mine.

"You'll just have to wait and find out," she said, eyebrow arched. "Won't you?"

## 12

## GABE

As soon as I walked into Big Sur's tiny post office, *everyone* wanted to know about the Hollywood People.

"I don't have much," I said, laughing and holding up my palms in acquiescence. "And Calvin has asked me to ask all of *you* to please stop spying on the models through the front window."

Gladys smirked. "I don't think that's a crime. Plus, my binoculars broke when I was watching my neighbor the other day. My only option is to hide in the bushes."

"Trespassing," I said, throwing a wink her way. "Definitely a crime, I'm afraid."

She rolled her eyes at me and continued stacking piles of mail on the desk.

"Your father wasn't such a rule follower, you know," she said. "And neither was Calvin's grandfather. They used to love when we spied on their goings-on."

That was something I seriously doubted.

Next to her, Gloria hooted. "You just like that one with the abs," she said. Then, turning to her customer, a red-faced tourist by the looks of it: "Stamps? Sending a package?"

As the customer stumbled through their answer, I leaned against the counter. If I had questions about how to properly court a woman, even for a day, these two would have the answer, but involving them would mean the Big Sur Channel would know *everything*.

But I could take that bullet for Josie.

"What bodice-ripping hero are you reading about today?" I asked.

"Feign innocence, Gladys," Gloria said. She turned to me, waving aside the customer like an annoying fly. "Sir, I'm not sure what you're referring to. My sister and I are simply lowly desk jockeys, proud to serve the United States Postal Service."

I bit my cheek to keep from laughing. "When do the two of you have your break?"

"Whenever the fuck we want," Gloria drawled. Gladys nodded seriously.

Behind them, Kevin threw his hands up in the air, exasperated.

"We do have about a dozen customers waiting in line. But I guess that's fine," Kevin said with all the sarcasm he could muster. He looked a little rough around the edges, and I guessed he'd had more to drink than me at the party last night.

"Great, we'll see you over there," Gladys said, nodding at the counter—which was literally five feet from where I was standing. In unison, they both put up their 'line closed' signs, grabbed their iced coffees, and slid over to the smaller counter.

"So I'm guessing you want to tell us the *real* gossip," Gloria whispered, sipping through her straw with wide eyes.

I shook my head, wondering if I was about to do something monumentally stupid.

"It's about a girl," I started, and before I could even get the next words out, I felt a presence by my side.

"Is it about the purple-haired girl?"

I turned to find Kevin hovering an inch from me.

"Christ, we need a movie theater in this town," I said, turning around and noticing that most of the customers were listening in. I shot the sisters a desperate glance, and Gloria propped a hand on her hip.

"Kevin, there's about *a dozen customers* in line, but I guess it's fine you're just standing here," she said.

"I'll just call your dad about it later," he said, scurrying back behind the counter.

I turned back around, glancing at my watch. "I need your best work, ladies," I said.

My heart was stumbling at the memory of the last time I'd had a conversation like this. Sasha had surprised me one day, asking for some space to 'consider our future.' I'd come to the sisters, totally in shock, trying to find a way to woo her back. I hoped romance and grand gestures would be the key to keeping her—and the sisters had whipped up something lovely. A moonlit dance on the beach, wine in a thermos, a picnic blanket on the sand. And yet when the three of us had planned it, the sisters had seemed… hesitant. Asking me questions, trying to pull out the things I loved, specifically, about Sasha. What made her my soulmate.

Gladys, specifically, had come right out and demanded to know why I hadn't just proposed to her already—it'd been almost seven years.

And I hadn't had a good answer.

Later when I came crawling back (Sasha had broken up with me on that same beach, and it was *awful*), they'd exchanged quick, mysterious glances as I told the story. They'd never specifically said 'I told you so,' but the loss of that relationship knocked me into an emotional tailspin for a long time.

And I hadn't dated a woman longer than a month since then.

"Details," Gladys said, snapping her fingers.

"Funny, weird, artsy, makeup artist from Los Angeles," I said. "Her name is Josie."

"What does she look like?"

*Like a punk-rock dominatrix sent to make all my fantasies come true.*

"A little... alternative," I said. Even though Big Sur was filled with alternative people, it was more 'I live off the land' and less 'I have a metal bar through my nose.'

"And her hair is only purple at the ends."

"Have you kissed her yet?"

"Absolutely not," I said, and dual sets of eyebrows raised in surprise.

"And how long is she here for?" They were scribbling down notes.

"One more night," I said as they scribbled. I tried to read what they were writing, but they shooed me away.

"Let the masters work," Gloria said, tapping the pen against her chin. I looked back at Kevin, scowling as he checked out customers. But they were all locals, and they were *all* listening.

"Does anyone else have something to say?" I said. "Or ask?"

Rex, whose family had owned a cattle farm for four generations, crossed his arms over his chest. "Is the purple-haired girl a Satanist? Kevin told me she had tattoos. Lots of 'em."

Next to him Rosalie, an old friend of Isabelle's, bit her lip in concern. I shot a glance at Kevin, who shrugged.

"At this point, I can neither confirm nor deny allegations of Josie's Satan-worshiping activities," I deadpanned, but no one laughed. I needed to give them a breadcrumb.

*Sorry, Calvin.*

"You know, Cal and Lucia, that super model, were getting kind of cozy, too," I said, already forming the apology I'd need to say later. Because of his grandfather's status, Cal was treated like a local. But emotionally, I wasn't sure if his delicate Silicon Valley sensibilities could handle the full force of the Big Sur Channel.

The customers erupted in excited chatter. I turned back to the sisters, who were smugly crossing their arms.

Sliding the paper my way, Gladys slammed her pen down and took a long, celebratory sip from her coffee. "You're heading to the florist, doll."

## 13

## JOSIE

I stared at the bouquet of flowers like it was a bomb about to go off.

When I'd opened my cabin door to a shy teenager, sheepishly holding a vase of irises, I thought Lucia had sent them.

But the card was from Gabe: *You don't seem like a girl who likes roses. So I chose something that looked most like a work of art."*

He was right. I hated roses—too traditional. But the periwinkle irises were cheerful-looking and unique, their bright yellow centers like something Monet would paint.

*Let me chase you.*

I'd stumbled home from Calvin's patio barely six hours earlier and tossed and turned all night.

Anticipation had kept me awake. Because Gabe was right—waiting made it all the more delicious.

Now, staring at his card, I couldn't stop the flutter in my stomach. Excitement and nerves.

I had a fucking crush.

Who I'd be seeing tonight *and only for tonight*. And it was okay. It'd been two years since Clarke. Surely my bruised heart could handle a little crush. Middle schoolers had crushes for fuck's sake.

Plus, this crush was going to drop to his fucking knees at my command tonight.

Really it was just a sex-crush.

Which was fine.

Another tentative knock at the door: the same sheepish teenager, this time with a bouquet of wildflowers.

"Again?" I asked, scooping the bouquet from him.

Another card. This one said: *I can't stop thinking about kissing you.*

Goddammit.

"How many more you got?" I asked, craning my neck around the delivery boy. In the distance, I saw another three bouquets lined up. All bright and colorful. All different.

"All for me?" I asked, and the messenger nodded.

"Yeah. I'm supposed to deliver them every half hour."

"Well, the cat's out of the bag, kid. Why don't you just give them to me now?"

He shook his head. "He said you'd say that. And he said I'm supposed to remind you that you're being chased."

Viking Man Bun was going to be my fucking kryptonite.

I rolled my eyes to the sky. Lucia wasn't going to believe this.

"Okay, then. See you in thirty," I finally said, closing the door in the kid's face.

*I can't stop thinking about kissing you.*

I'd spent the entirety of my first date with Clarke wanting him to kiss me. We'd met the day before, in line for coffee, and I thought he was cute. Like really fucking cute. I didn't go on a lot of dates back then, but when he'd asked me out, I found myself nodding like an obedient dog.

He didn't kiss me. Not on the first date. Or the second. Or

the third. I recognize it now as all part of his game. Clarke *loved* the game. Loved it when women were fawning and desperate for his affection. On the fourth date, I kissed him.

He was actually a terrible kisser, but I ignored that crucial detail.

One of many things I ended up ignoring.

But he'd always remind me that I'd made the first move: "I was just trying to be your friend. *You're* the one who took it to the next level," he'd say. He loved to tell this story to friends, to watch women swoon and men laugh. On the surface, it was an adorable story of how we met.

But as our relationship grew more intense—as red flags flared to life almost daily—it became a subtle jab, his way of reminding me that the stress and anxiety I now carried like a heavy cloak was my own fault.

*You wanted this.*

*This was your choice, not mine.*

As if I'd been stringing *him* along this entire time.

Before Clarke, I cultivated my independence dearly. I'd watched my four older brothers achieve their professional dreams without help from my parents, and I *wanted* that. To rely on myself. I paid my own way through beauty school, working the Clinique counter. Shared a two-bedroom apartment with four other women. I had a dream, and nothing would stop me from working for it.

Before Clarke, I'd flirted and kissed and danced with boys at clubs, but that was as far as I wanted to go. Marriage was something your parents did. I was too busy having my picture taken by the paparazzi with Lucia outside a club at four in the morning, too busy saying 'fuck it' to anything serious.

Three months into dating Clarke, as I left my apartment to move into his shittier one, I'd spend the day anxiously waiting for him to say "jump" so I could plead "how high?"

I got up and paced around the tiny cabin, finally throwing open the door to the view of the ocean to get some air. I'd grown up around the ocean, but this was different. No boardwalk, no rollerbladers or body builders or people blaring their radios on this beachfront... this ocean was raw and rocky. Dark thunderclouds threatened rain in the distance, and I shivered as I thought about what a storm would do to those waves. It was the same feeling I'd had last night.

*I can't stop thinking about kissing you.*

Big Sur felt like a beautiful danger.

The messenger stood awkwardly behind me with the remaining bouquets.

"Do you need anything? Coffee? Water?" I asked him.

"No, ma'am," he said, looking at his watch. "I'll just be here, waiting."

"Do you have a name?"

"It's Peter, ma'am. Nice to meet you."

I nodded as a flurry of nerves roared up my spine. Settling onto a rock, I watched the waves crash against the shore, over and over. I needed to get on set. I needed to distract myself with colors and textures and Lucia's calming presence.

I needed to fuck the ever-loving shit out of Viking Man Bun, toss those bouquets off this cliff, and get the hell out of Big Sur.

---

PETER and I walked through the forest toward The Mad Ones. The wind was picking up, slicing through the trees, and my delivery boy refused to let me carry the remaining bouquets.

"So I'm guessing you know Gabe?" I finally asked, picking my way gingerly over roots and leaves.

"Oh, sure," he said. "Everyone knows Gabe. And his family."

"Is he... like, is he a nice guy?" I asked. One thing I'd learned from Clarke. I only knew Clarke was nice because he'd *told* me, over and over again. But when you sought outside references—friends, coworkers, family—there were a scant few who could honestly say he was a good guy.

Because he didn't really have friends, and he was a total dick to his coworkers.

"*Gabe?*" Peter said with such incredulity I got a sick feeling in my stomach. *I knew it.*

"So he's an asshole," I said. "Also sorry for cursing. You're a child, basically. Or are you?"

"I'm seventeen," he said, lifting his chin the way all teenagers do when you refer to them as children. "And I curse all the time. And Gabe is the nicest motherfucker I know."

"Can you clarify this declarative statement? Do you have examples, experiences, et cetera?"

Peter shrugged. "Big Sur's a small town. *Really* small. And Gabe's family is like royalty here. But not... *fancy*; just, I don't know, everywhere. His dad was on the city council, and he's done a lot to help people. Gabe's brother and his girlfriend both teach at the elementary school. Gabe's sister lives in Monterey, but she and her wife are always out for community events, raising money. That kind of thing."

"Good examples," I said, impressed. "Go on."

"Gabe *is* Big Sur. He knows the history; he really cares about it. He's really nice and always wants to help, and he's funny, and all of my sisters think he's hot."

I was starting to wish I hadn't asked Peter for clear-cut examples. And I was starting to wonder if acting out my most secret sexual fantasies with a man who was also sweet, gentle, and kind was really that smart of an idea.

"Thank you, Peter," I said as we approached the bookstore. "I respect your honesty. Now I have to go to work. Are you going to give me the remaining bouquets or what?"

Peter pulled out a piece of paper from his pocket. Read it. Put it back. "Ma'am—"

"Josie, please. Let's not be so formal," I said, sardonically.

*"Josie,* Gabe said you'd say that as well because you're impatient and stubborn, just like him. And I'm supposed to remind you that—" he looked back down at the paper —"you're being chased. Get used to it."

I bristled, ignoring the strange sensations the words were eliciting.

"Do you want to come in and wait?"

But Peter shook his head, settling on a chair on the patio, taking out a book. "Only three left. Not so bad."

I lifted my eyes skyward and then walked inside the bookstore. Lucia was standing in the middle of the room, wearing a tiny robe, hands propped on her hips.

*"¿Dónde estuviste anoche?"* she asked with a sly grin.

I laid my black bag on the table, slowly unrolling my array of tools and colors.

"First, coffee," I said, indicating the makeup chair. She plopped into it obediently. "And then I'll tell you about my night."

## 14

## JOSIE

I flipped through my notebook and let the sounds of a hectic set wash over me. I was loving Big Sur, but I missed the rush of people and sounds and ideas that usually filled my senses.

"So, today, we're doing that white gauze-thing, right?" I asked, tilting up Lucia's face and turning around to the wardrobe stylists who were busily steaming layers of fabric.

"Yes," Ray said, immediately walking over and looking as overwhelmed as ever. "My inspiration today is..." he paused, thinking, as Lucia and I both sighed. "Summer-of-love wild child stumbles into this quaint book store. Looking for..."

"Sex?" I interjected since Shay Miller had a certain *predilection* for fashion that skimmed the edge of X-rated.

Ray snapped his fingers. "Absolutely. How'd you know?"

"Well, they're rubbing Taylor down with baby oil, so..." I said.

Lucia looked behind her.

"Can I get that?" she asked.

Ray rolled his eyes at us. "Just sex her up," he said.

I gave him a salute. "Promiscuous hippie, you got it," I said, unrolling my bag. Ray scurried away as I started to clean Lucia's face.

"Speaking of *promiscuous,*" Lucia whispered, and I shushed her.

"Later, *mija*," I whispered back. "When we take our break." I swept on a base foundation as Joanna, our hair stylist, began to weave tiny white flowers through Lucia's braids. "So sticking to Ray's subtle theme, I was thinking a sixties mod look for you today. Cat-eye eyeliner and a nude lip. What do you think?"

"You're the boss," she said, nervously coughing into her hand when Calvin walked by. He blushed furiously, then walked back behind the desk.

"Huh," I said, moving the sponge down her cheekbones, lightly covering her skin. "How ya doin', champ? Is there anything you need to tell me about *your* night?"

Lucia sat still as a stone as I worked. "Nope," she said, fighting, and failing, to keep from smiling. "I mean, I'll tell you when we take our break."

I pinched her, and she squealed. "You're fucking *feisty* today."

I grabbed a flat eyeliner brush, leaning close to layer on a thick strip of black across the top of Lucia's lashes. Gliding the black ink in a perfectly curved line was soothing. I did it again and again, flaring the line. I moved to her right lid and did the same thing, curling the eyeliner into that famous cat-eye shape.

"Open," I said, and Lu fluttered her eyes open, smiling up at me.

"Gorgeous," I said, and she was, her dark-blue eyes deepening beneath the black of the liner. I knocked some brightening powder into the palm of my hand, rolled a brush through it, and started dabbing along the inside of her eye.

"And I guess that party last night was *interesting* for both of us."

"It was an excellent opportunity to... get to know some people. Better."

I thought of Gabe, our night of teasing, silly conversation. I hadn't felt that... *buoyant* in a long time. Or that compelled to talk to a man I was just planning to fuck. Fuck and then leave.

Grabbing blush, I filled the palm of my hand with it, swirling the color. Held it up to Lucia's cheek. Another thing I used to calm myself after Clarke: blending. Something so subtle and almost magical about the quest for perfection. Right after the almost-wedding, I'd booked a now-famous model who was known for the patches of discoloration on her face and arms, and it became my ultimate goal to blend the perfect colors for her beautiful skin. Not hiding the differentiation but honoring it, bringing it to light.

She'd cried when she'd seen herself before her first runway show, and that moment had been the first tiny, jarring step I'd taken towards healing.

"Josie?" Lucia asked, reaching out to touch my wrist. I looked up, realizing I'd been lost in thought as I swirled pink powder obsessively.

And that's when Peter showed up with a bouquet of pale peonies, eyes wide and staring at Lucia in utter awe.

I exhaled loudly since Lu was never going to let this go. "I'm guessing those are for me?"

"Um... um... um," he said.

Lucia winked at him. He almost dropped the bouquet, but I caught it.

"Slow down, Romeo," I said, setting them on the table. Lucia reached forward to read the card, but I slapped her hand away. "You've got two more, right?"

He nodded, gulping.

"I'll see you in thirty," I said, nodding toward the door, and he walked backward toward it before tripping over a cord on the floor.

"Cute," Lucia said, giving me the kind of best-friend-look that said 'you are so full of bullshit.'

"Coffee break?" I asked since it would be better to just get it over with.

"Please," she replied.

---

OUTSIDE, it had gotten colder. Rain was steadily dripping through the trees. We huddled together beneath the overhang, shivering and wrapped in a blanket.

"So... the bouquets."

"They're going to keep coming," I said, wincing at the note of excitement in my voice. "Five total. One every half hour." I was desperate to see the note on the peonies.

"*Josie*," Lucia squealed, shoving my shoulder. "He's a total sweetheart. And he's got the hots for you, for sure. Did you go home with him last night?" She leaned in closer. "Did you go to the *bone zone*?"

I laughed, took a long sip of coffee. "Actually, I did not."

"Wait... *what?*"

"We just talked for most of the night. Flirted. It was... really sexy actually," I admitted. *Delay*, he'd said. *Wouldn't that make it sweeter?*

"So you *didn't* have sex. And he sent you flowers?" Lucia was incredulous.

"I believe his exact words were '*let me chase you*.'"

Lucia stared at me, eyes wide and slightly comical. "*And...*" She waited.

"*And*... we're seeing each other tonight. For like a... a date." I grimaced at the word.

"That's a good thing," she said.

"It's against the rules," I shot back.

"Rules-schmules. Just have some fun. We're leaving tomorrow anyway," she said.

I attempted to understand her rational thinking, but it was like listening to music underwater.

"What happened with *you* last night?"

Lucia shrugged, tossing her half-braided hair. "Oh, you know... got a little drunk and left Cal a poem by Mary Oliver at his bedroom door."

I spit my coffee across the deck.

"What is this, *The Three Stooges*?" Lucia teased.

"You have a crush on Cal," I exclaimed, forgetting that he was just inside.

"I sure don't," she lied.

The two of us looked away for a moment, both lost in thought.

"We've known these guys for three days. Shit, *I've* only known Gabe for *one* day. I'm really not sure what we're freaking out about."

"I'm not freaking out," Lucia said, and I half-shoved her out of the blanket. She was laughing, but as I stared out at the rain, anxiety rushed over me like a river. And with that—frustration. That even two years later, I couldn't allow myself to do *normal* things, like a casual date. A date without consequences. With a man I'd never see again.

It was safe. Gabe was safe.

I inhaled, and like a nasty weed, Clarke's voice appeared.

*What would Gabe think if he knew? If he knew you weren't good enough for me to marry?*

"I love you, Lu," I said, wrapping her in a hug. I needed my best friend.

"I love you too. And are you okay?" She asked against my hair. "Those flowers really upset you, huh?"

I pulled back, her gaze searching mine.

"I don't know," I said in a small voice, embarrassed when a stray tear slid down my cheek.

"Josie," Lu said, squeezing my shoulders and smiling kindly. "I think Gabe is a really nice guy. And I think he has a crush on you, even after one night, because you are brilliant and beautiful. I think it's okay to let yourself have fun with him tonight. Because, well, what are your chances of ever seeing him again?"

I lifted my chin. "Minimal," I said firmly. "And he's sexy as fuck."

"Thatta girl," Lucia said with a wink. "You deserve to get laid." I nodded, my walkie sputtering with Ray's voice, demanding to know our location.

"And you deserve a guy like Cal," I reminded her.

---

I DIDN'T LOOK at the cards on the remaining bouquets until later, as I was getting ready to head to The Bar.

The third one read: *make me wait.*

The fourth one: *give me everything.*

And the final card, clinging to a bouquet of black dahlias: *I'll beg for it.*

# 15

# GABE

I was entering the twelfth hour of the Longest Day Of My Life and wondering, for the hundredth time, why I'd suggested Josie and I *delay*.

I'd been on the verge of orgasm ever since Josie had wrapped those cool fingers around my shaft and squeezed. Every time I'd think I'd found *relief*—zoning out, in the middle of drying glasses, or sweeping the floor—I'd start to fantasize about Josie's pierced nipples.

How good they would taste.

The metal, knocking against my teeth.

The sounds she'd make.

And then the vicious cycle would begin again.

I checked my watch—for the fiftieth time—as I stared out the window at the nasty storm. The weather had been terrible all day, the news predicting a big storm, and the locals were hunkered down against the rain, drinking and gossiping.

There was a clap of thunder, and the lights briefly flickered off then back on again.

A tendril of nerves curled up my spine. Big Sur was no stranger to frightening storms, and The Bar had survived every one. But Big Sur was still a small, isolated town perched on a cliff overlooking the ocean.

Things could get bad.

"You think it'll get worse?" Ruth asked me as she pulled on her rain jacket to leave. She gave me a look passed between locals, a look that brought back other storms. The fear, the waiting, the town a helpless victim against the force of Mother Nature. The Bar had been an evacuation spot countless times, and as a child I remembered the moments, curled up on the floor with my neighbors, like a giant town sleepover.

"I'll admit I've been distracted all day. But this looks worse than I expected."

Ruth looked uneasy. "I agree."

"You okay to get home? Do you want me to drive you?" I asked. Ruth lived less than five miles away, but five miles down the winding curves of Highway 1 in this storm could be treacherous.

She reached up, patting my cheek. "Gabriel Shaw, I've been driving myself through Big Sur storms my entire life. Not going to stop now. And yes, I'm more than fine to drive."

I nodded as I held the door open for her. A blast of chilly air swept through, and just as Ruth left, another car pulled in. The door opened, and out stepped Josie.

And I suddenly remembered why I'd wanted to wait.

Because the world stopped.

The wind whipped her black-and-lavender hair around her face. As she walked toward me, she arched an eyebrow suggestively. In her ripped jeans and leather jacket, she looked like a hipster-biker-babe, *way* too cool for me.

Yet here she was.

"Gabriel," she said.

"Josefine," I replied, watching as she stalked past me confidently. Slowly slid her jacket down, revealing her bare back.

My fingers tightened on the doorknob, my eyes trailing up her gorgeous skin, the text and flowers inked there. When she got to the barstool, she half-turned her head—just a little—as if giving me a cue to follow her.

I obeyed.

I strode back behind the bar, grabbed a bottle of Jameson, and poured her a shot. Slid it toward her. Josie brought it to her lips, sipping.

Savoring.

Her eyes never left mine.

"I wasn't entirely sure you were going to come," I admitted.

"Well... the bouquets were a bold move," she said lightly. Behind me, Mrs. Manahan called my name, but I ignored her. Josie's finger traced the rim of the glass. "And your messenger didn't stray from his script."

I grinned. "I've known his family for years."

"He spoke highly of you," she said. "He said you were, and I quote, *the nicest motherfucker I know.*"

I threw my head back and laughed.

"You *are* nice. He told me all about how nice *everyone* in your family is. Gave me lots of specific examples."

I leaned across the bar, closer to Josie. Her dark eyes danced.

"So you were asking about me?" I said.

Her cheeks flushed—lightly, but it was there. "Please. I was just curious," she said. "No one's ever sent me flowers like that before."

"Too much?" I said, trying to respect the hard boundary she'd put up last night. *I don't date, Gabriel. I fuck, and then I leave.*

"I think you have customers," she pointed out. I could hear a handful of them grumbling to my left.

"And I don't care. Tell me: was it too much?"

"And I'm pretty sure you don't give the orders around here," she smirked, and my cock pressed against my jeans. *Fuck*, I wanted her orders.

We had a momentary stand-off.

"No," she finally said, "It wasn't too much. It was... just right."

Josie leaned a little closer, our faces just a few inches apart. Her eyes never left mine.

"I meant every word," I rasped. "Every fucking word."

Her breathing hitched. "Good."

"Gabriel Shaw, it's not like you to ignore your *fifth grade math teacher*." Mrs. Manahan banged her empty glass on the bar, and I rolled my eyes. Reached under for a bottle of red wine as Josie laughed.

"Please don't leave," I begged. "Stay right here?"

"I'll think about it," she said, biting her lip.

I walked backward, holding her gaze, until I got to the end of the bar.

"Sorry, are we interrupting a romantic moment in the middle of your business establishment?" Kevin asked as I topped off his wine as well.

"Oh, relax," I chided, grabbing two beers for Geoff and Fritz, whose eyes were glued to the television. "This round is on me, okay?"

Kevin and Mrs. Manahan exchanged a glance. "Two rounds," he said.

"Not a negotiation," I replied, then walked back toward Josie.

"Just to be clear: you're okay with the fact that half of Big Sur is watching us right now?"

"I am," she said, pulling her hair over one shoulder. "Plus, they can't hear what we're saying, right?"

We exchanged smiles.

I reached down and turned up the music. "Now they can't."

She nodded, tilting her head in recognition. "Is this Beyoncé?"

I shrugged and started drying glasses. "Maybe."

Josie's eyes narrowed. "You remembered."

There was a long pause while her eyes roamed up and down my body. I tried to appear nonchalant, but what I really wanted to do was sweep the glasses off the bar and let Josie have her way with me right on top of it. Right now.

There was another crack of thunder and an answering flash of lightning, but Josie didn't flinch.

"So what we're going to do tonight, you've never done with anyone?" she asked.

"No. Have you?"

She shook her head. "My sex life consists entirely of one-night stands. It doesn't leave a lot of time to feel comfortable enough with someone to... to explore something like that."

"When I was with Sasha, I actually never told her. Which is strange, saying it out loud now." I wanted to know *why* Josie wasn't dating seriously, but I didn't ask.

"Never felt like you could?"

"I guess... I guess not," I finally said, trying to make sense of why I'd so easily shared an erotic fantasy with Josie. But *not* with a woman I thought I'd spend the rest of my life with.

"Why does it excite you?" she asked.

I glanced down the bar toward the other customers. Turned the music up just a little louder. "Why does it excite *you*?" I shot back.

But Josie only sat forward on her elbows, crooked her finger at me. I leaned closer.

"You keep trying to tell me what to do, *Vikingo*, but it's not going to work that way."

She let the strap of her shirt fall down her shoulder, exposing the swell of her breasts.

"*Josie*," I growled.

"Why does it excite you?" she repeated with a sharp edge to her voice.

"Because..." I cleared my throat. I could see the outline of Josie's piercings through the thin material of her shirt. "Because I'm obsessed with making women come. I'm obsessed with the sounds women make when they orgasm. The way their breathing changes. The way they pant and moan..."

"Keep going," she said.

"Women deserve to be worshiped. *You* deserve to be worshiped, Josie. I want to worship you with my mouth. My tongue. My fingers. My cock, if you'll let me."

"If you *earn* it."

"If I... *fuck*, if I earn it," I continued, clearing my throat. I looked around, leaned closer to Josie. "And for the longest time, whenever I had sex, these ideas would come up. Images. Desires for them to take charge. Tell me *exactly* how to get them off. But I never... I never said a thing."

"Do you know where it comes from?" she asked.

"I think it's just... who I am. There's no source, just pure instinct." I swallowed roughly, looked down for a second. And when I looked back up, Josie's eyes were blazing.

"I feel the same," she said, fingers stroking along her collarbone. "I enjoy all different kinds of sex. I like giving and receiving. I would even let you dominate me if you really wanted to."

I saw Josie on her hands and knees. Purple and black strands of hair, twisted between my fingers.

"But if I'm being perfectly honest," she continued. "I think I'm going to get off on controlling a man of your size. Because even though you're massive, you're going to let me do whatever I want to you tonight."

"Yes," I groaned. "Yes, I am."

Josie smirked and bit her lip.

There was another long stand-off between us, the din of the bar fading away to the hush of stillness. Like I was back on the trail in the middle of the wilderness, that same quiet peace. And even though this moment pulsed with erotic energy, being around Josie made me feel at *ease.*

Behind us, the storm raged, branches scraping against the window.

"When are these people going to leave?" Josie asked, sitting back on her barstool and tossing her hair. I glanced at the clock on the wall. It was still early, and this would be all over the Big Sur Channel tomorrow, but I didn't give a fuck.

"I have been known, on occasion, to close The Bar early if there's an emergency."

"Storm's pretty bad," she shrugged.

"It really is," I agreed, reaching down to turn off the music. Turned to our audience at the end of the bar.

"I'm closing up early tonight. As in *now.*" I turned the lights half up, and the customers hissed angrily.

"It's *barely* midnight," Kevin said.

"And it's a *Wednesday,*" I replied calmly, crossing my arms across my chest. "I'll cover all of your open tabs. Don't worry about payment. But you all should really leave. The storm *is* getting worse."

I looked over at Josie, who was hiding a grin with her hand. I tossed her a wink.

"Come on, people," I said, coming out from behind the bar. "Let's get a move on. For your own good."

There was more grumbling, and at least two people said they were going to call my father.

"Well, you can go drink at his house then," I said, holding the door open.

Rain was pouring down in sheets, and I could barely hear people as they ran past me to their cars. I shivered, that tendril of fear briefly flaring to life again.

But then I locked the door. Turned back inside, and found Josie, perched on the bar, long, tattooed legs crossed in front of her. She crooked her finger.

"Come here," she purred.

## 16

# JOSIE

It was nice to be chased.

Even for a day. Even for just a night. That heady feeling in the beginning of a new relationship, when the complications of reality feel far away and the only thing you care about—the only thing you can *think* about—is the other person.

The flowers had been perfect. Romantic but not cheesy. Erotic but still mysterious. And sexy enough to keep me focused on Gabe all day, a heart-racing, butterflies-in-your-stomach feeling I hadn't felt in a long time.

I'd never experienced a tension so sweet.

And I'd never admit that I liked it. In fact, tomorrow morning, I'd be slipping away before Gabe awoke and returning to my slash-and-burn lifestyle, picking up men and discarding them an hour later.

As my Viking hustled customers out the door, I slid off my stool. Hopped up onto the bar, and crooked my finger at Gabe, who was waiting obediently across the room.

"Come here," I demanded, and in three long strides, he was standing in front of me. I spread my legs slowly, and he stepped between them. I twisted my fingers in his shirt and yanked him forward.

"Josie," he whispered, hands gripping my face. His thumb stroked across my lip. "I need you to know. This night is about you. Whatever you demand of me. Whatever you *need*. I want you to take it."

I responded by sucking his thumb between my lips, eyes locked on his. Gabe's expression grew feral as he growled low in his throat.

I'd never wanted someone more in my entire goddamn life.

"Then kiss me," I said.

And he did.

Although *kiss* would be an understatement.

My Viking *claimed* me, wrapping me in his arms like he'd just returned from battle. His big hands circled my hips, palmed my ass, and then I was lifted in the air as he walked me back toward the stairs, leading to the bedroom.

The kiss was endless. I twisted my fingers in his beard, nipped his lip with my teeth. His mouth was ecstasy. His fingers were on my throat, running through my hair, squeezing my thighs. Our tongues slid together, over and over, rough and teasing at the same time. Our moans collided in the brief seconds that we allowed ourselves to break apart. I felt my back hit a wall, my knees spread, and for one delicious moment, Gabe dragged the head of his erection between my legs.

His forehead landed against mine. "I need to go lock up the bar." He slid me down his hard body, lifted my chin. "I left something for you here. If you want... if you want to use it," he said, almost nervously. I was a panting, hot mess of desire, not even sure how I'd ended up standing instead of getting fucked against the wall.

"What... where the fuck are you going?" I demanded, breathless, pulling him down again for another heart-stopping kiss. His answering groan hit me low in my belly.

Then he tore his lips away. Backed out the door of his bedroom as he rubbed his palm against his mouth. "One minute, max. I'll be right back, gorgeous."

He left, and I caught my breath for a moment, attempting to orient myself, pretending I didn't get a thrill at the endearment. Spinning on my feet, I turned and saw what Gabe had left for me.

Clarke had laughed cruelly when I'd spilled this fantasy one night, a little tipsy at a hipster bar in L.A. *You don't have what it takes*, he'd said, and I'd believed him. Even though, before I met Clarke, that thought would have never even crossed my mind. Defeat wasn't in my vocabulary—I'd tirelessly obliterated every single obstacle in my way. And if I'd wanted to tie a man to my bed and dominate him all night long, I would have done it.

Yet Clarke's sneaky voice caused a swift wave of nerves. What was I *thinking?* Did I even know how to wield control over this Viking of a man?

But in the corner of Gabe's room, next to his bed, lay four long bungee cords.

For binding. Tying. *Restraining.*

And just that simple gesture of trust gave me a small shred of confidence to cling to.

Smiling, I picked up the cords, stroking my thumb against the fabric, and stood next to the window and watched the storm outside. Rain was pelting against the window, and the wind sounded hollow and harsh.

"Josie?"

I turned, slowly assessing my Viking.

"I need a safe word from you," I said, attempting to maintain an edge to my voice. Gabe's trust in me was exactly what I needed to make this fantasy come true.

Although it was also making me feel more *vulnerable* than I'd anticipated.

"Tell me what that does," he said, taking a step closer. I held up my palm, and he stilled.

"Makes me stop, regardless of what I'm doing," I said firmly since this was important. "Evens out the power dynamic. I don't want to..." I paused. "I don't want to do anything that makes you feel uncomfortable."

Gabe nodded, giving me a soft, gentle smile. "All right then," he said, glancing outside. "How about *lightning*?"

As if on cue, another clap of thunder shook through the walls, reverberating up my spine. I shivered.

"Good," I said. "Anything else you want to ask me?" I ran the cord through my fingers.

"What do you need first?" he asked.

I leaned against the window, flashed him a smirk. "Take off your goddamn clothes."

Gabe looked away for a moment, almost shy. Eyes down, then back up at me. I arched an eyebrow, crossing my arms over my chest.

He gave me a slow, lazy grin—and his fingers flicked open the first button of his shirt.

Behind us, the windows shook with the storm. But in this room, there was only furtive anticipation.

Another flick of his fingers, then another. Every button opened. And then Gabriel Shaw let his shirt drop to the ground.

He was a fucking *warrior*. Biceps like boulders, shoulders as wide as a house. Thick golden hair covered his chest, down his strong stomach. Gabe's muscles weren't fabricated in a gym. They were built with hard-work and honest exertion.

"You're beautiful," I said softly before I could stop myself.

"I think you're stealing my lines," he grinned. He reached up and undid his hair.

Magnificent.

Then, hands on his jeans. A snap, and they dropped. I sucked in a sharp breath. Thighs like tree trunks and black briefs that couldn't *begin* to hide the cock I planned on torturing all night.

I sauntered over. Held his gaze as he slid those briefs down his legs. I stepped closer. Tapped his stomach with my fingernail. His cock surged upward, thick and veined. Big. Deliciously so. I strolled around his body, examining. Taking my time with the naked Viking awaiting my commands.

Gabe's back rippled and flexed as I trailed my finger up and down the taut muscles. All the way down to the round globes of his ass.

"Am I… okay?" Gabe asked.

I stepped back around.

"You are," I sighed, "the most perfect man I've ever seen. Now, let me see you wrap those fingers around your cock."

He did.

"Show me how you touch yourself. Here, at night. In this bed."

Leisurely, I lifted my shirt over my head and tossed it away.

"Fuck, yes," he groaned, stroking himself. His fingers worked as I slid my jeans down my legs. His hand moved faster, arm shaking.

"You want to taste these?" I cupped my breasts, tweaked the nipples.

"Please," he begged, but I only shook my head. Worked my underwear down my legs, and Gabe swore beneath his breath. His breathing was growing ragged, motions less coordinated.

"Stop," I said.

And he did. Immediately.

I couldn't stop my smile of triumph. The fucking *power* that flowed through my veins was like nothing I'd ever felt. A man so willing to do my bidding that he'd deny his own orgasm.

Gabe's chest heaved. I dropped to my knees in front of him. Looked up, and rubbed my cheek against his cock. Starting at the base, I dragged my tongue up to the head. Swirled my tongue around it as Gabe shuddered.

"*Josie*," he bit out.

I sucked him into my mouth. He tasted so fucking *good*. The salty pre-cum. The unique, masculine scent of him. I twisted both hands at the base, dragging up, and his head dropped back.

"It's never felt like this," he groaned. "*Christ*, that's perfect. Oh, god, that's so *perfect*."

I hummed my approval, working my lips and my fingers faster, heard that ragged breath again.

I stopped.

Stood up gracefully, letting my tongue dance along the ridges of his stomach. Looked up at Gabe, expecting anger or frustration.

Instead, Gabe looked *happy*. I pulled him down for a kiss, and he groaned as our lips met. Groaned and snarled as I deepened the kiss, working him up. Pushing him closer to the edge.

Then I let go. Took a step back until I felt my thighs hit the bed.

"On your knees," I commanded.

With a wolfish, satisfied grin, Gabe's knees hit the floor, and I *swore* the floorboards rattled.

"Goddammit," he grunted, licking his lips. His mouth was level with my breasts. "Please let me taste you."

Twisting my fingers in his hair, I yanked his mouth to my breasts. He yelped in pain, then sighed in overwhelming pleasure. He nuzzled along my nipples. Circled his tongue around the edges before lapping. Sucking. Gabe was moaning louder than I was—and I was practically screaming. Because the piercings *did* make me more sensitive—made it feel like those same lips were on my clit. His teeth clicked against the metal, and stars shot across my vision.

"Does this feel good?" he asked, swirling his tongue,

I clutched at his shoulders to stay standing. "Almost too good."

Gabe switched his attention to my other breast, and as he lavished it with attention, I rolled my other nipple against my palm, wet from Gabe's mouth. The dual sensations had me squeezing my thighs together, seeking relief.

But then I remembered I had Gabe.

"Finger my pussy," I gasped.

His whispered *thank you* was almost too much. Until two of his thick, rough fingers curled inside of me, thrusting evenly. I looked down, loved the sight of Gabe's fingers working between my legs.

"Fuck *fuck*," I moaned, rocking against Gabe's fingers, holding his lips to my nipples. He continued his explorations, using his tongue, his lips, his teeth. All while finger-fucking me with dexterous skill.

"You're going to make me come this way," I panted, and his mouth left my breasts to roam up my collarbone. Along my throat, nipping at my jaw. I rocked harder, grinding my clit against his palm.

"Yes, you're going to... oh, *God, yes* I think... *Gabe...*" I wailed, suddenly needing his kiss.

I screamed against his lips as he fucked me through a

whirlwind of endless, pulsing sensation—an orgasm that knocked me back onto the bed, arms flung wide.

Gabe's fingers stayed inside of me, lightly gliding through my folds. *So* right—and I didn't even have to command it. I propped myself up on my elbows, staring down at Gabe between my legs.

"That was pretty good," I teased, still panting. "For the first one."

But Gabe was no longer in a joking mood. His eyes were pinned to my pussy, fingers moving faster now. I rolled my hips suggestively, and those dark eyes glared up at me.

"Then fucking *let me*," he growled.

"Let you... what?" I hooked my legs over his shoulders.

Gabe turned his head, nuzzled my knee. Kissed down my thigh.

"Please let me eat your pussy. *Please*."

I'd never seen a man so desperate to please me. My pussy was a goddamn *idol*, and Gabe was so willing to be on his knees and worshipping it.

I gave him a small, sharp nod, and then I was treated to the most blissful sensation of my entire life. Because Gabe Shaw didn't *just* lick my pussy. In absolute astonishment, I watched him devour me like his favorite fucking meal. I'd been prepared with a list of requirements: *harder there, less pressure, to your right*. The type of instructions I had to provide *every* lover if he wanted to get me off.

Yet there Gabe was, reading my body like a beloved book. Flicking his tongue in small circles, thrusting his fingers in a timed harmony, my pussy vibrating with the savage groans emanating from his lips.

And our eyes stayed locked on each other—something I *never* did because it always felt too intimate.

But we couldn't seem to *break* eye contact. And I wanted

him to see every single burst of pleasure on my face—every pant, every moan. When Gabe sucked my clit into his mouth, I clawed at the bed sheets. Pressed my thighs against his face. A third finger slid inside me, and the fullness plus the suction sent me rocketing into outer space.

I climaxed, and Gabe watched me.

I climaxed, and Gabe *saw* me.

Three sharp *claps* of thunder, the sound rolling through the room. Neither one of us moved. I reached down, pressed my palm against his face. He kissed my fingers sweetly, and my heart fluttered in my chest.

"Thank you," he said again, voice hoarse. But I could only nod, desperate to regain control of this night. Of this epic fantasy-session with a stranger.

Not two lovers.

"Up," I said, sliding off the bed.

My legs were shaking. Gabe looked up at me as I reached down, grasped his wrists, and yanked. He stood smoothly, towering over me.

I shoved him backward onto the bed. Grabbed one of the cords and secured his wrists to the headboard, over his head. Sitting back on my knees, I admired my handiwork: my bound warrior.

I felt like a *queen,* basking in the look of reverent submission Gabe was giving me. *Worship* couldn't begin to explain it, the way his body kept trying to arch toward mine. I ran my fingers up his chest, just over his heart, and yanked on a handful of his chest hair.

Gabe hissed in a breath, barely concealing a snarl.

But no safe word.

I yanked again. Threw my legs over the middle of his chest. Rubbed my bare pussy against him, letting him feel how wet he'd made me. Gabe pulled at the cords so hard I thought they'd snap in half, his biceps straining with the effort.

With a sly grin I turned around, facing his feet. Looked behind me and caught him staring at my ass hungrily. Bending down, I ran my tongue along his cock again.

The headboard shook.

"Gabriel," I moaned. "You're still not allowed to come. You know that, right?"

I teased my fingers around the head, then took the length of him to the back of my throat. Held him there and hummed.

"*Goddammit fuck Josie.*"

"What was that?" I whispered against him, taking a quick breath.

Then I took him deep again. I hummed against him, gliding my lips up and down.

This time, the whole bed rattled. And then a strangled: "I won't come, I won't... *Christ,* I'll wait."

I let him go with a *pop*.

"For what?" I turned back around, leaning down.

My hands roamed over his restrained biceps, the muscles flexing and jumping. I kissed along his neck, feathering my breath over his ear. The sound of Gabe's masculine groans, his head tilted back in pleasure, was so fucking erotic I was already balanced on the precipice of orgasm.

Again.

"Gabe?" I prodded, hovering my lips over his.

A crooked, sexy grin. "For permission. I come when you let me, gorgeous."

I kissed my Viking. Holding his head in my hands, I could feel the tremors of his muscles as he fought against the restraints. When we broke apart, the look of absolute trust on his face had my heart fluttering again like the traitor it was.

Of course I had what it fucking *took*.

So I grabbed the headboard and lowered myself right over Gabe's mouth.

He inhaled, then let out a guttural groan. "In case I didn't make it obvious before," he said, giving me a long, wet lick, "you taste like fucking *paradise*."

"I know," I sighed, letting my head fall back. "And you're going to fuck me with your tongue until I come on your face."

"Fuck *yes*," he growled as I snapped my hips, grinding against him, and it was so fucking *hot*. So hot to watch this giant of a man tied to a bed as I fucked his face. The bed rocked, his fingers gripped the headboard, shaking as I writhed above him.

Then his tongue plunged inside me.

And I screamed.

## 17

## GABE

There was no end to the pleasure.

My world was complete and total submission, burying whatever thoughts or demands that usually floated up when I fucked someone and instead letting Josie take it all.

My world was this bed and the intriguing sensations of rope against my skin. Pain and pleasure, denial and release.

I was *yearning* for her whispered "stop." Even though, at this point, my climax was on a goddamn hair-trigger. I'd never *denied* myself an orgasm before. Never experienced the strangely erotic sensation of being *so fucking close* and then... smothering it.

Yet that frustration was only making the experience hotter, letting my tattooed vixen use my body like a sex toy as the cord cut into my wrists and Josie's nails scraped down my chest.

Josie was straddling my face with a devious grin. She tasted sweet and musky, and I would have been content to stay here, just like this, until dawn. I plunged my tongue inside her, searching for her g-spot, and when I found it, she almost shot off my face. I worked that bundle of nerves with the tip of my tongue as she clenched around me. She spiraled into another orgasm—hands shaking the headboard—so I slipped back to her clit. Flicked her through the aftershocks until her fourth orgasm crashed over her.

Josie didn't move for a full minute, sitting back on my chest and piercing me with a look of complete and total sexual satisfaction. Her smile was lazy as she pressed her palm against my cheek. We were both out of breath, covered in sweat.

I was bound to this bed and rock hard with need—yet I felt weightless. Almost *effervescent*.

She was kissing me hungrily a second later, her body sliding down mine. I sensed her... *giving* me something before she sat back up. Smiled again.

"I really needed that," she said quietly, illuminated by moonlight.

"I really wanted to give it," I said. I'd never been more honest.

Her hands floated up towards my wrists, massaging the tender skin there. "You're still okay?"

"Never been better," I assured her. She kept massaging, working blood flow back into my tethered skin. Her hair cascaded across my chest, the rain cascaded down the window, and for a moment we were two sweet lovers, not practical strangers.

*Let those walls down*, I wanted to beg but swallowed the words.

Josie worked her way down my body, running her tongue along every inch of my abdomen, fingernails scratching down my ribs. I groaned, fighting the urge to thrust my hips. Let Josie explore.

Her lips descended on my cock again, and I sent a prayer to every god in the universe.

My cock hit the back of her throat.

"*Jesus,*" I growled, head back. The cord was cutting into my wrists.

But Josie only groaned with pleasure, speeding up her rhythm. Twisting her fingers at the base and gliding up in time with her lips.

"Fuck, I can't..." I pleaded, my orgasm beckoning. I wanted to come so badly. *So fucking badly*. But I also wanted to play this game, to be controlled by Josie in all the ways that made her happy.

"Please, fuck... *Josie,*" I pleaded again, my hips thrusting of their own accord. I heard her humming, then her fingers traveling up my stomach.

I looked down to find her eyes on mine.

"Josie," I whispered, seeking permission. "Josie, *please.*"

And then the sweetest miracle of my life happened. Because my tattooed vixen gave me a subtle nod of affirmation and sucked my cock between her lips again.

And I let go.

Light and sound danced and flared; a deluge of nonsensical sounds spilled from my lips.

And an orgasm *finally* swept through me.

---

When I finally opened my eyes, Josie was leaning over me with swollen lips and flushed cheeks. The hunger in her gaze was mostly gone, replaced with something deeper. An understanding. Our fantasy was over, but Josie remained my whole world, the shape of her fitting perfectly.

"Hey," she whispered.

"Hey," I whispered back, giving her a wide grin.

After a moment, she returned it, and an odd tightness came over my chest.

Josie untied the straps that held me to the bed. The liberation of my arms was intoxicating, and the only thing I could do was gather her to me, kissing her hair, her cheeks, her eyelids.

"I'm supposed to do that for you," she said sleepily, wrapping a leg around my waist and sighing with a deep satisfaction. "I want to make sure you're okay. That I didn't... hurt you."

"Too bad," I said. "And I'm more than okay. I've never been better."

"So you enjoyed that?"

"If by *enjoyed*," I kissed her cheek, "you mean *every cell in my body re-arranged itself*, then yeah. I enjoyed it."

Lightning flashed through the room, illuminating a vulnerability on Josie's face I'd never seen before.

"And I was... okay?"

The question was so absurd I wanted to laugh. Except she was *serious*.

I stroked my thumb across her cheek and tugged a curl of hair behind her ear. "I didn't think it was possible for my fantasy to be even better in reality." Her eyes softened. "Thank you for exploring that with me. For showing me what it would be like to be controlled by a gorgeous, sexy woman."

"You liked it?" she asked.

"*Loved* it," I said firmly.

Behind her, the clock was trying to let me know I only had a few more hours left with Josie—that the sun would rise, and she'd be off down the highway, back to L.A.

I ignored it.

"You turned my world upside down tonight," I whispered, pulling her in for a swift kiss.

"And you affirmed my suspicions that my *real* job should be professional dominatrix."

"I'd book you every night of the week," I said, and she laughed sleepily. "In fact, I think we should do it all over again in a few hours."

She tucked her head against my chest. "Gabriel, I just came *four times."* Her hands wandered down my back.

"I know, gorgeous." I said, against her ear. Already, her breathing was even and steady, body heavy against mine. "And I think you deserve even more than that."

# 18

# GABE

It was the thunder that woke me.

Or the lightning, like a knife slicing through the sky. Josie was still asleep, curled against my chest, but my heart was racing as I tried to put together why I'd been jolted awake. My nerves screamed with adrenaline. A quick inventory: I didn't hear anyone in the bedroom. Or the hallway. The windows were closed, and most importantly, Josie was clinging to me.

"Shit," I breathed out, wondering if it'd been a nightmare.

But then I heard it: the shrill ring of the emergency phone, the dedicated landline most people in Big Sur had to ensure they were informed during a natural disaster.

"*Shit*," I said again, jumping out of bed, still completely naked.

Josie stirred, and I smoothed the hair from her face, brushing my lips against her cheek.

"Go back to sleep, gorgeous," I whispered, and she gave me a sleepy half-smile.

And then I was moving, pulling open the bedroom door and half jogging down the hallway, half-formed memories of the last time I'd heard this phone ring already sliding through my brain. The horrific wildfire three years ago. The earthquake. The flash flood when I was fifteen that had almost washed pieces of Highway 1 into the Pacific Ocean. I tried to remember how much canned food and bottled water I had. Tried to make a plan for who might need rescuing.

"What happened," I said into the phone, already knowing who it would be.

"Gabriel," my dad said with a sigh of relief. "You're okay."

"More than okay," I said. "Here at The Bar. Nothing damaged as far as I can see… at least no human beings damaged."

"Which is the most important," my dad said with a quick, relieved laugh. "There were two massive rock slides about forty minutes ago. I'm going to need you to call the last ten businesses on the list. I've called the rest."

"*Fuck*," I swore. "Who's hurt?" My mind flew back to Ruth, patting my cheek before she left. To my brother Austin, who lived with his girlfriend Paige just down the road. To Kevin and Gloria and Gladys.

"No one, as far as the fire department can tell. The storm was so bad most people were at home, not on the highway. But the slide occurred at the entrance, and exit, to Big Sur."

My father's words slowly dawned on me: the worst-case scenario that most residents often feared. Highway 1 was the only access point for our town, and if both sides were covered in heaps of boulders…

"Okay," I said, my stomach jumping with anxiety. "How bad is it? What can I do?"

I heard voices in the background—my mother's. A whispered *he's okay* from my father. "Hey, Austin is okay, right?" I asked. "Do you need me to go pick up him and Paige?"

A shift, then I heard the phone go to speaker phone.

"Hey, big brother," came Isabelle's voice, sounding tired. "Maya and I are here with the baby. We'd decided to stay, ride out the storm. And we just called Austin and they're fine."

I let out a long exhale. "Well, good. Only issue is we can never leave Big Sur, but—"

"—that's basically your dream come true," Isabelle laughed.

"Yeah, yeah," I said, peering through the windows as a heavy branch ripped off the elm tree in the front of The Bar. I grimaced. "Happy to hear no one's dead."

"It missed the Mayor's house by inches. Same with Charlie's," my dad said. My heart lurched. Living in Big Sur was like that. You always had a dark understanding that, at any moment, nature could force its way through you.

"When are the road crews going out? And do they need extra hands?" I asked, looking under the bar for my work gloves.

"They're going out as soon as they can. And I don't think they'll need any help," my dad cut in. "Although, if you took over sandwiches and beers, courtesy of The Bar, I'm sure you'd be their hero."

I laughed, taking out a pen and a post-it note and scribbling the idea down. "Consider it done. I'll bring them lunch every day."

"Wait," Isabelle said, "I'm surprised you didn't hear it. The first slide wasn't more than a mile from The Bar. It's five miles from us, and I thought a train was coming through the living room."

I shifted on my feet uneasily since I'd been thinking the same thing. But Josie and I had both been out cold. I didn't usually sleep well with a stranger in my bed, usually tossing and turning, unsure of what to do with my limbs.

I glanced at the wall clock. We'd been deeply asleep, curled around each other, for hours now.

"I'm... you know, I'm not sure. Always been a heavy sleeper, you know?" I said, laughing nervously, knowing that I'd be grilled by both of them later. *Nothing* was a secret in our family, and god help you if you tried to keep one.

"Must have been some girl," Isabelle said, and I heard an *oof* as my dad shoved her out of the way.

"Ignore your sister," he said, "Although I know all about the purple-haired Satanist, and believe me, your mother and I have plenty of questions."

"Well, gotta go," I said quickly, holding the phone away from my mouth. "I've got natural disaster protocols to put into place, bottled water to find, you know the drill."

"Mhmm," my dad said, and I could hear the grin in his voice. "And Gabe—we're happy you're safe."

"Me too." I smiled, the relief continuing to course through me, lightening my heart.

I slammed the phone down, grabbed the protocol book. Looked up the first business, and of course it was The Mad Ones. Underneath, it still said *Robert Ellis, owner.*

Growing up, my parents used to drop all three of us off at The Mad Ones, knowing that Robert would keep an eye on us as we ran through the bookshelves. But, more often than not, Robert and Maggie would open the back doors and tell us to go play in the woods—plying us with lemonade and cookies when we'd run back hours later, exhausted but happy.

Those were some of my favorite memories growing up: falling half-asleep on the floor of The Mad Ones with my siblings. That comforting feeling of my parents picking me up and carrying me to the car.

And now the emergency phone was ringing, and Calvin was taking forever to answer.

"Um... yeah?" came his hesitant reply, finally. He sounded out of breath.

"It's Gabe," I said, not realizing how worried I'd been. "There's been a rockslide. Two actually," I said, quickly filling him in on the few details that I had. "I wish I had more to tell you, but you'll need to tell the Hollywood People they'll be stuck here a little longer than they'd initially thought."

And *Josie* was one of the Hollywood People. We'd both been set to say goodbye when morning came in a few hours, however reluctantly—at least, reluctantly, on my part.

But now...

"How long, do you think?" Cal asked, and I knew he was thinking the same thing. Whatever was happening between him and Lucia would have a few extra days to breathe.

"My dad thought maybe a week? Maybe less, but as soon as I know more, I'll tell you. The main thing for them to know is they are... we *all* are... essentially trapped."

"They're uh... not going to be happy about that," he said, and I heard him turning, the sound of people entering the room.

"Godspeed," I said. "And let them know whatever hint of internet connection they thought they had is gone for good."

I looked down my hallway where, through the open bedroom door, I could just see the bottom of my bed. A bed where Josefine was waiting for me.

"Oh, and Cal?" I said, suddenly nervous. "Can you let Lucia know that Josie is here? Um... with me?" Christ, now I sounded like Cal. I was a thirty-four-year-old man suddenly shy about talking about the girl he had a crush on.

A long pause, then Cal said, "Are, um, congratulations in order?"

I laughed. "Yes... yes, they are. I just didn't want Lucia to worry. And Josie's safe here. With me." That odd tightness again, right where my heart was. A desire to protect her—from the elements but also from whatever it was that lived inside her, causing her undue pain.

"Good," Cal said. "I'll come down tomorrow morning. We can, um... talk about a few things." Nothing more than that, but a note in his voice told me he had news to share.

"Looking forward to it," I said, hanging up the phone. I called the other businesses quickly, making sure everyone was safe, making sure they had what they needed. A few folks were low on water, and I promised I'd cart some jugs out as soon as I could.

A few folks asked about Josie, questions that I dodged unsuccessfully. But in exchange, they offered me a few juicy tidbits for the Big Sur Channel, which I took down to tell Gloria and Gladys later.

After the last call, I stood for a moment, watching more branches snap and skitter across the ground. A week ago, Big Sur had been drenched in sunshine, warmth finally seeping into the coast.

*Just like that.*

Our delicate ecosystem, snapping like the branches. Or rather, doing what it was supposed to do: destroy. Then rebuild.

I was suddenly keenly aware that I was naked and freezing and had some bad news to share with the vixen in my bed. Which, considering how skittish Josie had been, I wasn't sure she was going to take well.

I walked down the hallway, seeing the blankets move, hearing her stirring. Pushed open the door slowly to see her sitting up, long hair pulled over one shoulder. Legs tucked underneath her. Face wide and open.

"Josie," I said, rubbing my hand down my jaw, "I've got some bad news."

## 19

## JOSIE

Gabe was making me break my rules.

Every single one.

I'd come back to him for a *date*, even though I refused to date.

I'd gone back on my promise to *not* let him come, even though I'd originally planned to deny Gabe his orgasm all night long. But as I'd licked my way down his fierce, strong body, I was gripped by the need to unravel him fully.

Unravel he did—back arching, hips thrusting, binds straining. Yet I had no doubt that if I'd pulled back right before he climaxed—if I'd whispered *stop*—he would have. Because he was so attuned to the part of me that desired control. To the part of himself that desired submission.

Gabe came with my name on his lips, a litany, voice hoarse with pleasure. And thank fucking *god* we were never going to see each other again because his beautiful climax sent the hard walls of my heart tumbling down.

I'd remember this night, years from now, when I needed to. Needed to remind myself that the world wasn't as dark and hopeless as I'd convinced myself it was.

Then I'd let my Viking clasp me to his chest, and I *fell asleep* with him.

Even though I never stayed.

I fell asleep with my ear pressed to his broad chest, listening to the reassuring rhythm of his heartbeat. Letting myself, for the first time in two years, really *feel* this moment, this man beside me. Not just some stranger in the night that I'd taken home for mindless sex and second-rate orgasms. But *Gabe*: this funny, sweet romantic-with-an-old-soul who'd sent me peonies and irises so that I could feel, if only for a day, *cherished*.

A ringing phone had sent him racing to the other room, but I could only hear the low tones of his voice. Nothing specific. The alarm clock reminded me I needed to leave—soon—and I was torn between relief and regret.

"Josie?" Gabe said, leaning against the doorway.

I looked up at him: naked. Glorious. Kindness in his eyes. My bruised heart fluttered like a bird trapped in a cage. I knew there'd be no tomorrow for us. I knew it was highly unlikely I'd ever see this man again, but rational thought had fled my mind the moment I'd laid eyes on him.

"I have some bad news," he said.

---

GABE WALKED over to sit next to me on the bed. "How would you feel about... staying in Big Sur another few days?"

"What?" I asked, sharply. "What happened?"

"Everything's going to be okay, and no one was hurt, but there were massive rock slides along both sides of Highway 1. While we were sleeping. The storm dumped too much rain on the mountainside; the ground got too soft. It's happened before here, a few times, but not as bad as this."

It was taking a while for my thoughts to catch up. "Wait, this happened while we were *asleep*?" I pulled my knees to my chest, wrapping my arms around them.

Gabe nodded with a tight smile. "You fucked us into unconsciousness."

I couldn't let myself smile back. I was already supposed to be on my way, breezing through the door with a kiss and a wave. "Everyone's safe?"

"Everyone's safe. There was some damage to houses, and of course it'll take a while for the road crews to clear the debris, but—"

I was light-headed with anxiety. "So that's... wait, what did you say? The first thing?"

Gabe placed his palm on the back of my neck, squeezing. "The rock slides are cutting off entry and exit through Big Sur. We're connected to the rest of the world by Highway 1. Without that road, you and Lucia and everyone else will need to stay here until it clears. Stay here with... us."

I *knew* he wanted to say 'stay here with *me*.' And the part of me that was soft and weak—the girl that stood in her wedding dress sobbing in her best friend's arms, still expecting the groom to show up—wanted that badly.

"You got a better ETA on that?" I asked, moving back, moving *away* from Gabe. I pulled on Gabe's shirt, which was massive on me.

"Maybe... a week? Probably less. They don't know," Gabe said, reaching for me.

I flinched. I couldn't help it. I'd let this man have my vulnerability for one night, and *one night only*, and now I was going to be stuck here in the World's Smallest Town with him.

"I... I'm going to use your bathroom," I said, "I'll be right back."

And then I leapt over the pile of ropes and clothes and shut myself behind his bathroom door.

*You don't have what it takes.*

Clarke had always been good at manipulation, but that night he hadn't even *tried* to hide the cruelty in his voice. But like everything else he had done, it'd been easy to write it off as a misunderstanding (we had a lot of those). Or explain it away as a byproduct of his high-stress job, causing him to speak without thinking (he did that a lot too). And by the morning, after a night of crying in the bathroom, I'd convinced myself he didn't mean it.

And even though, just hours earlier, I'd done exactly what he'd said I couldn't do—done it *spectacularly*—here I was. Back in a bathroom, on the verge of tears. I needed my phone. I needed Lucia, my best friend.

But I didn't have those things, so I splashed cold water on my face. Took deep, slow breaths. Pulled my hair into a long braid, focusing on the motions of my fingers. Waited for my heart to slow.

The terrifying thing about Gabe was his kindness. Because Clarke had started off kind too, even a little compassionate. And just like with Clarke, I'd had this *feeling* when we'd first locked eyes. A feeling I used to trust, but now I knew where it led—to a relationship that would go up in fucking flames, burning down every single thing around it.

I needed to leave Gabe's house. And then avoid him until the roads were cleared.

I needed to re-set.

Re-orient.

Back to the Josie I'd been before a Viking warrior had stormed all my defenses.

I threw open the bathroom door, prepared to march out,

but there was only Gabe in sweatpants and a zip-up hoodie, hair tied back and a concerned look on his face.

He pressed a hot mug of tea into my hand, tilted his head. "Want to tell me why the thought of seeing me again has you freaking out in my bathroom?"

# 20

## GABE

She was like a skittish horse—eyes wide and staring at the mug of tea as if it was filled with acid.

"I need to leave," she said, stepping around me as though we hadn't just shared the most intense sexual experience of my entire life.

"Do what makes you feel comfortable," I said. "And I'll drive you if you want. But Josie... it's horrendous out there. Dangerous to be out on the freeway. There was just a *landslide* not two hours ago. You don't need to... we don't need to *do* anything. But if you want to stay here where it's safe, maybe even talk about what's happening between us, well... that's why I made you this." I held the mug out to her sheepishly. "Chamomile with honey."

Her eyes narrowed, glancing outside. On cue, another bout of thunder shook the foundations of The Bar, and she felt it, glancing down at her feet as the vibrations rolled through the floorboards.

"I'm sorry," she said, settling on the armchair across from the bed. But she took the mug, so that was a start.

"I don't, um... stay," she said. But then something in her

shifted. "I always leave," she said, firmly. Confidently. "I was prepared to do that, and then when you told me we were trapped..."

She took a long sip, avoiding my eyes.

"So what's going on? Just talk to me. It's not like we can go anywhere." I meant it as a joke, but her face hardened.

I was beginning to come to terms with the fact that Josie truly *did not* want to see me again. That we could be trapped in Big Sur for weeks and she'd go out of her way to avoid me.

"Things changed for me two years ago," she said. "I don't like talking about it, and I'm not going to talk about it, but it does mean that I live my life differently now. I told you," she looked up at me. "I'm a one-night-stand girl. I haven't slept *concurrently* with a person in a long time."

"Well," I said, smiling, "I also have not slept *concurrently* with a person in a long time. With some exceptions. I've dated casually, off and on. But nothing since my last serious relationship..." *Shit*, it was depressing to do the math. "Ten years ago."

Her face brightened in understanding. "So you get it, right?"

"Kind of...?" I trailed off. "Still leads me back to you, freaking out in my bathroom."

She rolled her eyes. "I wasn't... okay, *fuck*, I wasn't *freaking out in your bathroom*. I thought, maybe, and now I *will* be embarrassed if this isn't the case, but I thought, with the slide, and us being stuck here, and what we just did was so... you know *intense* and fucking amazing actually—" she shook her head, but I was stuck on *fucking amazing*. "—that you would want to keep seeing me."

A pause, and our eyes locked. Josie was captivating, wrapped in my shirt and drinking that tea like it was the best thing she'd ever tasted.

Of course I wanted to see her again.

"Because I don't," she said, and my hope popped like a balloon. "And I just think it's going to be awkward now, us seeing each other. Which maybe we won't. And maybe you didn't even *want* to, so now I've just embarrassed myself multiple times for nothing."

She tilted her head, rubbing her fingers against her collarbone. Those slender fingers were inked with tiny dots. A sun. A moon.

"I was just going to leave," she repeated. "As soon as the sun came up. Which it will any minute now. And, what we did *was* intense, and I'm so happy for it. Really."

Her gaze was so sincere it broke my heart.

"I meant what I said. It's been a... well, a rough couple years. Tonight put a few pieces into place for me. Of my puzzle. Is that weird?" she said.

God, I liked this girl, weird and all. "The Josie Puzzle," I said, nodding thoughtfully. "I know what you mean. Something was missing. Tonight, you found it. Right?"

"Yes," she said.

She started to get up, but I leaned forward, and something in my expression stilled her.

"Can I tell you what my intentions are?" I asked. "Or... *were*?"

Josie sighed, but then sat back down. "Okay," she said.

I didn't know what the fuck had happened to her two years ago. But someone *did* it to her, and I itched to know where that person lived.

"Well, since we can't really *go* anywhere, I was going to make you some delicious coffee, heaping with sugar and cream," I said and was granted a tiny smile. "Then cook chocolate pancakes for you and eat them in bed." Josie's entire body was softening toward mine. "And then..."

Her eyes flared with lust. Fuck, she *wanted* this.

"And then I'd see how many more times I can make you come."

Just like that, the delicious tension that had existed between us since our first meeting snapped back. Josie uncrossed her bare legs, and for a brief, heady moment I thought she was going to command me back to my knees.

"Then what?"

She re-crossed her legs.

I swallowed a groan. "Keep seeing you for as long as you're here. Explore what this is," I said, pointing to her. Pointing to the bed. "This connection that we have. I think it means something, don't you?"

She looked away, standing up to pull on her clothes. About to leave. I debated brutal honesty. Debated telling her that she was the first woman since Sasha where I actually felt a *spark*. More than a spark—Josie was a fucking *wildfire*.

Every member of my family was in a beautiful, committed relationship—except me, the one person *everyone* swore would marry his high school sweetheart and build a funky Big Sur life with her in a cute cabin in the woods.

But I hadn't. And I hated it. And now I was hurtling toward my forties with no partner in sight. It made me want to throw caution to the wind. Live in the *present*. Grab hold of a relationship that had the potential to be real.

"Don't you think that means something?" I asked again.

Josie shook her head. "No."

The last shred of my hope crumbled into nothing.

"I really don't," she continued. "Listen, as long as my car isn't like swept away out there, I'm going to drive myself home now. I'm—"

There was a war going on inside of her; it was evident in the bite of her lip, the shifting of her feet.

"Josie," I said, trying to pull it out of her.

Something seemed to break open for a second, and she walked towards me. Took my face in her hands and kissed me, long and deep. Then she pulled away before I could get my arms around her.

"*Josie*," I said again, not afraid to beg. I'd done it tied to the bed. I'd do it again.

"Last night was really important to me," she said, looking me straight in the eye. "But please don't read more into this than it was: a hot, intense fuck I'll always remember. With a sexy and sweet bartender who's going to make someone a wonderful husband someday," she said.

Then she kissed my cheek one more time and walked out the door.

I heard the sharp sound of her combat boots down the stairs, then the front door of The Bar slamming closed.

I fell back onto the bed. "Goddammit," I said to no one in particular.

The landline rang again, so I walked downstairs to the bar, staring at the mess I hadn't cleaned up last night.

"Big Sur Channel," I sighed. I knew who it would be.

"Gabe, it's Gladys. Did you know the Satanist is leaving your bar right now?"

"Yes," I said tiredly. "Very much aware." I sat up. "Also, I'm assuming you and Gloria are alive?"

A *pfft* sound. "Please. Gonna take a lot more than a rock slide to take us out."

A shuffling, then I heard Gloria come on. "If you need to come by the post office and drown your sorrows, I've got Hennessey beneath the desk right now."

I barked out a laugh, grateful for the temporary distraction. "Sounds good. I've got some gossip for you later, so I'll be in soon." I hung up the phone before they could ask more questions. But then it rang again.

"*Big Sur Channel*," I said, more irritated than I meant to be.

"Um... Gabe?"

"Calvin. My man," I said, smiling despite the terrible morning and the no sleep. "What's good?"

"Listen, I know it's... shit, not even nine in the morning, but do you want a beer?"

I sighed, thinking about the day that awaited me. The mess of the storm. And a heart that was slightly bruised.

"Yes," I said. "Yes, I do."

## 21

## GABE

"So... Josie," Cal said, gulping down the last of his beer. He'd just finished telling me about a "moment" he and Lucia, the supermodel, had shared last night, right before I'd called them about the rock slide.

It was comforting to know Josie and I weren't the only ones so swept up in the moment we never heard the gigantic rock slides that had almost destroyed my home town.

"You like her, I guess?" he said.

I was sorting through bottles of water and wrapping up sandwiches to take to the road crew.

I looked at Cal, debated giving him some half-version of the truth. But I was already almost two beers in, and that combined with about three hours of sleep and four hours of orgasm denial had me a little loopy.

"Josie's incredible. Last night was incredible. I'd be lying if I told you I wasn't just the tiniest bit happy they're stuck here. Does that make me a terrible person?" *Except that Josie doesn't want to see you.*

"Nope, because I had the exact same thought," Cal said, mouth tightening.

Both of us were silent for a moment.

"What about when they leave?" he finally asked.

"It'll fucking suck. And that's why we're not going to think about it. We're just going to live in the moment, content with the fact that two absurdly beautiful women want to be around us... for reasons no rational person can comprehend."

We knocked our beer bottles together.

"Live in the moment," Cal said, nodding. "It's what my grandfather would have said."

I grimaced at that, remembering my attempt to *carpe diem*. "Josie turned me down, actually," I said, shrugging like it was no big deal.

Cal half-spit out his beer. "Wait, you *didn't* have spectacular sex last night?"

I shook my head, memories from the night floating up unbidden, and I closed my eyes for a second. "We did. Have spectacular sex." I cleared my throat. "Kind of life-changing, I guess. Not to, you know, divulge too many details but... it was different with Josie."

"And you *do* want something more to happen? Even if she's just here for a few more days?"

I nodded, gulping the remainder of my second beer. Reached under the bar for another. Might as well get morning-drunk. "I asked her if she wanted to keep seeing me while she was here. Explore this... connection. See what it is."

"And?"

"She shut me the fuck down."

Cal knocked his beer against mine. "Familiar with that feeling, I'm afraid. It's why what happened last night with Lucia was so... *fucking bizarre*."

I laughed, feeling some of my sadness lighten with Cal's happiness. A lot of people would look at the two of them, a nerd with huge glasses and crippling shyness and a drop-dead gorgeous, famous supermodel, and never see a way they'd be together.

But I knew better. Because I had an inkling that the two of them were going to fall in love.

"You know my parents were exact opposites," I said, slowly peeling the label from my beer. "They met when they were ten years old. Neighbors, which is saying a lot in Big Sur, since our houses tend to be far apart from each other. But my parents happened to live in two houses that were connected by a small field, and they grew up together. Were best friends through middle school and high school. My dad was *desperately* in love with her from about fourteen or so. Never said a thing but really pined for her, you know?"

Cal grinned. "I'm already loving this story."

"And I love to tell it." I did. Their love story was the one I'd longed for my entire life. "Anyway, I guess when my parents were seventeen, another kid in school asked her to prom. She said yes, and when she told my dad, it absolutely destroyed him. He always thought they'd be together, but my dad was shy. And kind of unassuming. And didn't really think he deserved my mom. But that didn't stop him from being devoted to her. The thing was, they were classic archetypes. He was kind of the shy loner. She was a cheerleader, popular, should have had a string of boyfriends, but she never did."

"Why not?"

I shrugged. "She was also pining for my dad. Only said yes to that guy because she thought my dad didn't love her."

"Ah," Cal said. "There's a moral to this story."

"There is. Which is honesty. My parents would always encourage us to tell the truth. Share your feelings. You might..." My chest tightened, thinking about Josie. "You might not have the opportunity again."

Cal looked away.

"I just want to say though, as your friend... no one thought my parents were right for each other. Too different, too young. And they've been together for more than thirty-five years. I see that when I look at you and Lucia."

Cal reddened, squeezing his bottle so hard I'd thought it'd break. "Um... well, thanks Gabe. I don't... you know, it was just a moment. Nothing *extraordinary*."

"Liar," I grinned, and his answering blush confirmed my suspicions. "And," I said, coughing uncomfortably. "You should probably know. I, uh, had to give up some intel. On you and Lucia. To the Big Sur Channel."

Cal's head dropped to the bar. "Goddammit," he said.

"Been there before," I said, slapping him on the back. "And let this be your official welcome to Big Sur, California."

# 22

# JOSIE

I'd thought about Gabe all damn day.

I had fumbled through a day of shooting, feeling like a zombie, completely trapped in memories of our night together. Except not *just* last night. Every interaction we'd had over the past two days, all on an endless loop of happiness and pleasure. I was so obvious that every ten minutes or so, Lu would point a manicured finger my way and say, "Check out that *dreamy smile.*"

Which was saying a lot since she'd spent the entire fucking day with her own dreamy smile, floating on Cloud Nine after her *moment with* Calvin. Who was quickly becoming my choice for Lucia's soulmate.

I hadn't told her many details in the morning, needing time. Space. I hadn't been open or vulnerable with a man in a long time, and I ached all over with it—the way your muscles feel after your first hard run in years. Excited but trembling with exertion.

But I was now rounding out day two of thinking about Gabe Shaw nonstop, and we were stuck here in Big Sur with no known leave date. I wasn't sure what to expect from Ray this morning, but he'd been charged up by the storm and the land slide. We'd been behind schedule anyway. So instead of a few days off, where I'd planned to mope around Lucia's cabin and try not to think about Gabe, we were back on a grueling shoot schedule for the foreseeable future.

And now I sat, perched on the cliffs and watching a furious ocean. The sound of the waves echoed *Gabe Gabe Gabe* every time they slid across the shore.

I wasn't really a nature girl. I'd spent every year of my life in a concrete jungle—even when we went back to Mexico, we stayed near the urban sprawl of Guadalajara, where my parents had grown up. I didn't hike or run or crave the peaceful silence of the woods.

Yet there was something *about* Big Sur. As I'd driven Lucia and I up from the city on our first day, my eyes hadn't felt big enough to take it all in. The ocean to the left of me, a beautiful blue expanse. The fields of golden wildflowers, stretching down to the rocky beaches. To my right, a forest of redwoods and pines dotted with orange poppy flowers.

Gabe said he went to nature when his thoughts or anxiety got too strong, and I was starting to see why. A little. I still preferred a night out dancing to clear those thoughts, but now, watching the waves, I felt hypnotized into a kind of calm. An acceptance.

These waves had been here long before I was born. Would continue long after I was gone.

"Hey there, Dreamy Smile," I heard Lucia, walking up behind me. She held a blanket in her arms and a bottle of red wine.

"I could say the same about you," I teased, grabbing the blanket and wrapping it around my shoulders. Lucia curled up next to me, a vision against the dark storm clouds.

"Makeup looks good," I said, taking a swig from the bottle.

"Mm-hmm," she said, taking her own swig. "I only have the best, you know." She nudged my shoulder with her own. "Thought you might want to drink this wine and tell me some of your feelings."

"I like the wine part," I said. "And feelings about what?"

The waves whispered Gabe's name.

"Oh… the wild night you spent with Mr. Big Dick and how you might feel about it," she said.

"Okay, I'm *only* calling him Mr. Big Dick from now on," I laughed.

Lucia looked at me, smiling but waiting.

I looked away for a second. "Do you remember the night before the wedding?"

Beside me, Lucia stilled. She was President of the Let's Kill Clarke Club and despised talking about him.

Not that I ever really did.

"Of course," she said. "You wanted such a boring bachelorette party, *chica*."

I nodded. "You knew then, right? Or before?"

"What?"

I put the wine bottle to my lips. "Did you guess he wasn't going to show up?" The wine slid down my throat.

"Of course not. I thought *you* might not want to go through with it. It's why I tried to… *super awkwardly* offer to drive you away. From the wedding. From Clarke. I thought you might…"

"Wake up the morning of the wedding and see him for the psychopath he was?"

"He wanted you to be a certain way," Lu said quietly. "Liked turning you into his submissive little, I don't know, *doll*. He made you stop liking the things you liked. Made you stop loving yourself, most of all. I was so worried, I was sick about it actually, that he'd marry you and take you away. That I hadn't said something in time, and I'd lose my best friend. To, yes... a fucking *psychopath*."

She spit the last part of her sentence out, the angriest I'd seen her in a long time. "I regret it. If I'd said something earlier, you wouldn't have gotten engaged. Wouldn't have had to experience that bastard leaving you at the altar."

There was a ragged edge to her voice, and I knew she thought about that moment as much as me. There had been so much confusion that morning—I thought maybe, ultimately, it was just a misunderstanding. He could have gone to the wrong place. Overslept. Gotten the dates mixed up.

It's funny all the tiny rationalizations your brain can make in the middle of total shock.

But it was Lucia. Lucia who broke the news: he'd left her a message, letting her know in so many words that he wouldn't be there. And Lucia who held me in my wedding dress as I sobbed for hours—sobbed so hard I ended up being sick, throwing up until there was absolutely nothing left in my stomach.

And I'd never seen or heard from Clarke again.

I reached forward, holding her hand. "You know, and I mean this, that absolutely *nothing* about that time in my life is your fault." My voice caught a little at the end. "Nothing. It's Clarke's fault. He's the emotional abuser. He's the asshole that bailed on our marriage. You remember what I was like during that time—like I'd been *drugged* or something. The..." I grimaced, "*love* I thought I had for him was like a sickness. Captured my every waking thought. In some strange ways, I'm happy he didn't show." I paused, looking out across the ocean. "If he had, I think you're right. I would have never woken up and seen the light. Would have lost myself entirely."

We were quiet for a long time. "Give me that fucking wine, *mija*," I said.

"What does this have to do with Gabe though?" she asked. Ever the best friend, never forgetting the original point.

I shifted uncomfortably on the rock, not sure if I wanted to say my thoughts out loud.

Because I didn't trust them.

"I'm not going to judge anything you say," Lu said softly.

"You know, everything with Clarke was so... *intense*. Not on the surface. On the surface, he was easy-going. But in the reality of our relationship, behind closed doors, everything was cranked up as high as it could go. Our dates went by so fast, and then we moved in together before I knew it. Even the engagement—that was something we'd *never* talked about. He sprang that engagement on me, and it was a total fucking surprise. I remember saying *yes* and feeling what I thought was exhilaration. The penultimate romantic gesture—your boyfriend loving you *so much* that he just *had* to buy the ring. *Had* to make sure you would be his forever."

"All things I'm assuming he said to you when you brought it up later," Lu said.

I nodded. "But now I recognize that... feeling in your stomach, the weightless one? It was fucking *dread*. And fear. And the final straw. I was no longer in control of my life. Even as I loved Clarke madly and desperately, I knew—he would make all of the decisions for me, moving forward. There was like a war inside of me." I held my hands over my stomach, twisting them. "Rational and irrational thoughts. Love and fear. Pain and pleasure. I didn't know which thoughts to trust. I didn't know... and of course when I brought those fears up to Clarke..."

I trailed off, swallowing at a memory.

*"I love you so much I spent a shit-ton of money on a fucking ring for you,"* he'd said, in that tone I'd come to recognize. *"And no, I'm not afraid to spend the rest of my life with you, even if you think*

*it might be too fast. If our love is too fast for you..." he looked away, hurt. "If you have fears about our relationship, then that's not right."*

*"Having fears?" I'd pressed back, too aware of the giant diamond on my left hand. I actually hated diamonds, but we'd never talked about what I wanted. "Everyone has fears, mijo. It's marriage. It's a... it's a lifelong commitment. There's nothing* wrong *with having fears about that."*

*I'd looked away because we were suddenly locked back in a battle that had dominated our short time together: me expressing a feeling. Clarke telling me it was the wrong feeling.*

*"People in love don't have fears, Jo," he'd said. "So you either need to get on board and stop being afraid or..."*

*"Or what?" I said, hating the layer of desperation that coated my voice. I needed Clarke like I needed air to breathe.*

*"I don't know," he said dismissively. "I really don't."*

"When I brought those fears up to Clarke, he basically told me I was the one to blame," I said, voice firm, hating how memories of him could still seep into my conscious mind like a poison. How was that possible? How did he still have so much *control*?

Lucia squeezed my hand. "I'm going to take a big leap here. What is it about Gabe that reminds you of Clarke?"

I sighed, dropping my head onto my knees. "I don't even know why we're talking about this. I mean, I know we're stuck here for a few more days, but it's not like I'm going to see him again. Ever."

"Shit, you sound so *sad*," Lu teased. "Who says you'll never see him again? Or... I don't know, who says you can't have a wild, totally passionate fling for a week with a sexy bartender? I bet Mr. Big Dick could keep you *very* entertained while we're all stuck in this storm."

She waggled her eyebrows suggestively. I laughed, the

humor briefly clearing the tight feeling that was closing around my throat. I watched the waves for a moment, trying to make the jumbled mess of my thoughts into some sort of logical sense.

"That first night with Gabe, I was so fucking *attracted* to him. But then, instead of fucking, we... talked. And laughed. And he actually *listened*. And he gave me..." I held my palms out. "He gave me a fantasy I'd dreamed about for years. And none of this was expected. But it's been... what, forty-eight hours? And I feel completely turned inside out by him."

Lucia stroked my hair. "I get it, *chica*. You said something similar after your first date with Clarke."

Tears filled my eyes, and I wiped them away quickly.

"How can something so intense ever be healthy?" I asked in a quiet voice. I wasn't interested in another relationship with a person who was just going to burn me to the ground.

Lucia let out a long sigh, watching the waves with me. "Good question. And I'm not sure I can answer that. *You've* got to listen." She tapped the space above my collarbone. "It's in here somewhere."

"What?"

"The answer," she said firmly, wrapping us tighter in the blanket. "And for what it's worth, I think Clarke's goal... no, not think. I *know* Clarke's goal was to continually undermine you. Get you to doubt yourself."

A task in which he'd succeeded mightily.

"But he's not here. He doesn't have the privilege of being in your life any longer. And he's *definitely* not Gabe. And it's true that you don't know him that well but—" She turned, looking at me. "You could always get to know Gabe better. Of all the things in this world, happiness isn't something you should have to earn."

I swallowed back more tears, leaning against my best friend.

She hugged me. "Happiness is what you *deserve*. And I think you should reach out and take it."

23

## GABE

The next morning I filled my pack with sandwiches, laced up my hiking shoes, and headed out for the location of the first rockslide, about a mile from The Bar. As I hiked, leaves and pine needles crunched under my feet, releasing a unique blend of scents: Christmas morning and campfire nights. I looked up, craning my neck to see the tops of the redwood trees, and felt the power of standing under a living thing so old it defied imagination. Felt that same tug, right above my heart, towards this magical and beautiful place.

I'd gone to college in Monterey, less than an hour away, and not a single friend understood why I wanted to come back here. To waste the heady days of my twenties in a small town with almost no young people, no job prospects, and nothing to do.

But there'd never been another option for me. I couldn't explain it, the same way I couldn't explain my fantasy to be dominated. It just existed. Unending and unyielding. A piece of my DNA.

Despite my thoughts of Josie, the hike was peaceful. The

scenery beautiful. But when I turned the corner, coming out from the woods and onto the highway, the full impact of the rock slide—of the destruction and the terror—was a swift kick to the gut.

*My home.*

Boulders the size of cars lined the highway, having cascaded down the mountain, bringing smaller rocks, trees, branches and a river of mud with them. An ugly, jagged scar on the landscape—a landscape I knew had been slowly changing for a hundred years. Slowly being eroded by human beings, wildfires started by campers, global warming, and construction. I swallowed roughly, almost overwhelmed with my sense of anger and helplessness. The crew looked tiny against the immensity of the boulders.

I waved, suddenly feeling like my gift of sandwiches was inadequate. But then I saw Scott, an old buddy from high school.

"Gabe Shaw," he said with a grin, wiping dirt across his face. He whistled, indicating a break, and one by one the weary road crew began untangling themselves from the various pieces of equipment set up around the slide.

"I brought you a present." I slid the pack off my back, opening it up to reveal about 40 sandwiches I'd made and hand-wrapped in tinfoil this morning.

"I know it's not much, but we thought you guys might—" I trailed off, holding up a sandwich. Scott grabbed it from my hand before I could even finish.

"There *is* a God," Scott said, unwrapping it and devouring half of it in less than a minute. I laughed, greeting the crew members warmly and handing them as many sandwiches as they could hold.

"Listen," I said to Scott, indicating the massive boulders behind him. "I wanted to thank you for being out here. I know it's not easy. Or even that safe." I looked uneasily at the rocks balanced precariously above our heads. "But you're out here, doing the hard work that the community needs."

Scott shrugged. "You know I'd do anything for this place. But it's a big-ass fucking job though." He whistled softly. "We're honestly lucky no one was hurt."

"You're telling me," I said, glancing towards the cliff side where the smaller boulders had smashed into the ocean, which was currently angrily swirling in the stormy winds. It was the deadly edge of living here, the hair-raising risk we all took every day.

"The faster we work, the less effect it'll have," Scott said, interrupting my thoughts. "You remember the wildfire two years ago?"

I grimaced, nodding. Like all beautiful yet remote towns, Big Sur relied heavily on tourism, and when fires destroyed your picturesque views, people no longer wanted to pay to come here.

"I've been thinking the same thing," I said, unwrapping my own sandwich. "Tourists who are stuck here are going to be pissed, probably. And people who had already booked hotel rooms for this weekend will also probably be pissed."

It all had an effect; it all poked and prodded at the sustainability of our town.

Scott perched on a rock, taking off his vest for a moment. "I mean, there's nothing we can do except work as hard as we can, which we're doing."

"And the City Council meeting is next week," I said. "We can start talking about recovery efforts there. If we need to raise money, we can always do a fundraiser at The Bar. We've done it before."

Scott grinned wolfishly. "I don't remember much about the last fundraiser except I was drunk as fuck. The entire town was there. Gloria and Gladys, I think, danced on top of the bar? Austin wasn't wearing pants. Kevin puked in the bushes. And you and Sasha had gotten into some argument, right?"

He laughed heartily. I didn't. I *did* remember that night. My brother had a tendency to... unburden himself of clothing when he was drinking. And the whole-town fundraisers *always* turned into ragers.

"Fuck, how long ago was that?" I said, scratching my head. Sasha and I *had* gotten in a huge fight that night. But I'd just blocked it from my memory. She always felt that I was rushing her into commitment, but at that point, we'd been together more than five years, and I was dying to put a ring on her finger.

"Years, buddy," he said, chugging from a bottle of water. "Which is good. Town hasn't been in need for a while," he said, cocking his head at the rocks behind him. "But we never truly know."

"We sure don't," I said, staring at the top of the large hill where the slide had originated.

Terrifying.

When other people brought up stories of Sasha and I, they never painted us as the couple I thought we'd been. Like Gloria and Gladys, exchanging looks over my head as I explained the nature of our relationship. But I'd *sworn* she was The One. Sworn we were soulmates, traveling down a path towards a passionate and happy marriage.

What had they seen that I hadn't?

"So how's the Satanist?" Scott asked with a smirk.

"Not a Satanist," I said, shaking my head and laughing. "And it's not a thing. *She's* not a thing. Plus, they're only here until this slide gets cleared so... you wouldn't be willing to uh... slow down a bit? Clear this slide out slowly over a period of years?"

Scott laughed, and I hitched the now-empty pack onto my back. Rain was starting to fall lightly again, smattering against the rocks.

"Ah, I'd heard some things," he said mysteriously.

"Like what? And was it the twins?"

"You know it," he laughed. "Anyway, I heard this girl might be different. At least, that's what the Channel had to say."

I swore under my breath. "It's going to be hell the next time I see my parents."

"Aw, Gabe, it's only payback, brother. For all those years of gossip. Now *you're* the main attraction."

I clapped him on the back. "Yeah, yeah," I said, half-turning back towards the trail. "But I'll tell you now. There isn't anything there, man. It's not a thing."

Scott only nodded, whistling again to the crew lying tired across the rocks. "Whatever you say. And listen, thanks again for the food. Real act of kindness."

I shrugged with a grin. "Any time. Honestly. I can make a delivery again tomorrow if it would help? I'm supposed to drive some extra water over to Charlie's house. I can swing by and make sure you guys are fed too."

"Honestly, I think the crew would love that," Scott said, glancing their way. "It's gonna be a rough few days."

"Done," I said. "And not a problem. Maybe I'll even sneak a little beer into a thermos," I said, waving to everyone as I turned to go. "I'll see you tomorrow, hey?"

Scott laughed his approval before turning back to that gigantic mess.

I couldn't stop thinking about it as I hiked back. When you lived in a small town, these things tended to send shock-waves, and I definitely felt it. Already my mind was racing ahead to the next town meetings, of the money the clean-up would cost, the effect on businesses. I was so caught up in my thoughts, dodging the rain under heavy branches, I'd hiked back with barely a notice.

And when I pulled open the door to The Bar, the landline was ringing again.

It was Isabelle.

"Iz?" I asked, hearing the jagged exhaustion in her voice. "What's wrong?"

"Can you come and get this fucking baby?" she asked as Lola wailed in the background.

---

ISABELLE AND MAYA both looked like death warmed over.

"I brought coffee," I said, holding out large thermoses. Isabelle took one with grateful hands. I thought Maya was going to cry. Wrapping the two of them in a hug, I spotted Lola in her playpen in the corner, face screwed up in anger.

"So what's going on?" I said.

"Oh, nothing... just that our baby is trying to fucking *kill us*," Isabelle said, sinking into the couch with the coffee. Maya sat across the room, which I thought was odd.

I scooped Lola from her playpen and held her to my chest.

"She's been getting into the knives again?" I asked, but neither of them smiled. Lola gurgled softly, and I ran my palm over her soft hair.

"We weren't expecting to be... *stuck* here," Maya said, biting her lip. "So we don't have her things. And your parents have been *great*, but they've been busy since the rockslide, and we've been stuck in this *damn* house."

"And Lola won't sleep. Or can't sleep. Or *refuses*... fuck, I don't know," Isabelle said.

I grinned ruefully, rocking a half-asleep Lola.

"But look, she sleeps *for you*," Isabelle said helplessly.

"It's all good," I soothed. "I get it. You're exhausted and going stir-crazy. And of *course* I'll take her. I had some errands to run before opening The Bar anyway. We can hang out, have an Uncle-Gabe-and-Lola day."

Iz and Maya were both nodding like I was informing them they'd just won the lottery.

"From your reactions, I'm guessing that sounds good to you?"

Maya was already packing a diaper bag.

"*Thank you*," Isabelle said, standing up and leaning against me. "I think we just need to sleep."

"Do whatever you need," I said, grabbing the bag from Maya. "All I have to do is feed her. Change her diaper. Make sure she doesn't fall off of anything, right?"

"Something like that," Isabelle yawned. "Oh God, are we terrible mothers?"

I laughed. "Not at all. Remember that one time Austin threw a temper tantrum for a week straight and Dad threatened to leave him in the woods for the wolves to eat?"

"But Austin is a dipshit."

"And Lola is *just* a baby. And you're the parents to a six-month-old. They're like tiny psychopaths." I walked backward to the door. "Give yourselves a break. You're doing a wonderful job."

But they were already snoring on their separate couches.

I smiled, closing the door softly behind me. Snagged the car seat from their van. Buckled a sleepy Lola into my car.

"Hey cutie," I said, stroking her cheek. Drool dripped from her mouth as she giggled. "Looks like it's just you and me today, huh?"

---

LOLA WAS GOING to be the talk of the Big Sur Channel. Gladys and Gloria basically kidnapped her at the post office (I ended up having to bribe them with gossip to get her back). Ruth and Mrs. Manahan cooed over her at the grocery store. And now we were at the Big Sur Bakery, stopping for coffee and a bottle, and people kept coming up to exclaim over her cuteness.

To her credit, Lola *was* adorable.

I sipped my coffee and squeezed into the back of the room near the fireplace. It was packed, crowded with locals *and* tourists, and there was a low hum of conversation and laughter. Lola had a tight grip on my index finger, the windows were wide open to the rainy forest outside, and the server had just brought me an extra chocolate croissant because they'd baked too many.

"Great day we're having," I said to Lola, who tried to shove the entire croissant in her mouth. I laughed, whipping it behind my back and replacing it with her bottle. She took it greedily, milk spilling down her cheek. I had that sensation again, the gentle comfort of being in the place you love the most. Of Big Sur wrapping me in her arms.

But then I looked up toward the register and spotted Josie. And that gentle comfort was steamrolled by my intoxicating attraction to her. Immediately, there were whispers, several side-long glances directed my way, but I ignored them in favor of trying to both *stare* and *not stare* at Josie at the same time. She hadn't wanted to see me again—hadn't wanted to bump into each other while stuck here—and if I could have shrunk myself to honor her wishes, I would have.

Except I was a giant man squeezed into the corner with a six-month-old baby. I stood out. And any second she was going to look up and see me.

I hoped.

I mean... *didn't* hope.

"This girl's really got me twisted up," I muttered to Lola, who responded by throwing up on herself and knocking over my coffee. I laughed despite my confusion, lifting her from her high-chair and cleaning her against my chest as coffee dripped down my leg. And *that* moment—when I was covered in coffee and baby puke—was when I happened to look up and find Josie watching me.

## 24

## JOSIE

There ought to be a law that Gabriel Shaw—sexy bartender, hippie lumberjack, Viking with a man bun—should *never* be allowed to hold tiny infants against his broad, muscular chest. Should never be allowed to smile at that infant like she's his whole world, to laugh and tickle her as he cleans up her mess.

And definitely, Gabe Shaw shouldn't have been allowed to hold an infant that *looked* like she could be my daughter. The light-brown skin, the dark, curling hair. For the briefest moments, standing in line for coffee, nerves frazzled with sleeplessness, I had allowed myself a five-second fantasy.

*Oh, look. There's my adorable husband Gabe, holding our baby.*

Gabe looked up, eyes meeting mine, and every cell in my body softened.

*This* had been what I was fucking worried about.

I'd spent most of yesterday frantically trying to rebuild the fortress that protected my heart—the one Gabe had sent crumbling to the ground. And when I'd finally laid down to sleep, I was tortured by a nightmare I'd started to have after the wedding: that I was running down a long hallway, fleeing from *something*, but the walls were closing in. Pressing against my shoulders, squeezing my body. And just when I get to an open doorway, flooded with light, a hand grabs my wrist.

I hadn't had that nightmare in more than a year.

I didn't know if it was a response to Gabe—or the fact that Clarke's voice had seemed to spike in volume recently.

The nightmare had left me sleepless and anxious. I needed to get the fuck out of Big Sur's only coffee shop. Except I was *so* tired. So on edge. And in the midst of this crowded space, Gabe glowed like the sun in the sky.

Suddenly my feet were propelling me through the crush of bodies until I was standing in front of him and his tiny baby.

"Hi," I said weakly. Coffee was spilled everywhere, but Gabe didn't seem to care. "Do you want to share mine?" I held out my coffee with trembling fingers. "Although I should warn you, it's *real* coffee. Black, no cream and sugar."

A smile slid up his face as he chuckled. He took the mug from me, lips touching where mine had just been.

"I do want to share," he said. "And hello."

I sat gingerly in the chair across from him, mind flooded with memories of our night together.

"Who's this?" I asked, stroking the baby's arm with my finger.

"This is my niece, Lola." He looked down at her, waving her tiny fist my way. She was half-asleep. "Do you want to hold her?" he asked, and before I could even answer, I had an infant in my arms.

"Oh... I..." I swallowed awkwardly, startled by the sudden intimacy of holding a baby. She didn't even wake up, just turned her head against me, snoring softly.

My nerves lost a bit of their jagged edge.

"I think I needed to hold a baby today," I said.

"Lola is the cure to all of life's sorrows," he smiled, sipping my coffee. "My sister and her wife are stuck at my parents' house because of the slide. They called for backup, so I thought we'd have a day together. Let her hang out at The Bar. Take her first shot."

I laughed, tracing my finger around Lola's miraculously small ones. Trying to pretend I wasn't impressed with my Viking's love and support for his family.

"I'm sorry. About how I left the other morning," I blurted out. "And I'm sorry if that makes... me coming over here awkward."

He laughed, rubbing his hand through his beard. "I was desperately wishing you'd come over and trying not to be *totally* obvious about it." Hawk-sized butterflies beat their wings against my ribcage. "Also, you don't have to apologize. You didn't do anything wrong."

I looked back down at a sleeping Lola, aware I was blushing.

"Do you ever just get... too in your head sometimes?" I asked, refusing to meet his eyes.

"Absolutely," Gabe replied kindly. "You mentioned something happening a few years ago. Is that part of it?"

I traced Lola's cheek with my finger, then finally met his gaze. "Yes."

I didn't feel comfortable saying more, and luckily Gabe seemed to sense that, nodding at my answer. "You look pretty..."

"Exhausted?" I said, arching an eyebrow.

"You do. Did you sleep last night?"

I shook my head. "I did *not* sleep. At least not in the traditional sense of the word *sleep*."

Gabe grinned. "You missing the bright lights, city girl?"

I smiled since that was part of it too. I wasn't ready—would probably never be ready—to talk about what happened with Clarke. But I *did* miss Los Angeles.

"I miss the fuck out of it," I laughed. "It's the Best Place on Earth after all."

Gabe scoffed. "No way. That's *here*." He indicated the people around him.

"This small town in the middle of nowhere with *nothing to do*... that's your pitch? For Best Place on Earth?"

Gabe handed my coffee back to me, tips of his fingers brushing mine. "Absolutely. But I will hear opening arguments."

"*So* nice of you," I teased.

He laughed, nodding his head at me. "Go ahead, city girl. Make your pitch."

I thought for a moment, leaning back in my chair. "My parents are from Guadalajara, a huge city in Mexico. They married young and, as soon as they had enough money, immigrated to the United States. Specifically to Los Angeles because we had a few other family members who already lived there. In East L.A., where I grew up and still live, just a few blocks down from my parents. And my four brothers and their families."

"*Four* brothers?"

I flashed him a smile. "Yes. All older."

"I didn't know that," Gabe said.

"It's why I'm so independent," I said, tapping Lola's cheek. "Everyone always dotes on the baby girl in a family of all boys. Dotes and coddles."

"Ah," Gabe said. "Josefine Torres is not a woman who likes being *coddled*."

"Nope," I said. "Not at all. Although my brothers still do it. Growing up they were overly protective. Although," I said, tilting my head, "they also taught me how to kick some serious ass."

"You do have the look of a fighter about you."

My skin warmed under his appraisal. Although it had been my brothers who wanted to fight on my wedding day. They'd been livid with barely concealed fury and protectiveness. A trait of theirs I usually *despised*, but the day of the wedding was different. And as I clung to Lucia in my wedding dress, listening to my parent's fretful conversation in Spanish, it was wholly comforting to hear the numerous ways my siblings would make Clarke's life a living hell.

They never did, of course. In the end, I'd begged them not to. I was so confused and miserable that a small part of me still thought we'd get back together—after Clarke explained the simple miscommunication that led to him standing me up on our wedding day.

The things your brain will do to protect your heart.

"So they all live within spitting distance of you in East L.A.?" Gabe asked, and I drop-kicked those memories away in favor of the sweet Viking in front of me.

"Yes. And I love it. It just *works* for us. There's an ease to our neighborhood, the ability to stroll down the street and see your loved ones. Informally, not just around the holidays. Although my parents also 'stop by' often with some made-up excuse." I smoothed my hand through Lola's curls. "Even though we all know it's just that they miss me."

"What's East L.A. like?" he asked.

"It's almost an entirely Hispanic neighborhood, so I think for my parents they felt comfortable living there at first. Everyone speaks Spanish. It's culturally similar to Mexico. It has community. So they stayed. And then we all did. Different from Big Sur, where I get the distinct impression I'm the only brown person here."

Gabe nodded thoughtfully. "My sister's wife, Maya, is Black, and they've said before it's why they live in Monterey, not here. Not that Monterey is *that* much more diverse, but they feel like there are more people who look like her and Lola. And more gay couples too."

Lola's big brown eyes opened, looking up at me with complete trust. "I totally get it. Los Angeles is incredibly diverse, ethnically *and* culturally. I've never felt like an outsider there. Does that make sense?"

"It does. Although, if I'm being honest, I wouldn't have thought L.A. would have much *community*."

"Because it's a city?"

"I guess... yeah, I think of community as being fostered in small towns. Like Big Sur. Everyone knows each other, their neighbors. It's supportive."

I considered his point. "L.A. is huge. *Huge*, that's true. If you ever go there, you'll be overwhelmed with the sprawl and the smog and the freeways and just the enormity of it all."

Gabe grimaced. "It's why I'll never go."

"Never say never," I said softly. Then immediately wanted to shove the words right back in my fucking mouth. Because Gabe's face lit up so ardently... I knew what he was thinking. Hoping.

"You know, it's not so bad," I said, steering us back. "Because the trick to living in L.A. is to *find* that community, which usually exists in these pocket neighborhoods that become their own small towns. Suddenly, the city doesn't feel so big because your world is just fifteen city blocks of friends and neighbors."

We were interrupted by a server, dropping off another chocolate croissant and smiling broadly at Gabe.

"Popular guy," I mused, but he only shrugged, breaking the fluffy pastry into two pieces.

"They're all just here for Lola," he countered, but I knew differently. Gabe emanated the same energy here as he did on the patio that night—an energy that *welcomed*. People were desperate to be around him—it was obvious to me.

Gabe held the pastry out and I took it. It was warm and sweet with a hint of bitterness.

"Describe it for me," he said.

"What?"

"Your neighborhood," he said. "Because you've seen some parts of Big Sur already—"

"—Most of Big Sur," I interjected. "Right? I mean, how much more is there to see?"

Gabe shook his head in mock horror. "Josefine," he said.

"Yes?" I tossed my hair, very aware that I was now flirting.

Eating a croissant... sharing a cup of coffee... This was starting to feel like a fucking date.

"I'll *take* you to the best places in Big Sur," he promised. "You just tell me when. I'll take you wherever you want to go. Hidden waterfalls. Secret streams." A pause. "Private beaches."

Another searing fantasy: my back pressed against hot sand, Gabe's head between my legs, tongue on my clit.

I *wanted* to think about Gabe's cock. That perfect, thick shaft I'd taken to the back of my throat.

But I hadn't taken him inside of me. Something I was just now beginning to regret.

Because I'd never know that pleasure.

"Maybe," I hedged, attempting to claw myself back to higher ground. Gabe's eyes trailed hotly up and down my body. "What was... what was your original question?"

A sexy grin. "Tell me about your neighborhood."

So I exhaled and closed my eyes. Talking about L.A was something I could do.

I pictured a hot summer's night in my neighborhood.

"Sticky heat," I started. "*Mariachi* music blaring from someone's speaker, overlaid by the beats of a hip-hop song being played by someone else. A house party, probably, that will spill out into the street, and then everyone in the neighborhood joins in. *Abuelas* and little kids and even the loner down the street that no one knows. People walking around everywhere—people of every skin color and ethnicity. Languages you've never heard before. The smell of wet asphalt and that feeling when the entire night unfolds in front of you, like a dream. There's always something to do. New art or music or films or just sitting on your porch and people-watching for hours. Never bored. Never sitting still. Always *moving*."

I opened my eyes. Gabe's expression was filled with reverence. "That sounds beautiful," he said.

"A different beauty than Big Sur," I said, shrugging my shoulders, shaking off the intensity. "And not without its many issues. Namely that it's a hell of a lot easier to be a rich person there than a poor person. And it can be materialistic and fake and image-obsessed."

"Big Sur is slowly becoming a playground for the ultra-rich," Gabe said. "A vacation destination, a road-trip stop, not a community of residents."

I nodded. "We'd both love our home towns regardless."

"So this is probably a silly question but... you'll never leave Los Angeles?" Gabe asked, and there was no denying the plea in his voice.

"Never," I said. "Because of my family. But also I've spent ten years building a career there, a career that is very specific to Los Angeles. Technically, I could be a makeup artist in any big city but... I spent all that time building up a high-end celebrity client list. Referrals. My reputation."

I shook my head at the finality of it. Because I honestly did *not* want to move. But the more firmly I spoke, the more I wanted to reach across the tiny table, grab Gabe's collar, and yank him in for a kiss.

The contradiction was bothering me.

A lot.

"Family, career, community," Gabe said. "That's a pretty strong argument for staying in your hometown." His eyes landed on Lola.

"You feel the same way though," I said.

"Exactly the same way. Even if, ultimately, we disagree about which of our hometowns is the Best Place on Earth."

"Agree to disagree," I laughed, then stood to gently deposit Lola in his arms. My skin burned where it brushed against his. I inhaled his woodsy scent. "Here's your baby back."

"Do you have to go?"

"I... I mean yeah," I stumbled. "We're shooting today. Ray wants to get some storm shots."

Gabe lifted Lola up onto his shoulder, rubbing her back. She was *so small* against his chest, and it was doing things to me.

Strange things.

"You're good with her," I pointed out, gathering my things.

"I'd do anything for Lola," he said. "Anything."

I bit my lip; our eyes locked together. I wanted... I wanted...

Fuck. I didn't know what I wanted.

"You seem like the kind of person who would do anything for someone you loved." I was slowly turning away, even as I wanted to leap into his arms.

"I would," Gabe said. "For the person I loved? I'd give them *everything*, Josie."

## 25

## GABE

"A threesome?" Gloria asked, eyes wide with glee and wonder. She took another sip of her coffee which, not twenty-minutes before, she'd poured a generous amount of Hennessy into.

"I swear on my grandmother's grave," I said, laying my palm over my heart.

"I knew your grandmother," Gladys said. "Real piece of work. And don't tell your dad this, but if you think what *we* read is steamy, you should have seen her collection of 'vintage erotica,'" she said with exaggerated air quotes.

I shuddered. "I don't know if I need to know this."

"True story, though. True story," Gloria piped in, reaching under the desk for the Hennessey bottle. The three of us were in the post office although it was technically closed until the rock slide was cleared. A few locals kept wandering in there, ostensibly looking for updates from the Big Sur Channel.

"The mayor's son. Two other girls. All seniors, attempting to have a threesome in a car." I said solemnly. "I don't think it was... you know, *successful,* at least according to Angela."

Angela hadn't been a police officer for long, but for a glass of wine at The Bar, she'd gossip your ear off.

"What is this town coming to?" Gloria asked with dancing eyes.

Two dog-eared paperbacks were sprawled on the counter next to them. *Cold Bed, Warm Stranger* and *Wed to the Pirate Captain*. Both with long-haired heroes and wilting heroines on the cover.

"Who knows?" I shrugged. "But anyway, thanks for the tomatoes. And I'm happy to hear you two are okay."

I'd come by to make sure the sisters had enough water—which of course they did. Both had houses with veritable bomb shelters filled to the brim with water and canned food. When I'd asked why, Gloria had merely said, "The Apocalypse," and left it at that.

"You going to fill us in on why that Josie girl was fleeing your house the other morning like it was on fire?" Gladys asked.

"No," I said. "Unless you want to tell me about Angela having to tell you *for the fourth time* to stop taking pictures of the models at The Mad Ones."

"I do love that shirtless one," Gloria sighed, hands over her heart. "And we don't have television; you know that, Gabriel."

I laughed, grabbing the bushel of tomatoes Gloria had brought me. "Well, I should—"

"Details," Gladys interrupted. "What's the scoop? Josie didn't like the bouquets? They were too much? Or..."

She looked pointedly at the area of my crotch.

"*Gladys*," I hissed, holding the bushel in front of me. "Jesus."

"Well, then, what was it?" Gloria asked as Gladys snickered into her coffee.

"It's nothing. It's just... listen, I told you guys it was probably just going to be a one-night thing. And even though technically they're stuck here for a few extra days, she's still sticking to that."

"She sticks to her guns. I like that," Gloria said.

I liked that too.

"So I backed off." I paused. "Although we did have coffee together yesterday afternoon." Their eyebrows just about shot straight off their foreheads. "*Accidentally*."

It had also accidentally felt like a date. An experience that had my heart racing wildly for the rest of the day and a dopey grin glued to my face. Back at The Bar, I'd put on an old James Brown record and danced with Lola until customers showed up.

It was a small thing. But it felt like *progress*. Our connection wasn't momentary. Wasn't just lust-driven or random. It sparked between us like lightning striking the ground.

The only issue being that we'd spent that accidental date talking about how Josie would never consider living anywhere else except Los Angeles.

"And do you need any advice? Suggestions for *romance*?" Gloria said, tapping on the cover of *Wed to the Pirate Captain*.

"I'm not sure Josie is really *that* amenable to grand romantic gestures. Although she did love the flowers. So thank you for that."

They nodded, raising their mugs to me in a toast as I walked towards the door.

"Are you two going to be okay to drive home?"

"Oh, we keep cots in the back," Gloria said. "We'll just pass out whenever it's convenient."

I rolled my eyes to the ceiling. "Okay, then, well,"

I turned to go, but Gladys called out. "You'll find her. You know that, right, Gabriel? She's out there."

"Who?" I asked, even though I knew.

"Your person. You'll find your person."

I smiled in gratitude, but couldn't stop the roller-coaster-drop feeling in the pit of my stomach.

Because maybe I had found her.

# 26

# JOSIE

I unfurled my black bag of makeup tricks and instantly felt calmer after my accidental date with Gabe that morning.

We were prepping for a shoot in the rain, and by an odd twist of events, Calvin (who'd never modeled a day in his life) was going to be photographed with Lucia.

Who was a bundle of nerves—something I hadn't seen in years.

"You ready for this *mija?*" I asked with a sly grin.

"Born ready, motherfucker," she said.

I rolled my eyes, since I knew better, but there were people buzzing all around us, and I knew she wouldn't want anyone else to know why *Calvin* made her so nervous.

I turned back to my black bag, stroking my fingers down the assortment of tools. My career thus far had been one hell of a journey. I'd trained, studied, took tests and failed. Took tests and succeeded. Had scrambled to find clients while working multiple jobs (waitress, cosmetics counter at the mall, Sephora). All of that had led me to Lucia. Who led me to doing makeup for the models at the Victoria Secret runway shows. And then B-level actresses for award ceremonies.

And then celebrities for the Oscars. And now, I was doing makeup for the hottest fashion line in the world.

"Let's see," I said, pulling through a palette of bronzers and primers. "You're going to be in the pouring rain, so what's not going to melt right off your face as soon as you step outside?" I tapped my finger against my lip, thinking. "Maybe a subtle smokey eye and a nude lip?"

Lucia nodded, anxiously watching Calvin who was listening intently as Ray explained to him what modeling was.

"Cool, cool," she said. "You're the boss."

I laughed softly to myself, getting back to the task at hand. I grabbed a sponge and the foundation I needed, reached forward, and swept Lucia's hair up and out of her face.

"You're nervous," I said, moving the sponge down her cheekbones, lightly covering her skin.

"I heard through the Big Sur Channel you had coffee with Gabe this morning," Lucia said, ignoring me.

"The *fuck?*" I hissed, covertly looking behind me. "It's barely been two *hours*."

Her lips twitched up. "You're the talk of the town, babe."

"Cool, cool," I said, mimicking her.

She kicked me. Wincing, I coated Lucia's eyelids in a dark, gritty eyeshadow. Drew a thick strip of black across the top of Lucia's lashes.

"Open." Lu fluttered her eyes open, smiling up at me.

"*Hermosa.*"

"Do you remember what I said?" she asked.

I rolled my eyes with a sigh, turning back to find a brightening powder. I knocked some into the palm of my hand, rolled a brush through it, and started dabbing along the inside of her eye.

"You can still have a wild, passionate fling with a sexy bartender. Who has a big dick," she continued.

I laughed despite myself. "I remember what you said. And I also need you to remind me why I hate men, generally. And relationships, specifically. And that it won't work with Gabe, *especially*."

"Okay, I think I got it," Lucia muttered.

"Smart-ass," I said, laying down a strip of false eyelashes and pressing them into place. A memory was tugging at me: the morning of the wedding, my eyes closed as another makeup artist friend, Jazz, glued lashes to my eyes, speaking in soft Spanish with my mother who was holding my left hand.

And Lucia, holding my right hand, saying over and over, *You've never looked so beautiful.*

I swallowed hard, clearing my throat.

"These need to set," I said, even though Lucia knew that. This was probably the three-hundredth pair of false eyelashes I'd glued to her over the last ten years.

"Okay," she said kindly. "Sorry, I'm just still formulating the thesis you requested."

"You don't *have* to indulge my theatrics," I smirked, blending blush on my hand. I swirled the color, then held it up to Lucia's cheek.

"Got it," Lucia said, eyes still closed but a secretive smile on her face. "You hate men in general because two years ago, a terrible one used you. Emotionally manipulated you. Had you plan a fucking *wedding* for months. Stood you up. And you never saw him again." Her voice was quieter so the crew wouldn't hear.

The words hardened my heart. "That's right."

"Relationships, specifically..." she tapped her finger against her lips. "You hate men, in general, but you do use them quite frequently to get off."

"Their sole purpose," I said dryly.

"But Clarke..." she paused. "Clarke was not a good example of what I think a relationship could be. *Should* be. He gave them all a bad name." Her eyes fluttered open.

"You're going to fuck up the lashes," I said, reaching for her, but she grabbed my hand, holding it for a second.

"Which brings me to Gabe. I've thought a lot about this since we've arrived here in Big Sur. This place is... this place is opening my eyes to some things. Don't you think?" she asked, eyes wide and vulnerable.

I nodded slowly, thinking of the angry ocean, the dark, winding roads through the forest. The almost imperceptible calm I'd felt at night as I lay in my tiny cabin, listening to the wind and the waves. So different from the endless, frenetic energy of Los Angeles.

"I know what you mean," I said.

"I think... I think the longer you *don't* date someone who you might care about, the more you let Clarke win." Lu reached up to tap my temple. "I know he's in there, but he's not in charge anymore."

"*Mija*," I started.

"*Escuchame*," Lucia responded. "I'm not saying it's not complicated or that I have a clear answer of what you should do. But you, Josefine Torres, are the most bad-ass woman I know. Before Clarke, I watched you light the world on fire to get what you want. Is Gabe what you want?"

*Yes.*

"I don't know," I said.

"That's fair," Lu said. "It's only been a couple of days. But I just don't want you to dismiss your own bad-assery."

"That's not a word."

"Who gives a fuck?" Lucia said, leaning back in the chair and crossing her long legs. It was moments like this when it was easy to forget that my best friend was a famous supermodel. Even half-covered in makeup on the set of a photo shoot.

Calvin walked up to us, looking nervous as ever, about to join us in makeup. But then a wardrobe assistant grabbed him, lifting him out of his shirt. I narrowed my eyes.

"Cal has a nicer body than I thought," I said, suddenly distracted. What was *with* this town? Were all the men secret hunks?

"Mm-hmm," Lu said, similarly distracted. She was watching Calvin, fingers against her lips.

"How do you feel about him?" All I knew was that they'd shared a hot and heavy make out, they'd talked about books, and they'd been leaving secret poems for each other like goofy grade-schoolers. It was freaking adorable.

"Do you remember our Best Night Ever?" she asked suddenly, looking back at me.

I did. Every night Lucia and I tore it up in the city, we made it our goal for it to be epic and wild. But one night we'd hit the jackpot. Started with carnitas tacos from my favorite taco truck in East L.A. Drinks at our favorite blues club, Franklin Bell's on Colden Avenue. Stumbling down the road, we'd accidentally walked into a street fair, and Lucia and I had volunteered to be part of the fire-thrower display—holding hands and squealing as three sexy men tossed flames around our heads. Ended up at a club where, for real, Missy Elliott showed up for a surprise, pop-up concert, and we danced until we were breathless and covered in sweat. Were briefly stalked by the paparazzi as we'd snuck into KazuNori for late-night sushi. Then we snagged a 3:30 am showing of *Magic Mike* and hit our favorite diner for breakfast.

And then we'd honest-to-God shown up for work three

hours later: a twelve-hour photo shoot that I barely remembered because I kept sneaking off to sleep in the bathroom.

But it was... well, the Best Night Ever. My favorite combination of late-night shenanigans: part planning, part luck, part letting the warm embrace of a Los Angeles night guide you through chaos.

I grinned at the memory, feeling powerfully homesick. Exhilaration, spontaneity, a powerful feeling of being alive. The visceral texture of that night was something I could recall perfectly.

"Of course I do. Tacos, Missy Elliot, fire breathers."

"Every time I look at Cal, it feels like Best Night Ever," Lucia said.

"Wow," I said, applying blush to her cheeks, although she was already blushing. "All of that, just from looking at him?"

Her eyes turned back to me. "Every time."

I thought about Gabe and the exquisite connection we seemed to share. The way he seemed to really *see* me. His kind eyes. His desire to create a better community. His devotion to his family.

"Oh God," I said. "I think I feel it too."

---

THE NEXT MORNING, I woke up early and drove to a hiking trail in the Ventana Wilderness. Standing at the trail entrance, I looked through the forest: the branches dipping low, leaves heavy with moisture. The ground was drenched and muddy—pungently spring-like. There was no one around. No sound. No distractions.

Gabe had said he used nature as therapy, something I never thought I'd do. But I was entering my second day of sleeplessness, and I'd try anything.

Because I'd had the dream again.

Hallway closing in. A suffocating claustrophobia. A hand clamped on my wrist.

It was Clarke. I knew it.

And when I'd woken up, sweating, my heart galloping like a racehorse, it was thoughts of *Gabe* that comforted me. His deep laughter. The feel of his muscles flexing beneath my wandering fingers. His arms wrapped around me as I'd slumbered.

When I'd woken up, I wanted Gabe in my bed.

In so many ways, the fact that I'd used *Gabe* to get me through the night was more upsetting than Clarke's persistent subconscious presence.

My feet crunched over the ground as the trail wound through the forest. The after-effects of the storm were still present, and the mist hung like a fine curtain. The verdant greenery felt prehistoric. Ancient and beautiful.

I tried to find gratitude for this moment. This place. This unexpected week of pleasure I'd been granted. Like Lucia had said—I'd had a fling. I was allowed to *feel* things. To feel the complications of yearning for someone I'd never see again. It didn't mean I was going to end up, three months from now, waiting for Gabe to show up at our wedding.

And the rock slide could be cleared any day now—in fact, yesterday, at the coffee shop, could have been the last time I'd ever see Gabe.

Which was okay.

I inhaled the spicy scent of the pine needles. Tried to find peace in the bird song.

Except a rising tide of emotion was clogging my windpipe —so swiftly I had to sit down on a log, hands on my knees. Head between my legs.

*It was okay*. I was okay. The dream wasn't *real*. My wrists were free. Shoulders back. Nothing but expansive forest stretching behind me.

There was moisture on my cheeks, and I hurriedly wiped a stray tear. So *stupid*. I was just over-wrought. Homesick.

Actually, taking a lonely walk through the woods might not have been the best idea.

Suddenly there was a sharp *snap*, like ice breaking. Another one—distinctive, like a big animal moving through the brush. I jumped clear off the log, muffling a scream.

"If you're a bear, I will *fuck you up*," I shouted, looking around for a weapon.

But of course, it wasn't a bear. Or a cougar or a moose or even a large deer.

Because only in Big Sur could you wander through the woods and bump into the Viking you both desperately wanted to *fuck* and desperately wanted to avoid.

"Josie?" Gabe asked, hands up in surrender.

I let out a long breath. Propped my hands on my hips. "Oh, it's you," I said, trying for casual but failing miserably.

He gave me a mirthful look, an eyebrow raised. "Indeed. What are you doing here?"

"What are *you* doing here?" I shot back. On pure instinct, I was walking toward him. His half-grin spread across his handsome, bearded face.

"This is my hiking trail. I come here when I need to... sort some things out," he said, shrugging.

"Oh," I said as my feet took me right into Gabe's orbit. The tips of our shoes touched. I looked up, craning my neck, to meet his gaze. "Well. This national forest isn't big enough for the both of us."

Gabe chuckled. Then he reached out and hooked his pinkie finger through mine. "Can I say that I'm happy you're here? And… do you want to keep hiking?" A shy smile. "With me?"

Last night, in the depths of my insomnia, just the thought of Gabe comforted me back to sleep. Now in the middle of the woods, on the verge of panic, he arrived. Just in time.

It was okay.

*I was okay.*

"Yes," I said, allowing my finger to squeeze back.

## 27

## GABE

Walking through the wilderness with Josie, I felt more nervous than the night of my senior prom. I'd taken Sasha, who I was hoping would end up being my wife one day, but that felt like a relaxing day at the beach compared to how I felt now. Part of me had worried that our accidental coffee date was the last time we were going to see each other. My dad had called later that night and mentioned that the clearing was going faster than they predicted.

I was running out of time.

Although it wasn't like I had a plan. Josie had been explicit in her wishes.

But after yesterday, I had *hope*.

"So... you're sorting out some stuff, huh?" she asked. Josie looked beautiful in the forest. Her dark tresses in a high bun, her ears twinkling with piercings. She wore an over-sized sweater, black leggings, and boots. The play of the mist and the waning light made her look like a watercolor painting.

"Just thinking through some things," I hedged since of course I'd come out here to think of *her*. And I was pretty sure she knew that. "How about you?"

Josie bit her lip. "I'd remembered what you'd said. About nature as therapy. And I've... I haven't been sleeping well the past couple nights. I thought the woods might help."

I wasn't surprised she was seeking some help. When I'd come upon her in the woods, she'd looked pale and a little distraught. I thought about what she'd said, about being *too in her head*. Wondered what that meant.

I nudged her shoulder with mine. "You don't think I'm weird after all?" I lifted a low-hanging branch up for her as she walked beneath it.

"Not at all. Actually, I've been watching the waves by the cabins, you know, the ones by the bookstore?"

"Of course. They're beautiful. And that stretch of beach is so dramatic."

Her dark eyes brightened. "I think that's why I'm so captivated by it. Sometimes I just listen to the waves crashing against the shore. I'm starting to understand. The more I just let myself... *be* in nature, the more my tiny anxieties seem to quiet down. Not go away completely but..."

"Like a reprieve," I said.

"*Reprieve*. That's a great word for it."

We walked in silence for a minute before I continued. "I know it's different than how a lot of people live right now, being constantly stimulated and consumed with *stuff*. But I'm busy enough with The Bar. Between actually *running* it, then all the customers, finances, inventory... I usually end every day feeling like my brain is full enough without letting in anything else. I come out here, and there's this *quiet*. You can almost feel it on your skin. Everything just... clears away."

"That's interesting. You know, back home I'm almost never surrounded by silence. Not just the city, which is so loud and... sparkling," she said with a sigh. "But when I'm actually in my apartment, alone, I always have music on. Or the television.

Or a podcast. Or I'm talking on the phone. Thinking about that now... you're right. Every time there's quiet, my mind goes on overdrive."

"It's finally not overstimulated, so everything rushes back in. I know exactly what you mean. Sometimes, if I haven't hiked for a while, I put it off. Because I know the first hour my mind will be a fucking mess."

Josie nodded, looking down at her feet, thinking. We didn't talk for a few minutes, but I watched her looking around. Seeing the tiny details of the forest alive and all around us.

"*I went to the woods because I wished to live deliberately,*" I quoted. "*To front only the essential facts of life and to see if I could not learn what it is to teach and not, when I came to die, to discover that I had not lived.*"

A log, slick with moss, lay across a creek, and Josie walked across it gracefully as I followed her.

"Thoreau?" she asked.

"Yes. One of my favorite lines from *Walden*." We hiked up a slight incline, both of us starting to breathe more heavily. This was always my favorite part, feeling my body wake up. Muscles burning, lungs filling with air.

Josie looked thoughtful. "You have a really good life here," she said, but it wasn't a question. She looked at me with the same pensive expression. "Right? You own this great little bar. Live in the place you love the most, surrounded by family. I was just thinking about that Walden quote, and I don't know." Josie reached down to gather a bright orange leaf. She looked at it, and I imagined her artist's eye seeing things I never would. "I don't think anyone could say you weren't truly *living* here."

"Well... thank you. For what you said. I guess I can thank my parents and Robert, Calvin's grandfather, for that. Be honest. Be present. Go outside." I laughed a little. "Not bad life advice, considering."

"And love," she said, smiling almost sadly. "You'll have that too. And then your life will be full." Her eyes met mine, and I reached forward before I could stop myself, brushing a strand of her hair behind her ear. Letting the palm of my hand rest lightly on her cheek.

"Josie," I started, but she turned sharply, stalking toward a fallen redwood tree laying across the forest floor. It was a real giant, and I'd admired it every time I walked past it. Wondering when it had fallen, this mighty tree that had seen generations of life moving around it and through it. That had stood through lightning that singed the earth but also softly falling snow. Storms and sun, life and death.

And now Josie, running her hands up and down the bark like she was trying to memorize the texture.

"You think I can walk it?" she asked, turning to me with a new light in her eyes, the charged moment before seemingly forgotten.

"This?" I said, pointing. "I have a sneaking suspicion that you can do anything and everything, Josefine."

She looked startled for a moment, like she expected me to say she wasn't capable.

"Boost me up, mountain man?" she asked. I tried not to read into the slightly flirtatious tone in her voice.

"Of course," I said, walking over and kneeling down. I held out my hands, lacing them together and looked up at her. I liked this vantage point. I liked being at her fucking feet.

And I liked her looking down at me, lips poised to give me an order.

Her cheeks flushed, but she only said, "Thanks," before sliding her boot into my hands. I boosted her up.

"Can I use your head as a step?" she asked, placing her

boot on my head with barely constrained laughter. I joined her, trying to shake her off.

"No, you can't," I said. She pulled herself up the rest of the way.

"Well, you're no help," she said, looking down from her new perch, slightly out of breath and grinning. "And look, I did it," she said, standing up and spreading her arms.

"You sure did," I said. Josie looked like a goddamn queen up there. Tall, proud, overseeing her enchanted kingdom.

"What a bad-ass," I called up to her.

She gave me a goofy smile, flashing the peace sign. "I'll be down in a minute. I just want to walk up here. Entertain yourself, please," she said and then stalked down the log confidently. I watched for a minute, feeling the mist falling around me. Attempting to rein in the inevitable progress of my thoughts shooting towards the future. Wanting to ask Josie *why*. Or suggest *how*.

*Be present*, I reminded myself, breathing in the earth.

Letting her go.

## 28

## JOSIE

I was on top of the world. Standing on this giant, felled redwood, the sprawling forest all around me. Mist clung to the branches and to my skin in a gentle caress. There was bird song, the scent of dead leaves. And nothing to distract me. Not my phone, not the television, not music or art or work.

Just... this. My heart beating. The light layer of sweat beneath my clothing. I balanced, one foot in front of the other, and walked down the log, imagining it when it was alive, soaring into the clouds.

The hush of the forest was tangible. No sounds of traffic, no airplanes. For a moment, just like Gabe said, a rush of thoughts crowded my mind. *Is it okay that I'm having fun with Gabe? Is it okay that I want to kiss him? When are the roads going to be cleared? What will happen when I leave? Will I ever meet someone like him again?*

And then, like a burst of static in a silent room, I heard Clarke's voice.

*Do you think you can take that job?*

*Do you really think that's a good idea?*

*What if you're not able to do that justice?*

Clarke had a habit of endlessly underestimating me until I was able to do it on my own. Count myself out. It was the kind of subtle manipulation that started off as a mild irritant, almost unnoticeable. Before Clarke, I didn't give a *fuck* if other people thought I couldn't do something. But he started to say it so much that I came to believe it.

Until I didn't even have to ask his opinion anymore. I just stopped doing things.

Yet here I was, climbing on a fucking *redwood* tree, and I wasn't even afraid of falling.

The thoughts swirled together like a maelstrom. So I eliminated one of my senses and shut my eyes.

This forest wasn't capable of caring about my thoughts. This forest only knew how to do one thing: thrive. In all kinds of conditions and against all odds. It just... consumed nutrients and oxygen. Bathed in the sunlight. Let the rain streak down its sides. Rooted itself.

I was starting to understand.

"You like it up there?" Gabe called up to me, and I nodded, glancing down at him. My Viking was cute in his natural environment, leaning against a smaller tree like he was a second away from tearing it down with his bare hands.

"I love it," I said. "I can see why you love it here. In Big Sur. I know I can be kind of a Los Angeles snob, but... this place has a certain magic to it, doesn't it?"

I sat, dangling my legs off the side. Gabe reached up to help. His hands clamped around my upper thighs, then my hips, then my waist as I slid down the log. Slid down his big, hard body although his hands stayed respectful.

"You'll never leave this place," I said, voice thick.

Gabe was looking down at me, and for a moment, I

thought he might glide those hands up, under my countless layers, along my ribcage.

Instead he let go.

"Never," he said.

*There you have it.*

"I understand," I said.

He gave me a sad smile before turning back toward the trail. "Shall we, bad-ass? I mean, maybe you should lead the way." The humor was back in his voice.

I grinned back, grateful for the abatement: from his body, his heat, the gorgeous way his eyes crinkled at the sides.

"No way," I said, stepping back into place along the trail. "I'll always be a city girl at heart, which means my ability to lead us in a direction where we *don't* die—"

"—or get eaten by bears," Gabe said.

"True. Or get eaten—by *anything*—isn't something you should place much confidence in. But I can see why your childhood here was something you still hold so much respect for. This," I said, waving my hand around me, "is like living in a magical tree house but all the time. So much room for imagination and playfulness."

"It never leaves either. Even though I own a grungy dive bar with almost no windows, the feel of this place is always there. Always making itself known. Probably because the feel of the place is in the people, too."

"I love a good grungy bar though," I said, nudging his shoulder. "You know The Bar has a certain charm."

Gabe flashed a wry grin. "I love that place."

I laughed. "I know you do. You make it very obvious."

We paused for a moment to climb a steeper hill, and I realized I didn't feel nervous or weird about the fact that Gabe was witnessing me makeup-less, in workout clothes, as I huffed my way up hills, sweating and probably red-faced. Because I liked what we were doing, liked that he was showing me something that he loved—his tree house escape from the world.

I'd kept myself meticulous for Clarke, even when I wanted to just hang out in sweatpants. Meticulous, pretty, and always made-up.

"My favorite viewpoint is just up here," Gabe said. "Maybe another mile. Are you down for it?"

"Let's do it," I said. My body was relaxing into a mindless, comforting rhythm.

We were pleasantly quiet for a few minutes until Gabe cleared his throat awkwardly.

"Can I ask you a kind of intense question?"

I shrugged. "Sure."

"That first night we met, you told me you didn't believe in love. For yourself, although you believed it could happen for others."

"That's true. I do believe that," I said.

"Why? Did something happen that destroyed your ability to believe in love?"

*Destroyed.* That was a good word for it. Lies and half-truths swarmed on my tongue, but I surprised myself by being honest.

"I was engaged," I said and watched a visible reaction shudder through him. He turned his big body towards me, eyes wide with sympathy. "And I don't really like to talk about it. But it happened. And I'm not engaged anymore so..." I trailed off.

Butterflies flittered through my stomach, my body on high alert. I hated talking about this, only because the emotions and feelings I'd worked so hard to process would rear up so quickly, affect me as viscerally as they had on the morning of the wedding.

"Thank you for telling me," he said as we reached the view

point. Gabe turned to face me, emotions roiling in his expression. "And I'm really fucking sorry that happened to you."

"It's… it's okay," I said, distracted by his masculine scent. "It was two years ago. I've moved on. But it's the reason I don't do relationships. Or any kind of… intensity."

A stunning view opened up in front of us. A rich layer of dark forest and then the wide blue expanse of the ocean. It stretched on and on, so vast and so far-reaching, I had the oddest sensation that it must never end. Like ancient explorers, so sure their ships were going to pitch off the edges of the Earth. My throat tightened as I took it all in.

"I wish I had had a place like this. Back when… it all happened. The engagement."

Everything was roaring up again. Lucia, eyes red and face pale as a ghost, standing in the doorway. *He's not coming*, she'd said. So simple, those three words. Like we were meeting for a coffee and he'd gotten stuck in traffic. *He's not coming*.

"I've had my fair share of revelations at this spot. Sometimes it just makes me sadder. It's the vastness of the ocean, how small it makes me feel." He laughed softly. "And not many things make me feel small. But sometimes I'll hike up here, feeling lonely, and the ocean will make me feel lonelier." I looked at his strong profile; his full beard. That golden hair. "Other times it's my powerful reminder to keep on going. I mean, if this much *beauty* can exist in the world, how can I not be motivated to keep going? I know The Bar is just, well, a *bar* but it's really important to me. The legacy. Its role in the community."

"And I know what I do is just… makeup. Buying into all kinds of standards of beauty and product consumption. But—I just love it. It's simple but—"

"I understand," Gabe said. "You can't help what you love."

We stood in silence for a long time, and when Gabe finally

suggested we head back, I had to hide my face, covertly wiping away tears.

"Can I ask *you* a personal question?"

"Of course," he said, pulling the pack on and settling it across his broad back.

"Why do *you* believe in love so fiercely?" I asked.

"I guess... well, it's been modeled to me my entire life. Between my parents' relationship and my siblings' relationships, I'm just surrounded by people who have received this great privilege of falling in love. Of finding your soulmate, the person you're meant to be with."

My heart spun and twisted. You'd never know it from looking at him: this fierce Viking bartender was pining for The One.

"Makes sense," I said. "Our experiences were just different. You've had the beauty and happiness of love shown to you your entire life. I had the opposite, with my engagement. We view love in the same way; we're just coming from different experiences."

Gabe nodded, but he didn't look convinced. A drop of rain landed on the tip of my nose. "I wish that hadn't happened to you, Josie. I wish..." he trailed off. He was hiking faster now, but out of passion or fear for the rain I didn't know. "I just wish things were different."

And he didn't have to say more than that.

I knew what he meant.

## 29

## GABE

Josie had been engaged. And now she wasn't. A straightforward telling of what I was sure was a painful, horrible experience. I couldn't comprehend what it would be like to fall so deeply in love with someone you proposed *marriage*. And then... ended it.

But her hesitancy made sense now.

She was rebuilding her walls.

"You've had one serious relationship, right?" she asked me, yanking me back to the present.

I rubbed my hand through my beard, thoughtful. "Yes. I thought that Sasha would end up being The One. We'd met in high school, and I wanted that kind of relationship where a person has known you for most of your life. Has seen you through all the vital points, the ups and downs." I shrugged, suddenly uncomfortable with talking about it. "But I've been thinking so much about Sasha lately. About what went wrong. I was so convinced it was *her*. She wasn't... willing to give as much as me. To commit or... I don't know." I tugged on my beard. "I'm rambling, I know but..."

"It's okay," Josie said. "Speaking from experience, time

doesn't lend itself to memories of relationships, at least in my experience. Things become blurred. Intentions and actions aren't as clear as they were. But I'm sure you were a good partner."

I grimaced. "I was... younger. So I don't know for sure. I might have smothered her with romantic gestures."

"How so?" she asked.

I thought about the night Sasha and I broke up. "Looking back on it, I'd always seemed to want more commitment than she did. We'd lived together, in the apartment at The Bar, and I just assumed we'd get married and have children. But about a year before we broke up, she started pulling away, which only made me step up the romance."

"She broke up with you?"

"She did," I said, laughing grimly. "I wanted to get to the bottom of things, have a real conversation to figure out why she was pulling back. Planned this whole thing on a moonlit night on the beach with wine and food and blankets and flowers." I glanced at Josie. "She dumped me, right there on the blanket. And it was absolutely awful. Because it was a total blindside."

We were quiet for a minute, crossing a short log.

"Do you still see Sasha? It's a small town, must be awkward."

I shook my head. "No, she moved from Big Sur right after we broke up. Came and got her stuff and... well, I bump into her parents now and then. She's married, lives in San Francisco. I think she's really happy, which is good. And I've actually been thinking about our relationship more recently." I watched a bird jump from branch to branch. "Maybe we weren't in love the way I thought we were. I think I wanted to *be* in love so much, I ignored the doubts I had. Or the times I felt like... like there was an ocean between us. Our feelings, our conversations, our intimacy and sex... like trying to talk to each other under water. There was never any intensity."

Her brow furrowed at that word. "Maybe..." she bit her lip.

"What?"

"Maybe what you think is true love is really too good to be true. I'm not sure the kind of love you're talking about is healthy."

A smattering of raindrops hit my head and shoulders. I looked up at the clouds, recognizing that the never-ending storm we seemed to be trapped in was probably about to dump rain on us in the middle of the forest at least half a mile from The Bar.

"I don't agree at all," I said, hiking a little faster. She joined me, wiping a stray raindrop from her cheek. "I think we ultimately weren't right for each other. But I think when you find that person, your soulmate, it must be the most profound feeling in the world."

But Josie was shaking her head, and I couldn't read the expression in her dark eyes. She tucked her hair behind her ear, and I noticed the constellation of stars tattooed there.

"I think you've watched too many *Lifetime* movies, Gabriel," she said, but her levity sounded forced. "I think most people's relationships are not that happy. And that much intensity can be really dangerous."

*Dangerous*. Who was the fucking guy who broke off her engagement?

She glanced at me apologetically. "I'm sorry. I'm being a real fucking bummer about this. I just know from experience."

I nodded as the rain began falling heavier, no longer a fine mist but a steady drip. And getting steadier. Suddenly, it was like the sky unzipped itself, and a curtain of water fell down through the trees and directly onto our heads.

Josie squealed and made a feeble attempt to cover her face.

So I grabbed her, pulling her under a thick pine whose branches started a foot above my head.

The rain stopped, or so it seemed, the furry pine branches trapping the rain and keeping it above us.

"So in your experience," I continued, watching the rain pour down, "the relationship I want for myself is too good to be true? Not going to happen?"

She didn't answer for a minute. I turned to glance at her and was startled to find her staring at me.

"I don't want to speak for you or your future. I want you to find the person that you're... meant to be with." Pain flashed in her eyes but just as quickly disappeared. "But maybe those relationships didn't work out because you needed more from them than was realistic."

"Because I want intensity in my love?" I asked.

"Yes," she finally said. "I'm not sure that's real. I'm not sure that's *right*."

I thought about honesty. I thought about living in the moment.

"What about the other night?"

Her breathing hitched. The rain outside the tree increased in tempo, but everything was softness and light beneath the pine needles.

"What about it?"

"*Josie*," I said. "That was the most intense sexual experience of my entire life." Her nipple rings in my mouth, my teeth. Her naked, decorated body riding my tongue like her favorite sex toy. Her husky demands, the way she controlled my pleasure. "That was the most *right* experience I've ever had."

A long, winding silence. The two of us were separated by no more than an inch. Yet miles of mistrust and miscommunication—and whatever had happened with Josie's engagement —seethed in between us.

I wanted to close the distance. Desperately.

"I don't..." she started, biting her lip. "I'm not..."

And then we heard a startling *crack*, a flash of lightning. Rain crashed through the barrier of the pine needles, soaking us instantly.

"Gabe?" she cried, grabbing my hand. Not quite afraid but certainly unsure.

I looked out at the rain, then down at her.

"How fast can you run, sweetheart?"

"Depends on what's chasing me," she laughed.

I brought her knuckles to my lips.

"Because we're half a mile from The Bar. And I think we're going to have to make a run for it. Through the rain." I squeezed her fingers. "Think you can do it?"

A wide, loopy grin broke across her face. "Absolutely," she said.

And we took off in a sprint. Together.

# 30

# JOSIE

I wasn't a nature girl. I wasn't a runner or a hiker or a climber.

And I lived in Los Angeles, where it never fucking rained.

But suddenly here I was, hand-in-hand with my Viking and bolting through a rain-drenched forest in Big Sur, California.

We ran fast, Big Sur's magnificent beauty a blur of water. Trees swaying in the wind. The smells, the thrill of my legs flying over roots and branches.

I couldn't seem to stop laughing, and Gabe joined in, that rich, rumbling laugh of his muted by the thick falling rain. After the first minute, I stopped being cold, the hard sprint counteracting the chill, and instead I just let my lungs expand. My muscles burn. My fingers grip Gabe's with sincerity.

Because even though I wasn't a nature girl, I *had* been a little kid once, growing up in the abandoned parking lots and small front yards of East L.A. Had run and jumped and captured flags. Had forgotten that *kid* feeling of fleeing for fun.

There was no time to talk as we ran, but it was okay. We didn't need to.

And there was no time to talk when we reached The Bar, looking innocent and tiny in the woods. But it housed Gabe, and it housed four decades of memories, and it was the focal point of this weird community I'd landed in totally by chance.

And that was okay too.

Gabe pulled me down the hallway, our clothing dripping small puddles onto the floor. We were still laughing, couldn't seem to stop, and my body felt suffused with shimmering light.

"You can... um, use the shower if you need to?" Gabe said.

My teeth chattered wildly. We were standing in his bathroom, the same one I'd freaked out in not five days earlier.

"I've never run that fast in my life," I said as Gabe reached in and turned the knobs. Water sprang on, slowly starting to steam. "Or really... run. I've never really *run* in my life."

Gabe laughed. "You're a real Big Sur local now. Getting caught way the hell out in the forest during a rainstorm is something all of us have done. Usually people stop in at The Bar afterward to warm up with alcohol."

"That sounds nice," I said.

Gabe handed me a few fluffy white towels. I took them, laying them on the counter. We smiled at each other.

The scene was almost *domestic.*

Except Gabe and I *weren't* a couple. And I knew this was only going to make it harder for me.

So much harder.

But we were both breathing heavily. Gabe's wet clothing clung to every ridge and muscle. His eyes roamed my body as steam hovered between us and rain lashed against the roof. I felt, keenly, the inevitability of this moment. And even though it made me feel wild and out of control, I wanted to lean into it. Embrace the chaos.

"I'll just..." he said roughly, starting to back out of the room. So respectful.

So *submissive*.

"Take off your fucking clothes," I said before I could stop myself.

Gabe stilled, hand on the doorknob.

"Josie..." His gaze was questioning. Searching.

But I knew what I wanted.

"Take off your *fucking* clothes," I said, sharply.

A small quirk of his lips. A slight nod from me.

Slowly, he shook his hair out of his bun, and it fell around his face. He began to strip out of his soaking wet clothes right in front of me. Water dripped down his huge chest, the boulders of his biceps. The dark hair of his stomach, flexing with exertion. He stripped off his pants, and I was face-to-face with his powerful thighs. His thick cock straining upwards.

Already hard. For me.

How could I deny this man? Even if I didn't know for how long, even if we had no goddamn future in front of us, how could I deny my body this much *pleasure*?

"Get in that shower," I rasped, tearing at my clothes as if they were on fire.

"I want to see you first," he pushed back, literally, suddenly crowding me against the wall.

"Strip?" I taunted.

"Naked," he gasped.

I liked that. Liked Gabe desperate and on edge.

And I could make him desperate *so* easily. I hadn't felt particularly sexy all day although I'd felt strangely confident and empowered. But now, stripping out of my soggy, giant hiking clothes, I felt like goddamn Cleopatra. Off went the shirt, the pants, my soaking wet underwear.

Gabe dropped to his knees.

"Can I touch you?" His voice was brimming with reverence.

I nodded because I had no words. I had no words for my Viking on his knees, worshiping me.

"I think I'm becoming obsessed with your tattoos," he said, finger tracing the intricate mandala I had inked between my breasts. I shivered. His lips caressed the flock of birds flowing down my ribcage.

"Didn't peg you for an ink man," I said.

"I never was before," he said, tongue licking up my thigh until it reached the large tattoo of black and white flowers that hugged my left hip-bone. His tongue traced the first petal. A moan tumbled from my lips. "I liked them. Thought they were interesting. But on you, they're *mysterious*." His breath danced along my hip-bone, tongue tracing the next petal. Around and around.

"Oh... yeah?" I finally sighed, aware I should be wrestling back control, but I was mesmerized by Gabe's movements.

"That night we met—" *trace, trace, trace*. "I was so captivated by you. Wanted to unravel you. This—" He groaned, fingers splaying across my belly, moving up to my heart. Cupping my breast. "The first time I saw these, I wanted to lick every one." His tongue continued to move, and I began wondering if a woman could come from hip-licking. Because every intentional swipe of this tongue was pushing me higher and higher. "They're so beautiful on you, Josie. They say so much about you." His tongue inched closer to my cunt but was still focused on every delicate petal.

*Trace, trace, trace.*

"What do they say?" My knees were trembling. His other fingers began a tantalizing dance up my calf. My knee. My inner thigh.

"Hard and soft. Light and dark. Commitment and dedication. Because you wanted these beautiful flowers inked onto your body permanently. Always there as life goes on and you age and change. Even at eighty years old, your gorgeous hips will be covered with blossoms."

"And it'll look terrible," I said, trying to lighten the moment. Trying to ignore the fierce knocking of my heart against my rib cage.

"*Josie*," Gabe seethed, breaking the moment, almost breaking the scene. "For the love of *God*, if you're eighty years old and still not being worshiped by someone..." he stumbled, eyes traveling up my body to meet mine in a scorching gaze. "Please. Please tell me you'll let yourself be loved." But before I could push words past my dry, tightening throat, Gabe lowered his lips right to my clit. Not licking, not moving. Waiting, again.

"And *please* let me eat this sweet pussy. I need."

Nothing more. Just *I need.*

"Y-yes," I managed to stutter, and then my Viking devoured me. There was no other word for it. Two fingers slid inside. His tongue descended, fluttering in a maddening pattern.

"God, *Gabe*," I moaned.

He growled against my sensitive skin like a starving animal.

Licking and sucking, a maddening pattern, the same one from the other night. The same one that delivered three orgasms rapid-fire as I straddled his face.

That image alone had me gasping and clawing at the wall and then gasping and clawing at Gabe's hair. I rode his mouth, bucking against his tongue, and Gabe slapped his hand against the floor, the *cracking* sound like a gunshot. His cock was hard and straining, pre-cum soaking the head, but he didn't, or wouldn't, touch himself. Was still as restrained as ever, listening for a command.

"Get up off the floor," I managed to say.

Gabe pulled back, eyes on mine, eyebrow arched with interest.

"Yes, ma'am," he said with just a hint of a smirk. Stood, towering over me.

"And I'm pretty sure I told you to get in that fucking shower."

# 31

## GABE

It was happening again.

My world was shrinking to the shape of Josie and the sensation of unrelenting pleasure. All of my past sexual experiences had one singular goal. *Get off*. And I always gave my sexual partners as much pleasure as they wanted or needed. But the goal was *orgasm*. Release.

And sweet *fuck* that was the goal with Josie.

Except it also *wasn't*. The denial was becoming the ultimate aphrodisiac. Past orgasms felt wispy and paper-thin, like they'd never even happened.

Now there was a complex layering of need and desire, a tease and a dance. Orgasm denial and pain were suddenly things I welcomed and wanted.

I wanted to wait. To be punished. To give. My orgasms were no longer a headlong rush. They were a long, slow uncoiling.

And Josie's control wasn't harsh or unrefined but flowed gently like a stream.

I stepped under the hot spray of the shower, my body shuddering in the warm relief. Watched in rapt silence as Josie purred under the water, closing her eyes. I kissed along her neck and jaw. The sensitive spot between her throat and shoulder.

She shuddered and panted, palms gliding up my chest, finger tangling in my chest hair.

"Who's in charge, gorgeous?" I rasped as water rained down over our bodies.

She backed us into the shower wall.

"Me," she said firmly, reaching down to grip my cock.

I held her face in my hands, lips an inch apart. "Everything, Josie," I whispered. "I'll give you everything." I licked my tongue into her mouth, swiping my thumb across her cheekbone. "So tell me what you need."

Josie was leisurely stroking me, pupils dark with lust. My hands slid down her back and squeezed a handful of her delicious ass. I hooked her leg around my waist and ground against her clit.

"I get tested every month. How about you?"

"Same," I said. "I've always been clean. Careful. You?"

Josie nodded, stroking the head of my cock against her slick opening. "And I'm on the pill. A pill I take religiously."

I grinned against her lips. "What are you asking me to do?"

"Fuck me like this. No barriers. Just us. For our first time, I want... I want *you*."

She kept stroking, swirling, teasing. Every cell in my body screamed *thrust,* but I reined it back.

"Say the word." Josie rocked herself against the head of my cock, throat tilted, eyes hooded. "Or you can just keep doing that," I groaned and fucking meant it.

"Using your cock like a sex toy?" she taunted.

"Yes," I growled. "I... I like it."

"You like being used, Gabriel?"

I placed both of my hands alongside her head, staring down at her. Watching Josie, again, work herself to pleasure.

"When you do it, yes." My vision dimmed and darkened as I scraped my palms against her breasts, cock still trapped between us.

"How badly do you want to fuck me right now?" Her tongue traced the seam of my lips, over and over, before dipping in for a taste.

I experimentally thrust against her stomach, and she smacked me on the ass so fast I saw stars. And it only got me harder.

"God*dammit*," I swore.

"How badly?"

I leaned my forehead against hers. "A rock slide could tear this bathroom in half, and I wouldn't stop until you told me to."

"Then why don't you show me?"

"I'll hurt you," I said, momentarily tripping up on the double meaning. Except I wouldn't, I *couldn't*. But Josie was only shaking her head.

"All I want is to be fucked senseless. Fucked so hard I can't walk tomorrow. Or the next day," she said with a sly grin. "Do you think you can do that?"

Another spank, another challenge. She twisted her fingers in my chest hair and yanked.

In the space of a second, I grabbed Josie beneath her thighs and lifted her easily against the wall.

With a satisfied smile, she lifted her arms and looped them around the showerhead, baring her body to me. Her strong, tattooed legs wrapped around my waist.

I positioned my cock right at her entrance and paused.

Waited for her command.

Because it was more than just a sexy game. Of everything

we'd done, *this* moment was going to carve itself into my memories, the way water shapes a canyon.

I'd never be the same.

"Fuck me, Gabriel," she demanded.

The ragged moan Josie made when I bottomed out inside of her would stay with me for the rest of my goddamn life.

It was more than a sound of pleasure. It was a sound of total *completion*.

"Is this how you need it?" I asked, slamming back inside of her.

Shoving the wet hair from her face, I tilted her chin toward me so I could kiss her. And thrust again. With almost no finesse, no thought to the slow, teasing rhythm I usually started with.

I had instructions, and I intended on carrying them out.

"Your cock feels so... *fuck,*" she hissed as I kept fucking her in rapid-fire strokes. "And don't you dare stop."

Josie reached behind and dug her nails into my ass, breaking the skin. But never breaking eye contact. She held my gaze as her pussy clenched in time with my punishing rhythm. I took her nipples between my teeth, tugging on the tender piercings. Her sounds of pleasure were guttural and so *real.*

And every time I slowed, or faltered, she smacked my ass until I sped up.

And, *fuck,* I'd never been spanked before, but I was discovering nothing got me hotter. *Nothing.* I wanted to be used. Worked hard with a singular purpose. And it wasn't dehumanizing. In fact, the exact opposite was true.

I'd never felt closer to another person in my *life* as I did right now, taking Josefine against the wall with wild abandon.

Josie sucked my thumb between her lush lips, and I almost

lost it. But then she placed it against her clit and I rolled that tight bud in tiny, teasing circles.

Her hips snapped and shook, her orgasm so *close*. So I stroked her clit and fucked her with a fury. Suddenly, she was panting "*Gabe, yes please yes,*" with her head thrown back, her hands wrapped around my neck.

I fucked her against that wall like I was trying to break the damn thing down.

My goddess came with a *shriek,* back arched and laughing.

And as she spasmed beautifully around me, my vision filled with planets and stars and the entire *universe,* and in the center of it all was Josie.

My release was in sight, but I was still *waiting*. Being the ultimate audience to Josie's soaring climaxes over and over was becoming my new favorite drug. And when Josie left... when Josie left...

"Gabe," she whispered, breaking through my thoughts. She kissed me hungrily, and I breathed her in.

"Ask me anything." I was hard as a rock and slowly moving inside her.

"Again," she moaned, reaching down to grab my ass. "And *harder*."

## 32

## JOSIE

Gabe made me *insatiable.*

Which was saying something, since the orgasm he'd just given me had been a breath-stealing, heart-stopping, rearrange-my-cells type of climax. A quiet voice, deep in the recesses of my mind, was trying to get me to *stop.* But being with Gabe was like boarding a train you hoped *never* reached its destination.

Nothing else mattered as Gabe held me up against his massive body and walked out of the shower into his warm, cozy bedroom.

I was prepared to be fucked senseless, but instead Gabe slid me down gently, caressing the hair from my shoulders. Grabbed a towel and kissed along my collarbone as he rubbed the fabric across my sensitive, aching skin. Drying me. I giggled—I couldn't help it, and his answering chuckle was husky with need. The towel smoothed up my legs, my ass, my breasts. I was shivering and aching by the time he finished, curling his fingers around my neck and kissing me with real yearning.

"Now your turn," I panted, doing the same thing for him. I applied the lightest pressure to his shoulders, and he sank to the floor for me again. His body was a work of fucking art, and I felt myself memorizing the smallest details: the thick blond hair that trailed down his stomach. The light dusting of freckles between his shoulder blades. The guttural sound he made when I ran my tongue, lazily, from the crook of his neck to beneath his ear. His big palms slid around my waist, turning me, my back pressed to his front. He kissed a hot path along my throat as I arched back into his cock, fingers teasing my breasts, stroking my clit. As I moaned and sighed against him, I realized he was doing the same thing: memorizing me.

"Josie," Gabe whispered against my ear. "Get on that fucking bed." I nipped his jaw, and the low growl he made as I stretched out onto his bed had my eyes wide. In a daze, I watched my muscular, lust-filled Viking crawl up my body, holding himself over me with his strong arms.

Waiting for my command.

His hair was wet and loose around his shoulders.

I curled my fingers through it, sighing.

"Are you okay?" I checked in, letting my fingers dance down the ridges of his stomach.

"Never been better in my life," he said, softly. "Are you okay?"

I let my wandering fingers travel down the length of his cock then wrap tight around the base. Gabe's hands fisted in the sheets.

"Never been better in my life," I repeated, and he chuckled. I twisted my fist, dragging it up slowly. Exploring the smooth head of his cock with my fingers.

"What are you doing to me, Josefine?" he asked on a ragged groan.

I smirked, enjoying the heady rush.

"Teasing you," I said, jerking my fist up and down. "Controlling you." I sped up my movements and his arms shook. "It's like nothing I've ever experienced before, Gabe. You feel that, right?"

His lips hovered over mine. "I feel fucking *everything*, gorgeous," he growled.

I wanted Gabe off the leash. Unrestrained.

"Then show me," I whispered.

I licked my tongue into his mouth, and his answering groan gave me the confidence I needed to guide that perfect cock inside of me. Fully, until not another inch could fit.

We moaned together as he finally crushed his body to mine. I lifted my legs, and he took the cue, pressing my knees to the mattress, bringing us as close together as possible. He thrust once, eyes locked on mine, and I was already a goner—still tender and overly sensitive.

"Start slow," I said, and he responded with an agonizingly slow movement, pulling out every inch. And then snapping his hips forward. "But stay deep," I said, already breathless. His hair was falling all around us.

Gabe stayed still for a moment, cock nestled deep inside of me, and I rotated my hips, feeling him against my inner walls. A mewling sound escaped my lips, and Gabe shuddered with pleasure. I did it again—Gabe, still as a statue, as I shifted in semi-circles, stirring up my banked pleasure.

"*Fuck* that feels so good," he gasped.

I reached down to grab his muscular ass, pulling him deeper. On a groan, his head dipped between my breasts.

"Please let me," he begged, still *so respectful*, even though not moments ago, he had me pinned against a wall.

All I could do was nod.

Gabe's tongue darted out, licking around my piercings. I held his head there as I gave that perfect ass another ringing slap. He bit my nipple gently, and I slapped him again. The round muscles of his ass flexing under my palm.

"*Harder*," I groaned.

He knew exactly what I meant.

He began to fuck me, faster but no less thoroughly. Nipple in his mouth, hands holding me down, cock rubbing against my g-spot over and over. Gabe ravaged me, fucking me like a wild animal, the headboard smacking against the wall.

And yet there was no doubt: I held the reins.

I spanked him again, and he roared against me, hitching my leg up and over his shoulder, hitting an angle so deep I felt my eyes roll back in my head. My body arched up towards his, his hand slid under my back, holding me to him.

Keeping me.

Gabe was close, barely in control, and I was essentially a live wire, tiny orgasms already sparking their way up my spine.

I needed to see him. I needed to feel him.

I pulled his face up to mine and said, "Come for me."

For a moment, there was no time. Only Gabe's face in ecstasy.

He reached down to my clit and circled his fingers there, just once, so that I came with him, clenching around his cock, screaming and sighing with tears in my eyes.

And Gabe was still coming, his back muscles trembling and breath hot against my neck. And my name, a litany, tumbling sweetly from his lips.

I knew I had rules.

I knew I had reasons.

And I knew I'd be leaving Big Sur at any moment. Knew *all* of this and still.

Still I wrapped my arms around Gabe and clutched him to me, our lips crashing together for what felt like hours. Hands entwined, legs entwined, hearts fluttering together in the same hopeful rhythm.

## 33

# JOSIE

The rain was a soft pitter-patter against the windows in Gabe's bedroom. I was wrapped up in blankets, sitting up against pillows, and Gabe was giving me a foot massage.

He also looked sexy as hell. Old gray sweatpants, barefoot. Bare chest, his long hair drying around his shoulders. Big thumbs working their way into the balls of my feet.

I shouldn't want him again—not after he'd just fucked me into two orgasms so intense I had briefly lost my ability to form coherent thoughts.

Not after I watched his beautiful face in the throes of ecstasy.

But it was raining outside, and we were cozy and warm, and I was half-asleep from the orgasms and the foot massage and this deep-seated comfort... I didn't have the strength to overly analyze. Instead, I just let it all wash over me.

"This happened the other night," I said, nudging him with my foot. He'd been watching me with reverent eyes. "*I'm* supposed to care for *you* after sex. You're the submissive."

He shrugged, flashing an easy grin. "I guess I really like

caring for you afterward. It feels... right to me. All of it feels right to me."

"The fantasy?" I asked, curious.

"I'm not sure it's a fantasy," he said. "I mean, it's a fantasy in the traditional sense of the word. But I might... I mean..." He looked away, grinning bashfully.

"Gabe," I laughed. "You can tell me."

"I know," he said, picking up my left foot and starting to rub the insole. "I'm not sure I have the words yet. But the sex we have makes every other sexual experience I've *ever* had—and I'm not being hyperbolic—feel like nothing. Not just that the orgasms are more intense, which they are, but all of it. The... the headspace?" He looked at me. "Is that the right word?"

"I think you can use whatever word feels right."

He nodded. "Headspace. Like I feel comfortable serving you."

He blushed, just a little, and my heart did a weird little dance.

*Knock it off*, I told myself, firmly.

"It's interesting, because it almost doesn't feel like we're playing roles to me. It feels totally natural. And I've had this fantasy for as long as I can remember, so maybe it's less fantasy and more my true sexuality." He flashed me that grin again. "Interesting, huh?"

I swallowed against a rising tide of emotions. "I'm happy that, well, I'm happy that you've learned something about yourself. And maybe the next woman—"

"Don't," he said.

"Gabe," I started.

He shook his head.

I understood. The thought of him bringing home another woman, which he would, and... and doing the same things we had done. Handing her those ropes and begging her to tie him to the bed. I bit my lip at the sudden threat of tears.

"Either way," I said, covering. "That makes me happy."

"Do you feel that way, too?"

I was safe and warm. Gabe was safe and warm. "Yes. I've had similar revelations over the past couple days," I admitted.

Gabe lifted my foot, placing a tiny kiss on the ankle. "Good."

There was a knot in my throat desperate to be untangled. Words were clamoring to come out, and I wanted to let them. This could even be the last time we saw each other, and I didn't want Gabe to remember me as some heartless harpy who swept into his life and swept out without a valid reason. And just as I opened my mouth to tell him about Clarke, about what happened, that chilling voice of his swept into my subconscious with words he had never said.

But I heard them anyway.

*I would have shown up on our wedding day if you had been someone different. A different woman. A better woman. What will Gabe think of you when he finds out?*

"I should go," I said, voice shaking, as I removed my feet from Gabe's lap. "It's late, and we probably... well, we probably have a shoot tomorrow. If the road hasn't been cleared."

I started to pull on my clothes in the corner, a move I'd perfected over the past two years, while Gabe sat quietly on his bed. One hand rubbed down his jaw, and I *knew* he wanted to say something.

And I knew I had to get out of there before he did.

"Josie," he said softly. I zipped up my jacket and pretended not to hear him. "Why can't you let yourself have love that is passionate and soul-shaking? *Why*?"

I bent down, lacing up my combat boots. Turned my head an inch to see Gabe watching me with a devastated expression. And, *oh God,* now I was going to cry, and I really, *really* didn't want to do that.

"Listen," I said, standing. Backing up. "I know this... what we have," I said, indicating the space between us, "*was* more intense than a normal one-night stand."

"This wasn't a one-night stand, and you know it," Gabe said swiftly. "Tell me who hurt you. Tell me why you want to run."

"I was never supposed to see you again," I said, palms up and ignoring the second half of his plea. "It's why I... well, why I did things differently than I normally do. Starting with sleeping with you a second time. Which I *never* do."

"I understand," Gabe said. "The rock slide messed with your plan. Things might have been more... temporary if you hadn't gotten stuck here. But—"

"What?" I asked, hating the shake of my voice. Hadn't I just brought this man to his knees? I searched desperately for *that* Josie but couldn't find her.

Gabe reached forward, stroking his fingers against my palm.

"You love this," he said. "Whatever *this* is. This connection. This *intensity*."

Deep down, there was a small, delicate part of me that was starting to *open*—like a morning glory greeting the sun. Because with Clarke, our intensity had a sharp edge to it, a terrifying free-fall. I'd confused the adrenaline for love when it was really *fear*.

But this... was that it? Was it the same? Did Clarke ever make me feel so fucking cherished and interesting and captivating and *treasured*?

Had anyone?

Gabe's fingers circled my wrist. "What if... what if it was different between us?"

A long pause, lonely as a road at midnight.

"I don't know if that's possible for me," I said and meant it. "I really don't."

And then I stuffed my hands into my pockets, turned around, and left.

# 34

## GABE

An hour after Josie left, as I drank coffee and watched the sun rise through the forest outside my window, I got the call.

The rock slide had finally been cleared. The entrance—and exit—to Big Sur was wide open.

I hadn't slept after Josie's abrupt departure, and I couldn't put my finger on why I had so much anxiety churning in my stomach. Hadn't I known she was going to leave? She'd been open and honest about that from the moment I met her. And Josie didn't seem like the kind of person who changed her mind.

I had wanted, desperately, for the rockslide to be cleared so that Big Sur could be reconnected with the world.

But now I wanted to roll those boulders back down the mountain with my bare hands.

How, in a matter of a week, I could meet a woman who made me want to commit acts of destruction on the place I loved the most, I'd never know.

I distracted myself with planning a celebration at The Bar

for that night, letting the information float down the Big Sur Channel. Until Lucia called, begging the use of The Bar's kitchen to cook Calvin a surprise birthday dinner. Which I'd been happy to accommodate, especially since Cal had been sly and secret about their *obviously blossoming* relationship, and there wasn't anything I wanted more than for sweetly shy Calvin to find his soulmate.

Well, there was one thing—one *person*—I wanted more than that. But she was leaving.

So I'd changed things up and spread the word through the Big Sur Channel that if you wanted to celebrate that night, you needed to start early and be out of there by eight o'clock.

Which is how I ended up bartending to a bunch of drunk people at four in the afternoon.

They'd come in droves. Gloria and Gladys. Kevin looking especially harried. The Mayor. Ruth and Mrs. Manahan. Geoff, Fritz, and John sitting stoically in the corner, nursing their beers, and occasionally muttering about crop yields. Even my dad, Austin, and Isabelle were sitting at the bar nursing whiskeys and enjoying the revelry.

Scott and his crew were in the corner, sloppy drunk and grinning, taking shot after shot purchased for them by the locals. Every so often, he'd catch my eye, slur "We love you Gabe," and then go back to drinking.

A week ago, our town had been cut off from food, services, and the rest of the world with no idea when we'd be set free. Countless natural disasters hadn't gone as well, and the entire community seemed to wait with bated breath and crossed fingers, hoping and praying it wouldn't be like the others.

Miraculously, it hadn't been. The only side effect had been our own trapped crew of Hollywood People.

"Your dream is ruined, big brother," Austin said, grinning at me.

I was drying glasses, trying—and failing—not to think about Josie. But everything reminded me of her—even now, I kept looking towards the door, hoping she'd stride in wearing combat boots and ripped jeans, reach over the bar, grab me by the collar, and pull me towards the bedroom to have her way with me.

"Which dream is that?" I asked, nudging the whiskey closer to them. He and my dad looked like twins—both slight and shorter than me by at least six inches. I'd inherited my mother's genes—she had come from a family of giants.

"The one where everyone gets trapped in Big Sur and can never leave because it's the most perfect place in the whole world," my dad said fondly.

When I was ten, I'd had an actual dream that we could never leave Big Sur. My entire family was stuck there with all of our friends and neighbors. A nightmare, to some people, but I'd declared to my family that I wanted it to happen in real life.

A silly declaration that they *never* let me forget.

"True," I laughed. "Now the tourists can come back and ruin everything. And the Hollywood People will be on their way tomorrow morning."

"Taking all the excitement with them," Gloria said into her drink. "And their abs."

Austin and Isabelle shot each other a bemused look.

"Just how often did you spy on them?" I asked, running a towel along the rim of an old glass. I recognized it from when I was little—the curved handle with the slight chip on the side. It had once been Robert Ellis' favorite. I looked up, and my dad was staring at it with the same sad smile.

Gladys and Gloria exchanged a glance. "Who knows? I mean we couldn't go anywhere, so we'd just take the donkeys out for a walk, and... oh I don't know, lay in the bushes for a while. With our binoculars."

"Is *that* why you were late to work every day this week?" Kevin asked.

The sisters shrugged innocently, but my siblings burst into laughter.

"Guess you'll be saying goodbye to the Purple-Haired Satanist?" Dad asked.

I felt every single eye land on me, the sisters' heads swiveling like nosy owls.

"Carry on," I said, waving my hands at the crowd. "I don't want to hear about Josie on the Big Sur Channel tomorrow, you hear me?"

Dad snorted. "You can't control it, son. The Channel controls all of us," he grinned. "But lean closer, and we can talk more quietly about Josie," he said in a stage-whisper.

I leaned in. "She's leaving tomorrow, and I don't really want to talk about it."

"Are you going to make a grand romantic gesture? Ask her to stay?" he asked.

Austin nodded in agreement. Isabelle, however, stared into her drink.

I scoffed, rolling my eyes even though I'd spent the entire day thinking about doing just that. I wanted desperately for Josie to stay—wanted it so strongly it was like a physical pain.

"I don't..." I trailed off, thinking about what she'd told me. How she'd been engaged before, and whatever had happened had permanently altered her perception of love and relationships.

"I'm not sure a grand romantic gesture is what Josie would want. She has... a bad history with romance," I said, choosing my words carefully. "It might not go over well. Plus, what's my plan? Ask her to stay and give up her life in Los Angeles? I've known her for a week." Even to my tender, hopeless romantic's heart, that sounded much too intense.

"I did it for Paige," Austin said, pouring another finger of whiskey into his glass. "She was only supposed to be here for a six-month placement and then move back to the East Coast. And yeah, it was a *lot* to ask her and a *lot* to put on the line, but the thought of living my life without her wasn't possible."

"Yeah, but Paige also loves Big Sur," I pointed out. "Josie's only been here a week and has a whole life in Los Angeles. I know what you're saying, baby bro, but I don't think it's the same situation."

"Here's a question," Isabelle said, pinning me with a sharp look. "Austin, would you have moved to the East Coast if Paige had asked?"

"Absolutely," he said without even waiting a beat. No hesitation. He just *knew*.

"Gabe?" Isabelle asked.

Suddenly, I was floundering. I wanted things to be like they'd been this week—Josie and I floating in a world without consequences, having great conversations and going on hikes and having the best sex of my entire life.

"What?" I asked, stalling.

"Would you move to Los Angeles if Josie asked you to?"

"And leave The Bar?" I said, sounding defensive.

My dad shrugged. "Lots of folks could tend to The Bar."

"I know," I said. "But this place is everything to me. Our legacy. What it means. All the work I have left to do to have an impact here."

All three of them were silent, still staring at me. Because I hadn't answered the question.

"Make a grand gesture when you ask her to stay here,"

Gladys said, staring at me over the top of her (fifth) drink. "Gloria and I can plan it out for you."

I couldn't help but smile because making a grand romantic gesture was what I *wanted* to do. Wanted to sweep Josie off her feet and show her what a relationship was *really* about.

"What if it scares her away again?" I pointed out. "Like Sasha? I did the whole thing—the picnic on the beach. The romance. The wine. And she dumped me right there."

Gloria shrugged. "Maybe she wasn't the right girl. Seems to me this Josie, even though you've only known her a week, might be closer to The One."

I looked away for a moment, a battalion of contradictory thoughts fighting for dominance in my head. Josie, throwing up walls for a good reason, protecting her heart. A nagging, nasty feeling that if Josie turned the tables and asked *me* to move to Los Angeles… I'd say no.

And I didn't know what the fuck any of it meant.

Gladys reached over and grabbed my wrist, her sharp nails, crusted in fake diamonds, biting into my skin. "Listen, it's simple. Close your eyes and think of Josie."

I did. Thought hard. Of her laughter and quirky sense of humor. Her hands, tying me to the bed. The confidence that shone through her movements. Her shy vulnerability.

"What do you feel?" she asked.

My heart was full to bursting. "Warmth. Happiness. Joy," I finally said, letting my eyes open.

Gladys patted my hand, glanced at her sister. "I'd say a person that makes you feel *joy* is one worth fighting for. Do the gesture. Ask her to stay. There's no way she won't love it."

That feeling of joy suffused every cell in my body. Urged me to pick up the phone, dial Josie's number, and ask her to swing by late tonight after Cal and Lucia left.

She'd said *yes*, almost immediately and a little breathlessly. And the hope that blossomed in my chest felt as verdant as a spring garden.

Even as a smaller, darker voice urged caution.

But I ignored it.

"We're doing this," I said, and Austin let out a whoop.

## 35

# JOSIE

I was seriously starting to consider the possibility that my brain had split into two personalities. One part heard the news that the rockslide had been cleared, that we were free to leave, and wanted to dance the fucking jig. *No more confusion over Gabe! No more vulnerability! No more small-town country living!*

The other, louder, more obnoxious part of my brain wanted to curl up in Gabe's cozy bed and never leave. Just spend my days alternately tying him up and then having long conversations as we walked through the woods.

I mean, did I *really* need to make money?

In the morning, as I'd crawled back to Lucia's cabin, she'd sank in front of me, held my hands, and demanded a reality check. Things with her and Calvin had gotten serious quickly, and suddenly our week-long fun flings both felt decidedly different.

"Look at me," she'd said, and my eyes filled with tears. "You just met Gabe. One week ago."

"Right," I said, miserably.

"How well do you *really* know him?"

I sighed, petulant. "I guess... I guess I know him as well as you can know someone in a week. But—"

"No buts," she'd said firmly. "What conceivable future do you have with him?"

"None," I said, and the jig-dancing part of my brain cheered. "Which is why this is so terrible. I mean, my career is in L.A. My contacts are in L.A. There isn't a big need for makeup artists *here*. And Gabe? This place is his life. He's who everyone comes to for wisdom over a drink. For a kind word. He'll probably be the mayor in twenty years."

I was surprised that I could put what I was feeling into words. Because we hadn't necessarily *talked* about a potential future together, just delicately danced around it.

Except for this morning, when Gabe had held my wrist and wondered if we could be different together.

"Which means leaving here to move to Los Angeles with a woman he barely knows is just not in the cards, now is it?" Her eyes had that intense look she got when she'd held the same pose for six hours straight on set. And I knew this wasn't just about me.

"Lucia," I said quietly. "Who are you trying to convince here?" Because that girl was pining... *pining* for Calvin and refused to admit it.

She opened her mouth to respond but then closed it and leaned forward as I wrapped my arms around her. "I'm sorry. I just thought... with your history... I don't know. Do you want to be talked into something? Or talked out of something?" she said.

"I think I just want to be sad," I said, suddenly so awash in the feeling I could only let Lucia hold me as I felt it. I didn't cry, but I was *mourning* something.

And then our heart-to-heart had been interrupted by

Calvin, asking Lucia out on one last date. To which she'd said *yes,* regardless of the consequences.

She came back inside, grinning like a loon, and fell backward onto the bed.

"You're going to need to help me find the right outfit. Something that says: *I want to have hot sex tonight and explore our deep, personal connection. However, I do not want to think about our lack of a future.*"

"What about a romper?" I said dryly, tapping my finger against my lips. She laughed, turning to look at me.

"I know I'm making it harder," she said, biting her lip.

I shrugged, staring out the window. We had one night left here before we drove home at dawn. Could I do what Lucia was doing? Subject myself to equal amounts of pleasure and pain with Gabe?

"Josie," she started. "If Gabe called and wanted to see you tonight, wanted to talk about the possibility of a relationship, what would you tell him?"

"No," I said, firmly. "Because I don't *want* to live here. What I want is to live in a fantasy-dimension where Big Sur and Los Angeles are the exact same fucking place."

"Fair," she smiled. "But... what else? Because you seem conflicted, and I would be too. But what if tonight..." she sat up, grabbing my hand. "What if tonight we were *brave*?"

"Brave?"

She nodded. "Like we were talking about the other day. Something about Big Sur is *changing* me. It's all the natural beauty. The wildness. It makes me want to be *reckless*. Seize the moment. The day." Another smile. "Say *fuck* the future."

I remembered standing on top of that fallen redwood tree. The blissful freedom of the forest, how the gravity of nature seemed to mute my anxieties.

"Okay," I said. "So. If I was... being *brave—*" I said, and

Lucia nodded in encouragement. "I would... I would want to keep seeing Gabe. In a... relationship." The word felt heavy and awkward on my tongue. Lu's eyes widened. "Long distance," I finished. "Just... phone calls. Coming to visit each other. That kind of thing."

"Maybe one of you would end up—"

"No way in *hell*," I laughed. "We're both too stubborn to move. But... if I was going to *seize the moment,* then yes. I'd want a *light* relationship with Gabe. Limited. No strings."

"That's a big fucking deal, *chica,*" Lucia mused, eyes searching mine. Because it was. Not to some people, but to me it was the equivalent of staring down at a map and declaring the Earth to be *flat*. "To be honest, I actually didn't expect you to say that."

"Well, there's no possibility of us having a real future. Just a right *now*. And I'm... okay with that," I said slowly, expecting a veritable force of butterflies to take flight in my stomach.

But instead I actually felt... almost *normal.* Thought of Gabe rubbing my feet and grinning bashfully in his room. His trust in me. My inherent trust in him. If I was going to place the responsibility in *anyone's* hands, it would be his.

"I'm okay with you being okay," she said.

I bit my lip. "Me too."

Gabe called while Lucia was in the shower, which was probably a good thing.

"How are you?" Gabe asked, his deep voice so kind I *did* almost burst into tears. Just because.

"I'm good," I said. "Just... packing to leave."

There was a bit of a silence, and I could hear the rowdy sounds of The Bar.

"You've got company?" I teased.

"Oh, just the usual functional alcoholics that run this town —*ouch!* Gladys, that fucking *hurt*." Muffled sounds, then his voice was back. "Excuse me, my bar is merely filled with the lovely, law-abiding citizens of Big Sur."

I laughed, and I could feel him smiling over the line.

"Listen. No pressure at all, and you might not even want to see me, but Lucia is bringing Cal over tonight for his birthday —" he said.

"I know. Believe me, we've talked about it," I said, laughing.

"Well, so, after that I'm free for a couple hours. Do you want to... come by?" His shy hesitancy, so unlike him, shook me to my core. "I just thought, since it's your last night in Big Sur, we could just hang out in The Bar if you want? Totally casual. I'll even light the fireplace and kick out the law-abiding citizens."

I smiled, even though the rational part of my brain was chanting the word *NO* like cheerleaders at a high-school football game.

But Lucia and I were going to *be brave*. I could do it.

Right?

"Yes," I said breathlessly. "I'll be there."

---

FIVE HOURS and one-hundred outfits later, Lucia was standing in front of me looking like a blonde goddess.

"Thank you for the clothing montage," she said as I applied a coat of blood-red lipstick to her lips. Even off the clock, I itched to put makeup on people. "And for the support. And for not telling me that seeing Cal one last time tonight is only going to make tomorrow even harder."

"You're welcome. And thank you for not doing the same thing when I tell you that I'm also going to see Gabe tonight."

She gave me a little shove, and I giggled.

"Watch it or you'll smear," I teased.

"Lucky lady! You're just now telling me?"

I shrugged, trying to play it off. "It's after he helps you with your date."

"Small role," Lu said. "I'll only need him for, like, an hour tops." Her hands were on her hips as she looked out the window, checking for Cal.

My best friend was *nervous*.

"No, it's good," I said slowly, watching Lu. "He's a good friend to Cal. I like seeing that. Clarke didn't have friends the way Gabe does, didn't have relationships the way Gabe does. Gabe is... just really fucking *kind*."

Lucia's head whipped toward me, a strange look on her face "I think that's beautiful, Jo. Tell him what you're feeling. Just be honest."

I snorted. "I will if you will."

I stared her down for about thirty seconds before she said, "Fine. I'll do it."

"Pinky swear," I said, wondering what on Earth I was going to fucking tell him. Or *how*. Or even logistically what was *possible*. But I felt swept up in the moment, and the one side of my brain had beaten the other into silence.

"Let's go be brave," Lucia said just as Cal knocked on the door.

36

## GABE

"What if you lived in Big Sur?" I said under my breath for the fifteenth time. "What if you lived in Big Sur?" I kept practicing as I laid out the blanket, arranged the bouquets of peonies, lit the fireplace, placed dozens of tiny tea-light candles all along the bar, popped open a bottle of red I'd been saving for a special occasion (this one), laid out two wine glasses, and stepped back to review my handiwork.

The Bar looked *slightly* less dingy and a little more romantic.

*Not bad.*

"What if you lived in Big Sur?" I said again. I buttoned up my shirt. Re-buttoned it. Smoothed back my hair and re-tied the bun.

Calvin and Lucia had just left, and I felt oddly buoyed by their obvious spark and connection. In so many ways, they faced a similar situation. They came from two different worlds, lived in different places, but I felt like they were just going to make it *work*. Like you do when you think you might have stumbled upon your soulmate when you were least expecting it.

"What if you lived in—"

A sharp knock at the door interrupted my nervous rambling. My stomach twisted. My heart flip-flopped. I pulled open the door, and there she stood. Leather jacket. Ripped jeans. Combat boots.

*Dammit.*

"You made it," I said on a long exhale.

Her smile was like a burst of sunshine. "Did our two love-birds just leave?" she asked, walking in and shedding her jacket. Underneath, she wore an old *Dark Side of the Moon* shirt. Her hair was up in a messy bun.

I wanted to kiss her so badly.

"Just left. And they were adorable together," I said, laughing and heading towards my iPod. I slid through a few playlists before pulling one up.

"I know," Josie said, eyes bright. "Lucia's *never* been this excited about any guy she's ever dated. It's pretty amazing."

"And didn't I call it the first night we met?" I said, tossing her a wink.

She blushed prettily. "I don't have a memory of that," she said, sifting her fingers through her hair. "Not a memory at all."

I grinned, pressing play, and the sounds of Pink Floyd drifted through the speakers.

"Well done," she said, slowly turning. "And what is... this?" she asked, voice catching at the end. "Wait... did Gladys and Gloria tell you to do this?"

I rushed to pour her a glass of wine, leading her over to the blanket.

"No," I said. "Actually... maybe. Okay, yes."

*What if you lived in Big Sur?*

I couldn't read her expression—it was simultaneously open and guarded.

*What if you lived in Big Sur?*

Might as well get it over with.

"Yes, they did tell me to do this," I said, sinking down onto the blanket. Josie lowered herself gingerly, the firelight reflected in her eyes. "Because I wanted to talk to you about something."

She took a long sip of wine. "Okay. I kind of... well, maybe wanted to talk to *you* about something."

Hope was an effervescent thing, floating up and around me like dandelion seeds in the wind.

"Good," I grinned, attempting to keep my voice steady. "Because this is where I make a complete and utter fool of myself by asking you to stay here in Big Sur with me."

Josie's eyebrow arched but not necessarily in surprise. Then she took three large gulps of wine.

But she didn't say anything. So I soldiered on.

"Josie, I want to respect what you've been through. With... your engagement and whatever happened there. Which you don't need to tell me about. Now or ever. But I just want to tell you the truth. No games."

"Okay," she said softly.

I took a deep breath. "I really like you. For the past decade, when it comes to love and relationships, I've just been... floating along. Assuming it would eventually happen for me. Taking home strangers or tourists when I got lonely. Yearning for a connection I thought might never happen." I held out my hand, laying it gently on her knee. "And then you showed up. And I know we've only known each other for a week, but I feel a real connection to you. From the moment we met. And I can't explain it—I truly can't. Except that I can't stop thinking about you. Can't stop wanting to talk with you and make you laugh and walk through the woods and drink coffee in my bed together." I paused. "You want to keep dominating me? Making me submit to you?" My voice had grown raspy. "Good. I crave it now. Crave giving up total control to *you*. Because you deserve to have it, Josie."

I let out a long exhale. "How am I doing?" I asked sheepishly.

"Not too bad," she said softly, then chugged the rest of her wine in one gulp. "You may continue."

I laughed nervously. "Listen. You're supposed to leave tomorrow morning, but the thought of never seeing you again makes me feel like… like… well, like the world is coming to an end. And I *know* how that sounds… but please tell me you feel even a little bit the same way. You do, don't you?"

*God,* I was a nervous wreck. Hands shaking, sweat beading on my forehead. Josie's eyes fluttered closed for thirty seconds. A full minute. When she opened them, they were shining.

"I don't want to leave you, Gabriel," she finally said.

My heart grew wings and took flight.

"Okay. That's something to work with," I said, gently because she still had that same skittish look in her eyes—like she had on the night of the rockslide when she'd fled to my bathroom.

"So, can I share my idea with you?"

She nodded.

"Move to Big Sur. We'll figure something out. You could… shit, you could work here at The Bar. We could find you some place to live. And we could just try. To be together. My parents would love you. My siblings would *adore* you. You already know Calvin. I think we could build a community here. You could be a part of Big Sur. Like I am. But we'd do it together."

And I'm not sure what happened. Because her face had gone from openly cautious to *terrified* in a manner of seconds.

"What?" I asked. "What did I say?"

Her eyes briefly lit on the ceiling, then back onto me. She was so *beautiful*, features flickering in the firelight. "On the way over, I was practicing what I was going to say to you."

"Me too," I said and was rewarded with a smile.

"I was going to say… this is hard for me, but I wanted to see if you wanted to keep dating me. Even though I live in Los Angeles. Long distance. I'm not sure I can promise much more than that."

"Long distance? You wouldn't move here?" I asked immediately, then tried to take the words back. But it was the *truth*. I wanted Josie *here*. With me.

"No," she said. "No, Gabe… my entire life is in Los Angeles. A career I've spent nearly a decade building. A career I love. My family. Lucia. I fucking *love* that city. I told you before, I'm never going to leave it."

I shook my head. "I don't… sweetheart, I don't think I can do long distance. I mean, if neither one of us is willing to move to be with the other person, what's the end goal?"

"So you're not willing to move to L.A. one day if our relationship continued? Because you could easily get a job as a bartender anywhere. I mean, it'd take you a day. Tops." Her head was tilted in challenge.

"Of course I'm not willing to move. The Bar is my life. I *am* Big Sur. My family, we have a legacy here that I want to maintain. I know everyone… I want to live here forever…" I trailed off, wondering how this conversation had gotten out of hand. There were candles! And a fucking fire in the fireplace!

"Wait," I continued, threading my fingers through Josie's. "I feel like this isn't going how I expected."

"And how was that?" she asked, removing her fingers.

"I thought… I thought you would say *yes*. I hoped. I mean, I know it's complicated, but—"

"—what?" She interjected.

"I thought—" *Be honest.* "For a connection like we have, I thought it'd be easy. The sacrifice. For love, for *true love*, wouldn't a person give up anything? Even if it was hard? *Especially* if it was hard?"

Wasn't that what love was all about?

"We've only known each other a week, Gabe," Josie said. "I don't think we can be in love." My heart lurched as a look of deep disappointment flashed across her face. But what was she disappointed about?

"It's *something,* Josie. There is something between us I cannot categorize. It doesn't fit neatly into any box. And it feels like if you leave tomorrow morning, we're jeopardizing something that could be real, earth-shattering, mind-blowing love."

She stilled. "You really think that?"

"Yes," I said. "And I know how much I'm asking you to give up. I do."

"Do you, though? In order for us to have a relationship, according to you, I'd need to give up my job. My apartment. My friends *and* my family."

The words coming from her mouth made me sound like a selfish asshole. I started to argue but stopped.

Because it *was* what I was asking her.

"Gabriel," she said, drawing me back. Tears were silently streaming down her face. Immediately, I tried to reach for her, but she pulled away, shaking her head. "Can I tell you about Clarke?"

## 37

## JOSIE

Being brave fucking sucked.

On the long, winding drive down Highway 1 to The Bar, the singular beauty of Big Sur mocked me. The full moon, casting a pale glow on the roaring ocean. The night sounds of the forest. The peaceful simplicity. My headlights glancing along the dramatic cliffs.

So I'd practiced the whole way there, fortifying my heart for the inevitable.

*What if we dated long distance?*

Even as I wondered if I was being completely stupid. Who wouldn't want to give up their life to move to this idyllic paradise and let a big, sexy Viking take care of them?

But I'd *done* that before. And the worst had happened.

So here I was, surrounded by candlelight and bouquets of peonies, staring into Gabe's magnificently handsome face and telling him *no*.

More than that. I was telling him my truth.

"Can I tell you about Clarke?" I asked. His body went absolutely still like he was worried sudden movements would send me running.

"Yes. Absolutely," he said quietly.

"I don't... except for Lucia, who was there, I never talk about this. So it's not... I mean, it might not be the best telling." I swallowed around a lump in my throat as hard and sharp as a diamond.

"Okay," he said quietly. "You can just tell me what you want. No pressure."

I nodded and let the floodgate of memories open.

"Do you know what gaslighting is?"

Gabe shook his head.

"It's a type of emotional manipulation. A type of... abuse. Your partner or friend or loved one makes you feel like you don't have a grasp on your own reality."

*Are you sure you should wear that? Don't you think that opportunity is wrong for you? I'm not sure Lucia is as good a friend as you think.*

"It's subtle, so people don't realize it's happening to them, but it just wears you down until you believe everything they've implied about you. By the time... by the time Clarke asked me to marry him, I no longer needed him to subtly poke at my self-esteem. Or suggest my dreams were worthless. Because I was already doing that to myself."

A flurry of emotions were parading across Gabe's face, but he was still as a deer in a meadow. "And if you confront them, they use these... tricks. Verbal tricks. Persuasion... I can't, it's hard for me to really remember because Clarke was so fucking good at it, but if I ever pushed back on something he said or suggested that *he* was the problem, not me, we'd have a conversation, and by the end of it, I'd be the one apologizing and taking the blame."

*I'm only this way, Josie, because you make me.*

"Everything with Clarke moved too fast. Before Clarke, I wasn't really looking for a traditional relationship. I was young and hard-working and just wanted to fuck hot guys and build my career. Because I was the youngest daughter in a family of four sons, I was babied and doted on." I smiled a little. "Which pissed me off because my brothers kicked ass, and I wanted to as well. So I was like *doing it*, you know? On top of my shit."

"You lived alone?" he asked.

"I did after a long time of living five girls to a one-bedroom," I said dryly. "I was so fucking proud of myself. But the first time I ever brought Clarke home to my apartment, an apartment I paid for at the time by working two jobs, he took a look around and said '*is this it?*'"

My stomach clenched at the memory. "I know that's not a good example of it," I said hurriedly. "Because now, saying it, it feels so... *small*. But the weeks leading up to me showing him my apartment, he'd already been subtly undermining me. Trying to get me to see, eventually, that even though we'd barely been dating for three months, we should move in together. *Out* of my place and *into* his." I grimaced. "Does that make sense?"

"Yes," he said softly. "And you don't have to give me examples or prove it. I believe you."

"Okay," I said, feeling the tears streak down my face. "I hate thinking about it, so it's hard for me to say it all out loud..." I trailed off. "Also, and you can ask Lucia about this, but I was like a Stepford Wife-zombie by the time he proposed. I know that my friends and family had their doubts, or at least their concerns, but every time someone mentioned it to me, it was... it was like being ten feet underwater. I couldn't *hear* it. Plus, by then, every problem that my friends mentioned, he already had me blaming myself for. When he proposed to me, I thought it was too soon. Too quick. Not right. There was a part of me screaming about it."

"What did he say?" Gabe asked. He'd laid his palm on my

knee, a reassuring weight.

"Questioned my love for him, of course," I said bitterly. "Told me my feelings were wrong, a tried and true gaslighting tactic. Because it makes you question your sanity. Your partner becomes the only person who really *knows* how you should feel and react. I told him I was afraid, and he'd said, '*people who are truly in love aren't afraid. So if my love makes you afraid, something is wrong with you.*'"

Gabe's jaw clenched. "It's hard to have a relationship when you don't feel like you can share your honest feelings."

I nodded. "And it made me doubt every single... thought. Hunch. Feeling. Sixth sense. Down was up, and up was down. And the worst part was the *way* that I loved him. It was like a... a sickness. Everything with Clarke had to be rollercoaster-style intense. All the time. But it was just lies and manipulation. It's why I told you I don't want... could never *do* a relationship like that again."

There was a long silence. "What happened to your engagement?" Gabe asked. "And you don't have to tell me if you don't want to."

I took a deep, steadying breath. "We got engaged, rapid-fire. I planned a wedding in two months. Everyone was stunned, but like I said, I didn't believe them. And then, on the day of the wedding..."

*He said he's not coming.*

"Lucia and my mom and I had been getting ready for hours. Hair, makeup, the whole deal. Now, you couldn't catch me in a fucking white dress, but that's what Clarke wanted. A princess. So I was shoved into this white wedding dress about thirty minutes before the procession was supposed to begin. We wanted—*he* wanted—our first time seeing each other to be down the aisle, so the fact that he was missing went unnoticed the entire morning. He wasn't close with my family, didn't really have *real* friends, so I think he'd told the minister he'd be showing up right on the dot?"

"So no one had reason to worry," Gabe filled in. "They spent the entire morning thinking his behavior was normal."

Nausea invaded my belly. "And we... I was, well, with my mom. And now I remember how concerned she was. How worried, but she didn't let it come up on my wedding day. She just sat with me, held my hand, told me memories from when I was a little girl. We laughed and drank champagne, and the sun was shining everywhere..."

My throat hitched. And the tears continued to fall. "Lucia knocked on the door, and until the day I die, I will never forget the look on her face. She was *stricken.* Pale as a ghost and trembling everywhere. Clarke had left her a fucking *voicemail* on her phone and just said he wasn't coming. No explanation. No... no sense that what he was doing was a total and complete violation. He just didn't show. And I..."

Gabe reached forward, holding my hand, eyes locked on mine.

"I collapsed. I couldn't believe it for the longest time, even as Lucia held me in my dress. I sobbed for hours, probably. People kept coming in and whispering around me. At some point, my mother must have told everyone, which had to have been *terrible* for her. But I have no recollection of that. No memories at all except crying in Lucia's arms. And thinking." I laughed bitterly, and Gabe reached forward to catch a tear with his thumb.

"I kept thinking there was some huge mistake. A tear in the universe. A massively inappropriate practical joke. That he'd mixed up the date or... or went to the wrong address. I mean, we had a fucking rehearsal dinner two nights before where he'd given a speech about our life together. And it was smarmy and manipulative, but at the time, I didn't notice. Or didn't care. By then, I was addicted to the intensity and felt so goddamn *lucky* he had chosen me. Probably because he liked to remind me of that ten times a day. Every time I fucked up, by asking too many questions or doing anything that smacked of independence, he'd remind me that he could have had *anyone* in the world. But he'd chosen me."

Gabe kept wiping my tears away, and I should have stopped him but didn't have the strength. Plus, it felt *good*.

"I don't remember a lot except Lucia getting me home and staying with me for days. We were supposed to go to Bermuda for a week, so I didn't have work, but Lucia did, and she called and canceled every job she had. And when I couldn't get out of bed the next week, she called all of my jobs and told them I'd contracted some weird tapeworm in the islands." I laughed at the memory. "It was the first day I actually felt like a human being, listening to Lucia try to explain in vivid detail the size, shape, and specifics of my tropical tapeworm."

Gabe grinned, smoothing my hair from my face. "She was also the one who moved all of my stuff out of Clarke's apartment. Went one day when he was at work and grabbed everything for me. She let me stay with her for as long as I needed."

"She's a hell of a friend," he said.

"The best. It's funny, we talked about this just the other day, and she feels *guilty* about Clarke. That if she just could have convinced me he was a psychopath, none of this would have ever happened."

"Do you believe that?"

"Not at all. In some ways now... I'm grateful. I was so deep in it, so deep in his mind games, I sometimes wonder if I would have ever gotten out if he *had* showed up that day and we *had* gotten married." I shuddered. "And it's taken two years of healing and working on myself to be able to say that."

Gabe had moved closer, and I hadn't realized he'd wrapped his huge, Viking arms around me, holding me against his chest. Not smothering, or forcing, but folding against me just the way I needed.

"Did you ever see him again? Hear from him? Get an explanation?" He asked.

I shook my head. "No. I have never seen or heard from him. He's never returned my calls or texts; I've never even bumped into him on the street. And the only *explanation* is that he's a total psychopath."

"But you never got closure," Gabe pressed, arms tightening with tension.

I pulled back, staring into his kind eyes. "This experience has taught me that you don't always get that in real life. You're just left wondering, questioning yourself, hearing his..." I coughed, tripping on the words. "Hearing his voice in your thoughts."

Pain darkened his face. With the exception of Lucia, this wasn't something I ever mentioned out loud.

"You still hear him?"

"Yes," I whispered. "Not all of the time, less than before. But... he's there."

Gabe let out a long exhale, teeth set, jaw ticking. "I'm so sorry, Josie."

I shook my head, pressed on. "So I'm not trying to say you're *naive* or you shouldn't want this... this soulful, once-in-a-lifetime love, but it's why that thought doesn't appeal to me any longer. Do you understand now?"

The tension that rippled through his muscles was subtle but there. Gabe pulled back, brushed the hair from my cheek.

"You don't think it's real? What my parents have? Or my siblings?"

"I think what they have is *very* real. And I think they're lucky to have found a great love that isn't also toxic. And I'm not saying you won't find that. I just... Gabe, you told me that you wanted to love someone so badly it *hurt*."

"But not like Clarke," he said, shaking his head. "Not like... sweetheart, that's not what I meant."

"I had that," I said, forging on. "And it destroyed me. The person you see in front of you is... I'm *not* the same person I was before Clarke. There were days where I even questioned the very core of my being. Days where he had me convinced I didn't like art. Or dancing. Or my family. Or even being a makeup artist. He thought my job was *trashy*," I said, bitterness choking my throat. "And at the time of our wedding, I was starting to look into other careers."

Gabe's palm was stroking across my back. "I like this Josie though. I still *see* you. I don't see the things that Clarke did." His palm moved to my chest, spreading across my heart. "The moment I met you, I felt like I knew you. Not just because I feel this connection to you but because you put it out there. Everything about you screams *authentic*."

I smiled grimly. "It hasn't been easy. Finding her again. She was lost for a long time," I said.

And that's when the tears really broke, transforming into shuddering sobs that wracked my body. Gabe curled me into his chest, holding me tight, nothing but soothing words. Big hands stroking my hair. No judgment. No qualifying. Just there.

After a long time, I finally pulled back. The reality of our conversation, of what we were *deciding*, was like a punch to the gut. It must have hit Gabe at the same time because his features twisted with pain.

"Tell me what you want to do," he said.

I steadied my voice. "Long distance. Phone calls. Coming to visit, that kind of thing. And I don't have any idea after that. We'd just be... living in the present, probably without a future together. But after Clarke, it's... well, it's what I can offer."

Gabe dropped his head in his hands.

"You don't want that," I said, stating a fact.

"We're back at the same crossroads, gorgeous," he said, voice muffled. When he looked up, his gaze was so vulnerable it fucking *hurt*. "Because I want you here. With me. *Now*. I don't want to explore this over the phone. I don't want to..." A long pause as he looked into the fire. "Josie, I don't want to fall in love with you and then have no future together. If we date, even casually, it's going to happen. It's already happening for me."

His ears were pink, cheeks flushed. I wanted to crumple against him again, kiss away the pain of this shitty situation.

"What is?" I asked softly because I was a goddamn masochist.

"I'm falling for you."

The tears were back now, half-joy, half-heartache, because I'd known it too. The only way I'd *ever* consider even a casual relationship with someone right now, after Clarke, was if I was stupid in love.

"Then move to L.A."

Gabe shook his head. *No*.

"This was what Clarke wanted," I reminded him. "Wanted me isolated and depending on him. No friends. No family. He only offered his love to me by making me sacrifice everything. It was conditional. I was lucky. I got out. I saved myself and have spent the past two years healing." My voice broke.

"I know," he said, trying to reach for my hand again.

"You don't," I said, pushing back to the very edge of the

blanket. "And I just asked you to do the very same thing—to give up your job, your family, your hometown. And you wouldn't do it."

I stood, grabbing my things. I needed to leave now before I never left.

"Gabe," I prodded. "You wouldn't do that. Would you?"

# 38

## GABE

I wanted to find Clarke and beat him to within an inch of his life.

Actually, no.

I wanted to build a time machine and travel back two years, to right before Josie met him. *Then* beat him to within an inch of his life.

And then take Josie on that first date instead of Clarke.

"Gabe?" Josie said again. Pushing me to answer a question that *should* be easy.

*Yes. Let's try and date long distance. And maybe, if things go well, I'll consider moving down to Los Angeles.*

*That* was the answer.

But I couldn't make myself say the words. And didn't that make me the world's biggest hypocrite?

"You won't, will you? Move to Los Angeles?" Resignation was written all over her face.

I swallowed roughly, hating myself. "I don't think so. No. I'd hate it there."

"And I'd hate it here," she said softly.

"But every day could be like this," I said, leaning forward, indicating the candles and light around me. "I wasn't lying, Josie, when I said my entire goal in life was to be someone's husband. To make them happy. Josie, I'd worship you every fucking second of the day. Any way you wanted. Flowers and candles and foot massages and—*Fuck*... you want me on my knees every night, sweetheart?"

Her pupils darkened, and I felt my cock harden at the thought. At the memory of kneeling before Josie like she was a goddamn queen.

"I'd *live* on my knees for you." I cupped her face in my hands, swiping away a tear that was sliding down her cheek. "Please, Josie, I want to give you a beautiful life here in Big Sur."

"It's too much," she said, half-sobbing. "It's... you're asking too much of me. Right now. All I can offer you is a long-distance relationship that has nowhere to go. But there's value in that too, Gabe. We wouldn't be together forever, but we'd be together for a little bit."

"No," I said, shaking my head. "I can't have you for just a little bit. I *need* you."

Josie bit her lip, nodding her head like I'd just affirmed something for her. "Okay, then." She stood, and I thought my heart would fall right out of my chest.

I stood with her, but she was already shrugging back on her jacket.

"Please, don't go," I said. I was openly begging now. "Please. Josefine."

She walked up to me, leaning up on her tiptoes to press a small, sweet kiss against my lips. I tried to hold on, but she backed away just as quickly.

"Thank you for being honest with me. Thank you for listening to my story and... and really *seeing* me. I know this isn't what you wanted, but I feel forever changed. By you. By this place." Her smile was so sad I felt the world tremble. "I'll never forget you, Gabriel Shaw."

"*Josie*," I pleaded, and later I'd wish I'd said something, *anything*, other than just say her name over and over again like some lovesick fool. That I would have said *yes* to what she was offering me instead of forcing what I wanted on her.

But I didn't. Instead, I watched as Josie walked out of The Bar, out of Big Sur, out of my life.

Leaving me with flickering candles and wilting flowers and a fire that burned too hot and too bright.

## 39

## JOSIE

"I'm either incredibly stupid. Or I just protected myself from yet another horrific heartbreak," I told Lucia as we drove at ninety miles an hour back to Los Angeles.

We'd traded driving duties several times during the six-hour trip because one of us kept spontaneously bursting into tears, and that was *not* a good frame of mind for driving.

"I'm with you," Lucia said feebly, curled up against the passenger side door. I'd never seen her so low, her usually frustratingly flawless complexion looking pallid. We were flying through the Central Valley, everything around us flat and impassive.

I kept repeating to myself, over and over again, that I'd done the right thing.

"You think I did the right thing, right?" I asked Lucia for the fiftieth time.

She'd left Calvin the same way I'd left Gabe, and both of us couldn't have been more miserable.

"I mean... ultimately, *yes*," she said. "I do. I just wish... I just wish Gabe had been more open to what you were proposing. Why double-down and *force* you to make a choice? It just doesn't make any sense."

"Because he's a stubborn son of a bitch," I said grimly. *A sweet, kind, funny Viking that would have done anything to make you happy*. But I'd dated Clarke. And even as my sweet Viking swore up and down that what he was asking wasn't the same kind of manipulation, I couldn't be sure. "And because Clarke has to ruin things for me even two years later."

"Don't say that," Lu said softly. "This was your decision. You listened to your instincts, and your instincts said it was too rushed and too soon."

"Which they should have said when Clarke asked me to move in with him. *Marry* him."

"And that wasn't your fault. He was a fucking psychopath. But you're listening to yourself again, Josie. I know this is a terrible time to say this, but as your best friend, that makes me happy." She reached forward, grasping my arm. "You're trusting *you* again."

I sighed. "That's true. That was my goal after all of this. To find… to find *me*," I said, voice cracking at the end. I swallowed down the tears.

"What did it feel like to tell Gabe about Clarke?" Lucia asked.

I searched my feelings, and with the exception of nausea—which always happened when I thought of my wedding day—I felt oddly… liberated.

"It felt good, actually," I finally said. "It felt good to have someone really listen. Like a great unburdening." The volume of Clarke's voice ebbed and flowed, but the *story* of what happened to me felt heavy as shackles, weighting me down.

"I feel lighter." I looked at Lucia. "That's progress, right?"

Lucia nodded. "Yes," she agreed. "That's real progress, *chica*."

"I'm fascinated with Gabe," I continued. "Attracted to him. Loved spending time with him and, *if* things were different, would have considered a very slow relationship with him."

"But they're not," Lu said.

"They're not," I repeated. "And I can't help but feel my only other option is to be horribly heartbroken a month from now."

"So you did the right thing," Lu said. "Right?"

"Right," I said firmly, driving on through the night.

A few hours later, the skyline of Los Angeles reared up in greeting, the two of us giving little *whoops* as we entered the Valley. We rolled down the windows and breathed in the smell of the city: smog and people and smoke and yearning. I took us right to our favorite taco truck.

"Big Sur doesn't have *carnitas* tacos on every street corner," I pointed out.

"True," Lu said. "Or all-night dance clubs."

"Or Saturday street fairs."

"Or red carpet events."

"Or everyone that means the most to me," I said firmly.

She nodded. Across the parking lot, a cute guy flashed me a grin. *Cute* cute. Tattoos and scruff and a sinful smile.

And suddenly my slightly joyful mood came crashing horribly down around me, everything up in fucking flames.

Because I was going to have to go back to picking up strangers. Dating guys like *that.*

Guys who weren't Gabe.

"Oh my God," I said, suddenly, sinking against the car, head in my hands.

Lu knew, stroking my hair as large, wracking sobs worked through me.

"I know, *chica*. I know," she said and let me cry in the middle of the street on a hot Los Angeles night.

# 40

# GABE

*One month later*

Dimly, I heard the sound of the front door open and footsteps approach. I was lying in front of my new home—the fireplace—and engaging in my new favorite activity: replaying all the stupid things I'd said to Josie the night she left.

The footsteps got closer, but I wasn't worried. It was probably Calvin, who'd been coming by most nights to drown his sorrows about Lucia. He and I would switch off on lying down based on whose turn it was to pour the drinks.

"Cal?" I said, opening one eye and wincing at the light.

I'd had a lot to drink last night. There was a sniffling sound then another. I sat up, body protesting with the movement, and came face-to-face with Isabelle.

"Iz?" Tears streaked down her face as she sank to the floor next to me, Lola pressed against her chest. "What happened?"

Isabelle hiccuped, flashing me a watery smile. "I just need my big brother for a minute. Is that okay?"

And then she collapsed against my chest, baby and all, and cried for a long time. I held her and Lola, told her everything would be fine—a sure lie, since I wasn't sure what had happened or if it could even be fixed.

"I'm going to go to the bathroom for a minute," she finally said, wiping away tears with the sleeve of her sweater. "And then we can talk, okay? Can you watch the baby?"

I nodded as Isabelle walked away. She looked pale and deeply unhappy. If I'd taken the time to look in a mirror recently, I'd probably see my own pallid expression reflected back to me.

Lola seemed unperturbed, crawling on the floor and trying to eat something that looked suspiciously like a cigarette. I snatched her up quickly before I needed to pump her stomach.

The Bar was *not* baby-proof.

"What's going on with your mom, huh?" I asked Lola, her wide, dark eyes peering at me curiously. I stroked her cheek, and she grinned at me, drool running down her lip.

The unconditional love I felt for my niece put a small dent in the month of heartbreak. We bounced around the room a bit, me pointing out random objects and Lola either laughing or crying at them. We skipped the penis paintings, of course, but she was inordinately drawn to the glasses and the sharpest of my knives.

"Gonna be a little killer, huh?" I asked, grabbing the butcher knife she kept trying to touch and putting it out of reach. I lifted her high in the air, and she squealed with delight.

"You're great with her," Isabelle said, sneaking up behind us. She blew her daughter a kiss before standing behind the bar and grabbing a towel.

"Easy when you're in love," I said, sitting on a bar stool with Lola in my lap. A look passed over Isabelle's face.

"You want to talk about it?"

A long exhale. "I do. And, actually, I want to go on a fucking hike."

I arched an eyebrow. "Well, then, let's do it. I'll grab the carrier."

I dug through the closet until I found it, strapping it to my chest as Isabelle placed a squirming Lola inside.

"When was the last time you went hiking?" she asked softly as her fingers tightened the straps.

"All the time," I lied. "Gotta get that exercise, you know?"

"Mhmm," she murmured, unconvinced. "You know, Cal called me a few days ago."

"Why?" I asked, trying to sound nonchalant. Attempting to lace up hiking boots was hard with a baby on your chest.

"Oh, you know… just to let me know that you haven't been outside since Josie left and that all you do is lie in front of that fireplace, groaning."

I scoffed but stopped at Isabelle's sharp expression. "I'm not… I'm not just *groaning*." I paused. "Sometimes I *exhale sadly*."

A twitch of her lips. "I think we both need this."

We stepped outside into the misty November of Big Sur, turning toward the trail that extended behind my house, boots crunching over pine needles and pine cones. I hadn't been outside *once* since Josie had left—something I'd never done before. Since usually nature was therapeutic, the silence letting me process my emotions.

And I'd been avoiding it. Because I knew what my emotions were: anger, frustration, embarrassment, *yearning*.

I didn't want to think about that shit.

But as soon as we entered the forest, I felt something slide back into place. A crucial missing piece. It must have shown on my face because Isabelle reached over and squeezed my arm.

"There's my big brother," she smiled, dipping under a low branch.

We fell into place along the old trail, the forest alive and verdant around us. Lola seemed to love the woods, her little hands reaching out to grasp at every living thing we passed.

"So," I said slowly. "Tell me what happened."

"Maya and I had a huge fucking fight. A bad one."

"Seriously?" I asked. "But the two of you were just in here the other day. For another date night. You looked—"

"Fine?" she interjected, shrugging a little. "Probably because we were. Or are. Nothing's... *damaged* beyond repair or anything. But some things have been kind of bubbling beneath the surface... and this morning, they all boiled over."

"About Lola?" I guessed.

Isabelle's shoulders dropped as she sighed. "Having a baby is hard. I think Maya and I wanted to be parents for such a long time, but we never *talked* about it. All the big and little ways that your life changes. Our entire lives have been thrown off track. We don't sleep. Our jobs are up in the air. We never have time to ourselves. Sex is completely out of the question."

"You've had sex?" I teased.

"Yes, big brother. A lot of it. Unlike *your* virginal self," she said, smiling now.

I placed my hands over Lola's ears. "Don't corrupt my niece. She'll never know about my sordid past."

Isabelle laughed for real this time, filling the woods with the happy sound. "It all amounts to this... like a *seismic* shift to a relationship. And I just wished we had... I don't know, read some books. Or made sure we were on the same page about certain things." Isabelle looked away. "I'm happy we live in Monterey. It's best, I think. But you know Maya's family lives in Texas. And I know you guys are only an hour away, but..."

"It's isolating," I said, remembering how they looked during the rockslide when I'd picked up Lola. "You said you've been feeling isolated."

Another sad shrug. "We're both on maternity leave, so we only see each other, no other adults, all day. I guess I thought our friends would come over more. Mom and Dad have been great, obviously; it's just..."

"Different?" I offered.

There was so much honesty and hurt in Isabelle's eyes.

"Yeah. Different. Not bad. Never *bad*. But not what I envisioned in my mind, if I'm being honest. Which is hard. So much of motherhood is about these *moments*... of happiness and love. And I have those moments. And so does Maya. But we're not having them *together*. I've never felt so separate from her." Isabelle's voice cracked a little. "We were always so connected. On a deep, soulful level. And now I feel so separate from my wife. It's awful."

I'd always thought of Maya and Isabelle as true soul mates. Anyone who knew them would think the same.

"It's hard for me to imagine the two of you fighting like this," I said, stomach clenching.

Isabelle laughed again but not bitterly. "Oh, Gabe, we fight all the time. Just like any other couple." She tilted her head at my confused expression. "Just like Austin and Paige. Just like Mom and Dad."

We stepped over a tiny stream filled with moss-covered rocks. "Which is also hard for me to believe if we're both being extra honest today," I said. The scent of the pine cones and the feel of the mist on my skin was hammering away at my thoughts about Josie.

"You know why, though, right?" Isabelle smirked.

"Um... I don't," I said, unable to stop from smiling back at her. "Why?"

"Because the Shaws are stubborn assholes, that's why," she said, pointing a finger at me.

"Hey, why are you pointing at *me?*" I laughed, smoothing my palm through Lola's curls.

"Because you're stubborn too, Gabe. We all are. And the hard truth of the matter is that *all* relationships require compromise. Which is not something that comes easy to us. It was one of the biggest things Maya and I would argue about in the beginning. That I always like to get my way, and I never thought to think of things from *her* perspective."

I nodded, even though I found it hard to believe that these three couples I'd held up on a pedestal my entire life struggled so frequently.

"I know what you're thinking, Gabriel," she said with a knowing look.

I looked down at Lola. "That my niece is so adorable I want to physically *eat* her? And why is that?"

She grinned. "I say that all the time. I mean, how terrifying for a baby, huh? All these massive humans around you, saying they want to consume you. *Especially* you. You're the biggest person she's ever seen." Lola held tight to my fingers, her delicate breathing in sync with my own.

"Also, you just deflected," she laughed.

I shrugged. "Yeah? What was I thinking then?"

"You're surprised that Maya and I fought, that couples even have fights. Especially Mom and Dad, who fought a lot more than you allow yourself to remember."

That uneasy feeling returned to my stomach. "Okay. Maybe I was thinking that. It's not a judgment. I just don't want you and Maya to get a divorce."

Isabelle exhaled. "We're not going to get a divorce. She needed some time today. And I needed some time. Actually, we probably just both need to fucking *sleep.* I'm not in favor of big fights like this, and we *rarely* have them. But sometimes... like I said. It's a compromise, always. In a million different ways, at a million different times. And *that* is the hard work of being in a committed relationship. Even if you're soulmates," she said, reaching forward and touching my arm. "I believe in love, just like you. How could we not with Mom and Dad as our role models?"

"It's what I've always wanted. They just seemed so *content* every moment of the day. With each other, with all of us."

"And they are content. Blissful, even. But I think... I think you and I have different ideas of what a soulmate is."

"How so?" I asked.

"I've never felt so disconnected from Maya as I do right now. And I'm kind of pissed at her. And hurt. But of all the women in the world, *she's* the woman I made a commitment to. A commitment to love her forever. And, most importantly, to *fight* for her. Which is why we're giving each other a day to cool off, to process, and then sit down and begin the hard work of repairing what's broken." She waved her hand in the air, driving home her point. "The difference being, I wouldn't do that for someone I *wasn't* supposed to be with for the rest of my life."

I nodded, taking it all in. Isabelle was right, and maybe it *was* the stubborn asshole in me, but I did believe loving your soulmate would be easy. Like breathing. Or, that kid feeling of climbing on your bike and speeding down a hill without a fear in the world, only this buoyant joy. *That's* what I thought it would be like: simple and joyous.

That's what I thought I was proposing to Josie, the night she left.

"Sometimes I forget... but Sasha and I fought. Quite a bit, I think," I said. "Which isn't easy for me to admit."

Isabelle bit her lip, stooping to pick up a fallen leaf bursting with orange.

"There is another difference," she said. "And you have to figure this out on your own. But there's... how do I say this: healthy fighting? When you're working through things that are important to the both of you. But then there's... well, the fighting you and Sasha did. The kind that signals the relationship *isn't* right."

"You don't think we were right for each other?" I asked. "We were so alike. Had a lot of the same goals and values. I thought we had the same dreams." I hated the hurt in my voice, still there after all this time.

"Maybe on paper?" Isabelle said, shrugging. "But were you in love with her?"

I opened my mouth to answer, but whatever I was going to say got stuck there. An image of Josie floated up: of her and I, laughing, as she told me she hated macaroni and cheese. The comfortable playfulness between us, the ease, even though at that point, we'd only known each other a few hours.

Had I ever felt that comfortable with Sasha?

"Of course I loved her," I said firmly, but it felt like a lie, and I wasn't yet sure why. "The problem was on her. She didn't love me back even though I would have made a great husband for her."

"*Her* problem?" Isabelle hit my arm.

"Yeah," I said.

"Stubborn asshole," she said, shaking her head. "You're

just like the rest of us. And you're going to need to work on that if you want to be that good husband you've always talked about. Plus," she said. "Here's an idea. 'Husband,' 'wife,' 'boyfriend'... these are just words. They mean jack shit without actions behind them. Try just being a good *listener*. In the beginning of our relationship, Maya always said I didn't listen to her, always forcing my own thoughts or ideas onto a situation. But *listening—*" she reached over, patting my ear, "is what's going to be the difference for you. I promise."

I looked at my little sister, exhaustion etched into the lines around her face. Her hair wild and held back with a chip clip. Baby drool on her shirt. She was such a wonderful mother—and now, suddenly, she seemed to be soaring past me in both wisdom and maturity.

"When did you get so smart?" I said.

She laughed wearily. "Not sure if I'm that smart. Just been through a lot."

I pulled her in for a side hug, and the two of us walked in companionable silence for half a mile. The silence was edging its way in, and my thoughts were anxiously trying to stop it.

"You want to talk about Josie?" Isabelle finally asked, and I groaned in response. She nudged my shoulder. "I bet I can help."

"I'm not sure what you could help with. Things with Josie and I didn't work out, and I'm pretty sure I ruined my chances anyway." I shrugged grimly, watching a small bird flit from branch to branch.

"Hmmm," Isabelle said, tapping her finger against her lip. "What did you ask her? The night she left Big Sur?"

I shuddered at the memory. "I asked her to stay here with me. To move here, officially, and be in a relationship."

"You did *what*?" she said, smacking me on the arm. Again.

"Hey, *ow*," I said, ducking away from her. "I just did what Mom and Dad always told us to do. Be *honest*. And I was. That was what I wanted out of our relationship, and I asked her for it. I didn't think… I didn't think it would backfire so spectacularly. I thought Josie would want to sacrifice for me." I paused. "I thought true love was sacrifice. Isn't that what you were just saying about Maya?"

"Yeah, except what were *you* sacrificing?" she prodded, hitting the nail right on the goddamn head.

I sighed. "I know. I know what you mean, and I'm not sure why I stumbled. Because she called me on it. She said I could move down to Los Angeles, and I… well, I said no."

Isabelle gave me a curious look. "What type of relationship had she proposed? Or did she want to stop seeing you altogether?"

"Long distance," I said. "Nothing real intense or serious. Josie had…" I paused since it wasn't my story to tell. "Josie was in a bad relationship a couple of years ago. Someone who manipulated her. Emotionally abused her. I think it makes it hard for her to trust people."

Isabelle grabbed my arm, stopping me, and pinned me with an angry look. "So why would you ask a woman who'd been through *that* to leave her life and her job after only knowing you for a week?"

The blinding clarity of every stupid thing I'd done and said hit me like a ton of fucking bricks.

I stopped under a large redwood tree, eyes to the sky as everything came roaring back. Thought of Josie, balanced on that fallen log, reclaiming something she'd lost.

I put my hands over Lola's ears. "I'm such a fucking fool."

"Yeah," Isabelle said. "A big ol' lovable fool." She looped her arm through mine and kissed Lola on the cheek. "It's the romantic in you. You've always been this way, and I watched Sasha take advantage of that, Gabe. Of your big heart and endless kindness. But real relationships, even ones built for soulmates, are not that easy. Mom and Dad fought to be together. Fought to stay together. Went through plenty of tough and challenging times that we never saw. Because we were kids and were too young to understand the nuances."

"I know," I said. "Deep down, I know this is true."

"So why did you ask Josie to make that choice?" she asked softly.

"Because..." I started. I was mentally wandering into some uncomfortable territory. "Because maybe I'm not willing to make that same sacrifice. Because deep down, I *do* think Big Sur is the most magical place on the planet, and it's hard to imagine anyone else feeling differently. And that *does* worry me. That I asked her to do things for a potential relationship that I wasn't willing to do."

I felt vaguely nauseous at the thought. Sure, I wasn't Clarke, but hadn't I asked her to give up her life for me? And offered nothing in return?

"What if you just took some more time?" Isabelle asked. "Why the rush? Why the ultimatum?"

"If neither one of us is ultimately willing to move," I said. "Then I didn't see the point of prolonging the inevitable and making it even more terrible when, I don't know, six months from now, we're still in the same position with no solution. It sounded like a recipe for a broken heart, regardless. And that week between us has been incredibly intense. I can't really explain our connection, but it's more than just sexual. There's a spark between us I've never truly felt before. I thought it was... fuck, my heart? The universe? Trying to tell me that Josie was my soulmate. And I did... love the idea of having this one week together, falling head over heels for each other, and making it work. A real love story, like Mom and Dad." I let my eyes close in pain. "And actually, that sounds terrible when I say it out loud."

Isabelle had stopped in the middle of the trail and was just watching me. Waiting for me to come to the conclusion she'd come to forever ago.

"Why?" Isabelle asked.

"Life... and love isn't that simple. And it's a shit thing to do to Josie. Making her choose like that." I was nauseous again, and I actually worried I'd puke into the wildflowers.

"I wasn't born knowing this, Gabriel," Isabelle said. "None of us are. But meeting and marrying Maya has taught me an endless amount about love and life and relationships. I told you, in the beginning, our main argument was about my stubbornness and inability to listen. I always thought I *knew* just what she needed. Wanted to be the one to give her what she needed. And over and over again, I hurt her feelings. Dismissed her needs, really. Totally unintentionally, and it came from this deep well of love for her. But still. It was hurtful. I had to own that. Plus, I'm a fool too," Isabelle continued. "Just ask Maya. She would concur." We laughed together. "So I'm not trying to say I know every damn thing about love. Because I *definitely* don't. But my ultimate advice?"

"Let's hear it," I said.

"You're still hung up on her?"

"I've thought about her every moment of the day since she left." Which was painfully true.

"And you'd like to pursue a relationship with her?"

"Absolutely," I said firmly.

"Then t*alk* to her. *Listen*. If she wants to still be with you, take it one day at a time. I think you'll be surprised when a solution ultimately *does* make itself known to you."

---

We walked for a long time after that until that same quiet, serene feeling started to invade my cells. Until I could start to see *clearly* again, my vision no longer mired with the grief and regret of the past thirty days.

If I really wanted a relationship with Josie, what was I willing to do?

## 41

# JOSIE

It was a Saturday night in L.A., and like the last four Saturdays since I'd left Big Sur, I was staying home.

I sipped a glass of wine on my porch and tried to find some peace in my neighborhood. As usual, people were *out*. Walking around, talking. Children played a complicated game in the street right in front of me. Friends from high school and distant relatives waved as they walked by, calling out in Spanish.

And I was fucking miserable.

I'd thrown myself into work until my fingers cramped and I only dreamed of gold-flecked eye shadow. Tried to go to my favorite bars or clubs only to end up leaving after five minutes.

Everything felt wrong wrong *wrong*. Like I was walking around in the wrong body, skin tight and joints aching. On particularly morose evenings, I'd find myself driving out to Long Beach and watching the waves, which continued to echo *Gabe Gabe Gabe* as they rolled across the shore.

Next to me, my phone rang, and I picked up, already knowing who it would be.

"*Buenas noches*," I said.

I heard Lucia sigh on the other end. "Oh my God, *you're still miserable.*"

I rolled my eyes, kicking my legs. "*Si,*" I said sardonically. "I'm still wallowing."

"You going out tonight?"

"Nope."

A long pause, and I could hear her shifting around. "What can I do, *chica*? I hate seeing you this way."

A few kids rode by on bikes. I envied their careless laughter.

"Nothing," I said, blinking away tears. "It's okay, really. It'll pass. I just miss Gabe, but we don't have a future together, so at least there's an end point to this."

"It'll pass," she repeated but didn't sound convinced. "Or... there's another option."

We had spent hours on the phone about this—her, dutifully allowing me to wallow in that secretive way you can with your best friend because they won't judge you, won't tell you there was a *reason* why you never took men home twice, laughed with them, went hiking with them, or explored hidden fantasies.

Because when it was over, it felt like your heart was being hit by a truck. Repeatedly. And then lit on fire.

So she let me wallow—although recently she'd been gently suggesting solutions. All of which I kicked right to the fucking curb.

I wanted to wallow.

"It's been a month," I said, waving when I saw my mom walking down the street heading toward my house. "I'll get back out there soon. Until then..." I trailed off.

Lucia made a noncommittal sound.

"Hey, I think my mom's here. Can I call you back?"

My mom was slowly walking up the path to my house, and I couldn't read her expression.

"Give her a kiss for me," Lucia sang.

"Uh-huh," I promised. "*Luego*."

My mom walked up, perching a Crock-Pot on her hip.

"What's that?" I pointed.

"*Pozole*. I thought I'd bring it by and see if you were still heartbroken over that man. The one with all the body hair."

"*Hirsute*," I said automatically, ignoring the pang when I remembered the night Gabe and I had met. "And I'm not heartbroken." I stood up, pulling her in to kiss her cheek. "*Entra mama.*"

I gestured toward the open door, and she followed, tut-tutting at the clothes on the floor and the twelve pairs of black boots lying everywhere.

"You should see Miguel's house, though," I said, hands on my hips.

She smiled at me and plugged in the Crock-Pot and began prepping the soup in a bowl. She grabbed a ripe avocado from my counter and began to slice it.

"What's this for?" I asked, sliding up on the counter and watching her work. There was more gray in her hair than the last time I had seen her. "Not just my heartbreak?"

"*Si*, your heartbreak," she said, looking at me with kind eyes. I had to swallow sharply to keep from crying. "Last week, at your *tía's* party, you looked like a ghost, Josefine."

"I've been working long hours," I explained, which was true. Anything to dull my thoughts. "You know how it is. It's already awards season, so my client list basically doubled."

She nodded. "I know, *mija*. I know how hard you work." She pressed a hot bowl of *pozole* in my hands, garnished with avocado. The smell instantly transported me to dinners when

I was a kid. My mom always made *pozole* when it rained. "But this is different."

I took a sip and felt, for the first time in weeks, a sunburst of contentment. "This is really good, *Mama*."

"Of course it is. Now eat your soup and talk to me."

I rolled my eyes, feeling like a teenager again. "I don't... I don't know what more there is to say. I told you what happened. We're not going to work out. You don't want me to move all the way up to Big Sur, do you?"

Her eyebrows shot off her head. "Of *course* not. And I'm not saying you should. I *am* saying that it's been two years, Josefine. Two years since that monster messed with your head. And maybe..."

I took a fortifying sip of soup, sensing what was coming.

"Maybe it's time to trust again."

My head fell back against the cabinet, my eyes closed. For weeks after the wedding, every member of my family, plus my parents' church, brought food for me. Like after a funeral. Like Clarke had *died*. They came by, wearing black and with distraught expressions, and pressed stews and enchiladas and casseroles into my hands. Marriage, especially in the predominantly Mexican East Los Angeles, was a way of life in this community. It was sacred and traditional.

Your groom did *not* leave you at the altar.

Between Lucia caring for me and my family and neighbors' endless gifts of sustenance, I'd felt *loved*—a feeling I had recognized as having all but disappeared while I was with Clarke.

"What does Gabriel make you *feel*?" She asked me, disrupting the silence. I bit my lip.

"Happy. Silly. Wanted. Cherished." I paused. "Safe."

"Safe?" she pushed.

I nodded.

She brushed a lock of hair behind my ear. "When did you ever feel safe with Clarke?"

I looked away because we both knew the answer.

"What if he's not real, *Mama*? In the beginning, I felt completely swept up with Clarke too. *Exhilarated*. I'd never felt that way before. And now, here comes Gabe, seemingly too good to be true, and I have no idea if he's just a Clarke—but in disguise. I have no idea how to—"

"Trust," she finished for me, taking my empty bowl and filling it with more soup. The scent of pork and chiles filled my tiny kitchen. "What does this say, *mija*?" My mom placed her palm over my heart, which was beating recklessly.

"Last time I listened to my heart, I ended up sobbing in a wedding dress," I said softly. "My heart can no longer be trusted." But she was shaking her head swiftly.

"You underestimate yourself. You underestimate your *heart*. I think it knows," she said fiercely. "I think it knows this time what's real."

---

LATER I WAS BACK on my porch, this time with tea, listening to the city sounds. My mom had left an hour ago, and I still felt mixed up and strange, like I wanted to cry and laugh in equal measure.

And when my phone rang, I picked it up, not even checking to see who it was. I was expecting Lucia.

"My mom says hi and also wants you to remember that she loves you like her own daughter," I said, taking a sip of chamomile.

There was a long pause on the other end, and then: "Josie?"

It was Gabe.

"Oh... *Gabe*?" I asked, sitting up swiftly and sloshing tea on my arm. "What are you—Wait...?"

In my ear, he chuckled softly, and all the hair on my neck stood up. "To be honest, I didn't think you'd pick up. So now I'm *extra* nervous."

I didn't say anything for a moment, still in a state of shock.

"Um... how are you?" he finally asked.

"Fine," I lied. "How are you?"

"Fucking terrible," he said, and I burst out laughing, twisted up by the awkwardness and Gabe's brutal honesty.

"I'm happy you get so much joy from my misery," he teased. "But it's true. I'm fucking miserable."

"Oh," I said, voice shaky. "I see." *Same here*, I wanted to declare but wasn't entirely sure what was happening.

*Was this real?*

Gabe cleared his throat, and I tried to picture where he was. Maybe in The Bar. Maybe in bed. Rubbing his thick fingers through his beard, plaid shirt straining at the buttons across his chest.

"Josie," he started, "I want to apologize to you. For what I said. For that last night you were here."

"Apologize?" I parroted.

"Yes," he said grimly. "I'm not calling to beg for you back or anything. I know... I *understand* where you're coming from. But I do need to apologize for what I said the night that you left. For what I asked you to do. Sacrifice your life for a guy you barely know no matter how strong our connection."

"You were swept up in the moment," I said, feet trying to get purchase on what felt like quicksand.

"I'm not making excuses. I'm calling to say *I'm sorry*. For putting you in that position and making demands of you. Like Clarke."

I looked toward the smoggy L.A. sky, eyes filling with tears.

I blinked them away rapidly.

"You're nothing like him, Gabe. And I'm sorry I said that that night. That wasn't fair. To equate the two of you. You're like... night and day. And I mean that," I said.

"But I'm still sorry," he pressed on. "I might not be like Clarke, but... I behaved like a hypocrite. And a little bit intensely. I just..." he trailed off for a second. "I've spent my whole life idolizing love and the relationships I was raised around. Idolized love but never seemed to find it. Because I didn't really know it or understand it. I'm learning that now... and I'm not perfect. Part of me wanted to drive down to you today with a marching band and a flock of fucking doves."

I laughed, and he did too. "I would have hated that."

"I know, Josie. And not long ago, I might have known that and done it anyway."

"In love with the idea of love," I said. "That's you, Gabe."

"Yes. And I'm not telling you that to make excuses. I wanted you to know that's what I thought *you* needed. Even though you'd been telling me what you needed since the moment we met. And I didn't listen. And for that I'm truly sorry."

The heart was a mysterious organ. But so was the brain. Because, for the briefest of moments, I remembered after the wedding—how much time I'd wasted fantasizing about receiving a call like this from Clarke. An apology. Or an explanation. As *if* that could have undone the catastrophic damage of that day.

And then I realized: that was the first time I'd thought about Clarke in four weeks. No memories. No flashbacks. *Definitely* not his voice, whispering from the shadows. I'd been so consumed with trying to unravel the complicated knot that was *Gabe*, it was like my subconscious had no room left for abusive ex-boyfriends.

I pressed my palm over my heart. "I forgive you," I said, and I could picture Gabe smiling into the phone. "And thank you."

"I'm just happy I could hear your voice, Josie," he said softly.

The end of this call was dangerously in sight—and I was suddenly desperate to keep him on the line. I closed my eyes and located the source of reckless exhilaration, pulsing beneath my skin. There was no fear, only a bright light of hope.

"Me too," I agreed, laughing a little. "And I promise I haven't been lying around L.A. being angry with you. Not at all. That time with you in Big Sur was... really life-changing. It's still affecting me, even though it's been a month. I can't stop... thinking about it."

Gabe cleared his throat roughly. "This has easily been the worst month of my life. I've just been lying on the floor, groaning. The Big Sur Channel is convinced you cast some kind of witchy spell on me."

"Well, I *am* a purple-haired Satanist," I replied. "I'll lift the spell soon. I promise."

"Please do because I can't go on like this," he said, and it was hard to ignore the serious undertones in his voice. "Gladys and Gloria have been bringing me what they call 'Heartbreak Gifts.'"

"And what are those?"

"Bottles of Hennessy, their liquor of choice, hidden all over The Bar. I found one the other day in my bathroom cabinet. With a little note that said, 'Chin up, loser.'"

I laughed so hard I sprayed tea out of my mouth. "Stop. You're *joking*."

"Serious as a heart attack, gorgeous," he said, the endearment sending an illicit thrill up my spine.

"Since we're sharing heartbreak stories, you should know I haven't even been able to go dancing," I said, and Gabe gave a shocked gasp. "I've also been going to bed at a reasonable hour. *And* I contemplated going for a hike the other day. I mean, a hike through downtown L.A., but still."

"Are you *unwell*?"

More laughter, contagious now. "Maybe *you* cast some kind of spell on me?"

"I put a potion in the coffee," he said calmly. "It was in the cream and sugar."

"Shut up," I teased, and I heard a settling sound, like he was sinking into a chair. I kicked my legs up onto the banister of my porch, leaned my head back. A few stars twinkled, so different from the brilliant Milky Way of a Big Sur sky. "So... tell me what's been happening on The Channel since I've been gone."

"How many hours do you have?" he laughed, and I bit my lip as my cheeks flushed.

"As long as you want, Gabriel," I said softly.

---

THREE HOURS LATER, and I was curled up under the covers, head on the pillow and phone still pressed to my ear.

"Okay, but I *really* have to go to bed now."

"Me too," he laughed. "But we've been saying that for the past hour." He yawned loudly, which set off a chain reaction of yawns between the two of us. "You should go to sleep, Josefine."

"Don't tell me what to do," I smiled, loving the sound of his amusement. "But I do have to be awake in... *fuck*, four hours for a twelve-hour photo shoot, so..."

There was a long, tempting pause, and then Gabe said, "Maybe I could... call you again sometime?"

"Please," I said, before he'd even finished talking. "How about tomorrow night? Which is technically tonight?"

"I'd like that," he said.

And I would have given away my worldly possessions for my sweet Viking to be tucked into this bed with me.

"Good. I'll talk to you in, like, fifteen hours," I promised, knowing that I wasn't going to sleep now, too keyed up and happy.

"Sweet dreams, gorgeous," he murmured and finally hung up.

---

THAT NIGHT LUCIA and I called Best Night Ever, when we'd stumbled into that street fair after tacos and blues and whisky, I'd enthusiastically volunteered us to let those fire-dancers toss molten-hot rods of flames around our heads. She hadn't really wanted to do it, but I'd been fearless back then. Welcomed the delicious flare of heat, the slight threat, the heady adrenaline that made my heart race inside my chest. I hadn't been able to stop laughing, even as Lucia screamed in terror.

That night, deeply asleep with fingers curled around my phone, I dreamed of the fire-dancers. Felt powerfully *alive*. Euphoric even. Laughed in delight as the fire flew past me because somehow I just *knew* I couldn't be hurt. Felt wrapped in cozy safety even as my skin tingled with elation.

And in the morning, as I blinked through the hazy sunlight, I realized I hadn't been dreaming of the fire-dancers at all.

I'd been dreaming of Gabe.

# 42

# GABE

*One month later*

Josie and I talked on the phone every single night for an entire month.

During the day, we texted constantly. She sent me silly selfies and pictures of her clients. Snapped photos of gauzy sunsets over the L.A. skyline and walls of vibrant graffiti near her house. A video of her nephews running through her backyard. The sprays of magenta jacaranda that grew around her banister.

Josie was bringing me into her world, bit by bit.

I didn't have a fucking plan. Our future was shrouded in mystery. And yet I woke up each morning grinning and spent my days enchanted with our conversations. Yearning for the next one.

I was okay with that. More than okay—I'd never been more blissfully happy.

Josie had had a shit day at work—a busy photo shoot with an asshole creative director and two entitled, whiny clients. I'd made her laugh with stories from The Bar, but there'd been a ragged edge to her voice. So before our call, I hiked out to the overlook at Pfeiffer Beach, sneaking under the guardrail (a skill of every Big Sur native) and filmed a short video of the waves beneath the moonlight.

Pfeiffer Beach was my favorite place in Big Sur, and I regretted never taking Josie here. A cove of rocks surrounded a small beach, and a tiny waterfall endlessly splashed against the sand, digging a hole that had been reformed and reshaped for a millennium. Gently carved by water. Beyond it lay the rugged coast of California, and on clear days, you could often see whales in the distance.

Tonight I was filming the silvery reflection of the moonlight and the endless rock of the waves, thinking the sound of it might help her sleep. Or that seeing her phone's tiny screen bursting with nature might bring her some serenity. I'd gone hiking every single day that we'd spoken, even if I could only find a free fifteen minutes, even if it was pouring rain, and the Ventana Wilderness seemed to breathe and expand into my lungs as I strode beneath the canopy.

In the silence of the forest, Josie remained the center. No regret, no sadness, merely an acceptance of this time that we had. The *present* in all of its simple beauty.

When I got home, I sent her the video, praying the myriad of technological upgrades I'd had Calvin input for me would get it to her. He'd set up a signal booster and a Wi-Fi hot-spot, and he'd found me a cell phone that hadn't been designed in 1998.

The Bar was slowly entering the twenty-first century.

And I was okay with that too.

My phone *pinged,* and when I swiped my thumb across the screen, I expected to hear Josie's voice. But there, in miniature, was her image instead.

"Is it okay if we video chat tonight?" she asked, and the

force of *seeing her* for the first time in eight weeks slammed through my chest.

I also had no idea what I was wearing or what I looked like. "Of course," I said, trying to covertly glance into the mirror over the bar. *Was there food in my teeth? Had I even showered today?* "Although, to be honest, now I'm a little nervous."

"Why?" she asked, smiling prettily. Josie was in yoga pants and a giant shirt that had Boyz II Men on it. Hair in a braid. No makeup. Curled up in blankets on her bed.

"Because you look absolutely beautiful," I said.

She bit her lip. *I* wanted to bite that lip.

I wanted her to bite *me.*

"And I have no idea what I'm even wearing right now," I laughed, looking down at my appearance. "Do I look normal?"

"You look like a real-life version of the Brawny lumberjack," she said dryly.

I laughed, loving the way her smile flashed in return. "Is that a compliment?"

"*Si*," she promised. "And I guess... talking on the phone has been amazing, but I... I miss your face." Her finger reached out, stroking the screen. I couldn't believe this was happening, and my heart raced at the thought of what this meant.

*Maybe she'd be... maybe soon.*

"Seeing you is... I mean," I stopped, struggling to find the right words. "Seeing you is really powerful, Josie."

She nodded, clutching the blanket around her shoulders. "I keep thinking I see you in L.A. The bearded man-bun thing is kind of hot right now, and there's like a million copies of you walking around the streets."

I scoffed. "I've had long hair since I was sixteen. How can it be *really hot right now*?"

"Just a trend," she grinned. "Although, as the Original, it clearly looks the best on you." She winked.

My heart fluttered like a teenager's, flirting with a crush.

"About once a day I think I *see* you. And it's like..." she cleared her throat, shifting on the bed. "Well, I really wish you were here right now." Those dark eyes captivated me. "And I loved your video. It's why I wanted to call you. That was really thoughtful, Gabe."

I shrugged. "I thought maybe you could listen to it tonight, and it might help you sleep a little."

We stared at each other for half a minute, moon-eyed and goofy. "Hey, can you show me your house?" I finally asked before I did something stupid like declare my undying love.

"*Yes*," she squealed, climbing off the bed. "I forgot you haven't seen it."

"Nope," I said. "Not at all."

"I bought it more than a year ago. I'm really proud of it," she smiled. "But I'm not going to show you my bedroom because it's a wreck."

There was a husky tinge to her voice. I wanted to ask her if she touched herself in that bed. Touched herself and thought of me.

She slowly panned the camera around her kitchen, which was the most Josie-looking room I'd ever seen. Her appliances were old and pastel-colored; the floor was black and white tile. The windows were wide open, and every single available space was covered in either art or photographs. I spotted a Polaroid of Josie and Lucia, looking years younger, hugging each other and laughing in front of the Hollywood sign. Black-and-white photos of family members; funky art in a rainbow of colors.

"Tell me what you do here," I said, and she turned the

camera back around, scrunched up her face, tapped her finger against her lip.

"Drink endless cups of coffee with my mom. Or Lucia, usually after a night where we haven't slept," she said, laughing. "I cook for my brothers a couple times a month, and all of us squeeze in here, wives and kids and all."

"Do they ever cook for you?" I asked.

"*Fuck* yes," she said. "Actually, they're better cooks than me."

I laughed as she showed me her tiny backyard, lit with string lights and filled with mismatched furniture. I could picture her there on summer nights, surrounded by those she loved. Her community. I felt a twisted pang when I thought about how swiftly I'd dismissed *this.* The life she led before Big Sur.

"This is my living room," she said, passing a room that was just as cozy and colorful as her kitchen. Framed photos hung on her wall, magazine covers of her clients, an interview she'd done for *Style Magazine* with Lucia. In the two years since the wedding, Josie seemed to fill this house with every ounce of her personality, and it only made me fall for her more. Could picture us entwined on that very couch, every inch of our bodies pressed together.

"And this is my favorite place," she said, opening the front door to her porch. There was a swing and more chairs, and she'd hung miniature, glowing globes from the ceiling that cast everything in a soft glow.

"I sit out here all the time. Watch my neighbors. See what's going on. Actually, I'll probably get a call from my parents any minute now."

"Why?" She'd flipped the phone back toward her face, and I desperately wanted to cup her cheek.

"Because I'm outside, in my *pajamas*, talking into my

phone," she teased. "This neighborhood is *filled* with busybodies, Gabriel. I'll have to answer to them eventually."

"Ah," I said, stroking my beard, "The Big Sur Channel is alive and well even in East L.A."

"*Especially* in East L.A.," she laughed. "There's a Gloria and a Gladys in every town. Even big cities."

"You know I'm not even sure the sisters know video chatting is possible. Really takes their perversion to a whole new level."

Josie arched an eyebrow. "In their house, I bet there's a grainy, out-of-focus video of the Hollywood People that they watch on loop."

"Oh, *definitely*. Also, they came by yesterday to swap out the penis paintings."

"No," she said with mock horror.

"Yes," I replied. "And replaced them with another slew of paintings *also* of penises."

"Let me guess. They're all doing things."

I laughed, walking across The Bar to show her on the video. "This one's wearing a bow tie and a top hat. Who knows why. *This* one I think is like... a financier? Maybe a banker?"

Josie frowned. "That one doesn't look very happy."

I leaned in closer. "You're right. Fucking miserable."

"What else happened today?" she asked, wrapping an arm around her legs and laying her cheek against her knee. Josie gave me a toothy, sweet grin. I was falling hard for both sides of this girl. The fierce bad-ass who'd strapped me to a bed. And this softer, gentler woman who was just starting to reveal herself to me.

I didn't know what this meant. Any of it. Except if felt like fucking *progress*.

"Settle in, gorgeous," I said. "Because tonight I had to moderate a semi-drunk argument between Ruth and Kevin about the separation of church and state. As related to pornography. Per the request of Gladys and Gloria."

Another smile. Another laugh.

Big Sur and L.A. were feeling closer and closer.

---

Two weeks later, I carried a six-pack over to my parents' house for family dinner. Kissed Lola. Hugged Maya, Isabelle, and Paige. Punched Austin. Let my parents hug me and check me over for signs of injury.

"I'm really okay," I laughed, sprawling in one of the dining room chairs. "It was an *emotional* pain I was dealing with that first month. You remember, Dad. When Mom was going to the prom with that other guy, and you thought you'd lost her. It was that same, gut-wrenching agony of unrequited..." I coughed, tripping over the words. *Lust, like, love*. Because now, after I was done closing down The Bar, Josie and I video-chatted every night, and the intimacy of *seeing* each other, of exposing the other person to the moments of humor, frustration, wonder, that make up your day... my feelings for Josie were spiraling beyond intense captivation and powerful lust.

That gut instinct I'd had, that Josie and I were going to *be* something to each other, was turning out to be right.

At least, I hoped so.

My parents shared a look that spoke volumes. "You couldn't pay me to go back to that time," he said, squeezing my mom's hand. "Meanwhile, your mom was going through something similar, and I had no idea. Our houses were one-hundred yards apart, and both of us were lying on the floor, wallowing."

"Hey, that's how I found Gabe that one day," Isabelle pointed out, tossing me a wink.

Maya leaned her head against Isabelle's shoulder. I arched an eyebrow Isabelle's way. I hadn't seen Iz in a month, but the last time we'd talked, she had mentioned that she and Maya were starting to regain their balance. Find some peace with motherhood.

"I'm a great wallower," I shrugged. "What can I say?"

"I saw you at the farmer's market, talking into the phone as you walked around," Austin said. "Was that Josie? Were you like... showing her the fruits and vegetables?"

Every woman at the table pinned me with a wide-eyed gaze.

"It was a Saturday. We were... showing each other around our respective hometowns. You know. East L.A. has a bustling farmer's market as well, and I wanted to see it. Had to return the favor."

*You're a fucking goner*, Isabelle mouthed at me. I grinned.

*I fucking know*, I mouthed back.

"So you're video-chatting now?" My mom asked, opening up another bottle of wine and giving us all another generous pour. All the doors and windows in the house were open, and the rich green of the forest pressed inside. "That's a good sign."

Lola reached for me and I leaned over, scooping her up from Maya's arms. She was eight months old now and getting bigger every day. "I think so."

"You're listening," Isabelle said, and Maya gave me a knowing smile.

"I'm trying," I said as Lola giggled against my chest. "I'm really trying."

# 43

# JOSIE

*Two weeks later*

Last night, I'd had another dream about Gabe.

A *sex* dream.

We'd been video-chatting and texting and talking on the phone for more than two months now, and although we sometimes *gently* flirted, our conversations stayed sex-free.

Probably because I could feel Gabe *yielding* to me, waiting for me to call the next step.

Which was beautiful and kind and sensitive, and *God help me*, it only made me want to fuck him more. My intense attraction to him hadn't waned a bit—only increased—but I think we both knew that sex, even video sex, would push us towards the next ultimate step.

Figuring Things Out.

And this morning, I woke up feeling turned on and wanton. Confident. I felt like the Josie I'd been *before* meeting Clarke and the Josie I was now had finally met. Converged into a woman I could feel proud to be. Strong but vulnerable. Trusting and kind to myself.

Unashamed of my scars.

Clarke hadn't interrupted my thoughts for three months. My client list had exploded. L.A. had never been more beautiful to me.

*And* a bearded Viking was willing to be in a relationship with me set to my terms.

He'd compromised and listened and bent to my desires. But I knew what Gabe wanted.

Me. All of me.

And I wanted to show him that I was listening too.

I rolled over in bed and sent him a text.

*Tonight, when we see each other, what if we did something different?*

Gabe responded almost immediately.

*What do you have in mind, gorgeous?*

My heart raced, arousal pulsing beneath my skin.

*I want to watch you take off all of your fucking clothes*, I sent. *Then I want you to take that thick cock of yours in your hand.*

I waited twenty seconds. Then: *And I want to watch you stroke it.*

A full, tortuous minute went by, where I frantically tried to convince myself I hadn't pushed the envelope. Rushed us. Maybe I could tell him I'd taken an Ambien and was sleep-texting. Or that Lucia had hacked into my phone and was sending joke texts to all of my contacts. The three little dots appeared and disappeared in an agonizing dance of despair.

And then, finally: *So sorry. I literally fell out of my bed, face first, when I read these messages. Took me a second to float back down to Earth. And I might have broken all of my bones.*

I'd never experienced the exhilaration of sky-diving before, but suddenly felt like I *might* know what that joyous, weightless feeling might be like.

*Poor baby,* I wrote, grinning like a loon.

*Not poor anything*, he responded. *Ready, Josie. So ready.*

*For what?* I sent, toes curling in anticipation.

*To beg for it*, he said.

I fell back onto the bed, sighing with happiness, heart singing.

And so turned on I couldn't see straight. Lazily, I let my fingers trail down my belly, pressing between my legs. Pretending it was Gabe.

*Good*, I finally said. *When I call you tonight, you better be naked and on your knees.*

*Fuck. Yes.* He responded.

---

IT WAS the longest work day of my entire life, only made brighter by the continual text exchange between Gabe and me. Which was no longer unusual—we talked constantly now—but this one had the added benefit of being flirty and sexy. I smiled so much my cheeks hurt. Updated Lucia every few hours—she couldn't stop sending the heart-eyes emoji to me and just "!!!!!!!!!!!!!!" over and over.

When I got home, I pulled on a sexy black nightie. Dark lipstick. Curled my hair and poured myself a big glass of red wine. Slipped on a pair of stilettos with a deadly looking heel.

And then I called Gabe.

It was like the day Gabe sent the bouquets all over again—that delicious anticipation of seeing the other person. Your thoughts crowded with desire and yearning. Butterflies shimmered in my stomach, and my heart was a wild, untamed thing.

And then the video screen clicked on, and I saw him.

Arousal slammed through me like a gale-force wind. My Viking, every single one of his brawny muscles on display. He was on his knees with his hands behind his back, stretching his chest. The muscles of his arms and shoulders rippled with strength.

And his heavy cock, standing straight out from his body.

Suddenly, I knew where this night would lead.

"Gabriel," I purred. He lifted his head and gave me a filthy, entirely *un*-submissive grin.

"Josefine." We stared at each other for a full minute, and even through the screen, even a hundred miles away, I could feel his hot, caressing gaze on every single inch of my skin.

"You followed my instructions," I said, taking a sip of wine and spreading my legs for the camera.

His throat worked, stomach muscles flexing. "Yes, ma'am," he rasped.

"Good," I said, approving. "Now, take your cock in your hand."

He did, slowly wrapping his fingers around the base. I nodded and he gave it a slow, leisurely tug. Gabe groaned, low and intense, and if I was ever going to orgasm just from a sound, *that* sound would be it.

"It's been a long time since we've seen each other," I said, letting the straps of my lingerie slip down my shoulder. "Why don't you tell me every single dirty fantasy you've had these past months."

"Who said I had dirty fantasies?" he growled, fingers working.

"Stop," I said shortly, and he did. Flashed me a rueful smile.

"Smart mouth," I teased, fully exposing my breasts. His fingers twitched but didn't move. I cupped my breasts in my hand, smoothing my thumb over my nipple piercings, and there was that sound again. It was so *hungry*.

"Now you can keep going," I said, and his fingers flew. "And tell me, Gabe."

"I thought about... you on your knees."

I spread my legs wider. "Keep going."

"You... on your knees. Sucking me off behind the bar while I served customers. But you don't... you don't let me come. For hours."

I bit my lip, loving that my Viking loved being denied as much as I loved denying him.

"Interesting. What else?" I demanded.

"I thought about taking your ass," he finally groaned.

I swallowed a moan. Because of *course* he did.

"That's not very nice," I chided.

"I'd make it nice," he panted. "So nice for you. Use my tongue and my fingers until you beg for it."

I squirmed on my bed. "What else? And don't you dare stop."

His movements were becoming frantic, and every pulse of his fingers I *felt*. He was racing toward release, and so was I—even though I wasn't even touching myself.

"Christ, Josie, I thought about so much. So fucking *much*. I thought about how your pussy tasted. Thought about that sweet clit and the way you screamed when I tongued you. I thought about being tied up for you. Strapped to the fucking bed. I thought about... fuck, I even thought about fucking you with another fucking man. Giving you that fantasy you've always wanted."

Tilting my head, I spread my legs as wide as they could go, completely exposing myself to Gabe's starved gaze. Another groan and a husky curse.

"Gabe," I prompted.

"We'd do it... we'd do it however you wanted it. However you'd *make* us do it. Eat that sweet pussy while he eats your ass. Suck my cock while he takes you from behind. Knowing you, you'd make me watch while he fucked you, while he worked over that gorgeous cunt of yours."

"That's absolutely goddamn right," I said, so fucking turned on by this fantasy. "And you wouldn't get to come."

He shook his head with a small smile. "No, Josie. You'd torture me all night long, gorgeous."

"I like that idea," I said softly, sensing he was close.

Torn between denying him more—or taking the leap.

"Josie, fuck, I'm going to come." His voice was strangled with need.

"And?" I taunted.

"I don't... can I? Please?"

My Viking, on his knees and begging for it, just like he promised. And in the midst of this erotically charged moment, the complete and total trust this man had in me flared in my chest like a match being struck.

"When, Josie?" His head was back, throat exposed, arm muscles bunching with exertion.

I leaned in closer, wanting to make sure he heard me.

"I don't know, Gabriel. How soon can you get down here?"

## 44

## GABE

Speed limits became a malleable concept to me. Even though I'd never once broken the law. Never even gotten a parking ticket. But flying down the freeway, going God-knows-how-many miles per hour, I was okay with the fact that this might be the first night I ever get pulled over.

Because I was driving to Josie.

Six hours away. I'd thought about it a lot these past two months, remembering Isabelle's advice. That if we took it one day at a time, a solution to our long-distance problem would reveal itself.

It hadn't yet, and the six hours was part of the problem. That and the fact that we were both self-employed and never took a day off—certainly not for a twelve-hour round trip drive to see each other.

I'd left a frantic voicemail for my parents, asking if they wouldn't mind coming out of retirement for a couple days to watch The Bar for me. And even in the middle of the night, I received a joyous "YES" texted in response—which surprised me.

Except I also realized that in the past decade, I'd *never*

asked someone to fill in for me at The Bar. Suddenly, my life was starting to make room for Josie—to stretch and grow and find space.

And maybe, if I *listened* even more, we'd find a way. Because here I was, at four in the morning, racing to the tattooed vixen who had beckoned me.

There was no way I'd be able to give her up now.

Two hours and two coffees later, the sun rose behind me as I approached the famous Los Angeles skyline. It was a vibrant dawn, streaked with rosy pinks and plum purples, and all of it reflected off the glittering skyscrapers.

I gaped like a kid down long, palm-tree lined boulevards with buildings that raced toward the sky. There was a hum of *people* that Big Sur didn't have, and as I turned off down Highway 1, I coasted through Santa Monica and Venice Beach and saw surfers and body-builders and rollerbladers. The beaches weren't as dramatic here as they were in Big Sur—they were welcoming and soft. And as I drove east toward Josie, I was greeted with rolling hills and smoggy traffic and kids walking to school.

If someone could create a place that was Big Sur's exact opposite, Los Angeles would be it. I had expected to hate it the moment I'd arrived, but instead, I felt suffused with wonder and excitement. Because the truth was I almost *never* traveled. Never saw things that were new, even though I was surrounded by Big Sur's magnificent beauty every day.

But even that could stop feeling amazing if you weren't paying attention.

Even though I hadn't slept, I felt wild with reckless energy. I drove past a large sign that said 'Welcome to East Los Angeles.' I rolled down my windows, and a blend of Spanish and English sifted through as people walked to the bus and opened their storefronts. I passed huge murals: a brightly lit

Virgin of Guadalupe, Frida Kahlo, and the colors of the Mexican flag. Josie had told me how important this city was to her heritage, how her parents had sought a place in America after they left Mexico where they could rebuild their community.

I felt another stirring of discomfort that I'd so easily asked Josie to give up this place that reflected the prism of her Mexican-American heritage. That I'd demanded she move to Big Sur with its population of nine-hundred people.

I needed to make things different between us. Better.

And before I knew it, I was pulling in front of a light blue cottage, covered in magenta jacaranda, and Josie was sitting on her porch swing. Everything came roaring back: our separation; the long, sweet re-kindling; the aching erection I'd had for going on six hours now.

When I stepped out of my car, I had the strangest sensation that the path of my life was about to take a sharp left turn into something new and beautiful.

And as Josie raced barefoot across the wet grass and launched herself into my arms, the only feeling I felt was gratitude.

## 45

## JOSIE

I'd had a sexy plan that I'd concocted during the six hours it took Gabe to drive down from Big Sur. I was going to drag out the delicious torture, making him beg until he lost his voice. The fantasy had done the trick—distracting me (and arousing me) as I tossed and turned, unable to sleep.

But then he was suddenly standing there. In Los Angeles. In *my front yard*. With his kind smile and even kinder eyes. No longer a ferocious Viking sent from another world to seduce milk maidens before he charged into battle.

Just Gabe. Here to fight for *me*.

So instead I launched myself into his arms, squealing as he lifted me easily. I wrapped my arms around his big shoulders and kissed him for what felt like days. His hands tightened around me, one palm gliding up my back to tangle in my hair.

"I've seen a lot of things in my life, Josefine," Gabe said against my lips. "So many beautiful things, and, sweetheart, *nothing* is as beautiful as you are."

We were moving backward through space, up my front

steps. My front door was kicked open, then slammed shut, and then my back was shoved against the door with a solid *thud.*

"I need to know what you want," Gabe said as he kissed and licked along my neck just under my ear. I was already floating in some kind of pre-orgasmic bliss.

"Why?" I panted, loving that sex between us was always one long, delicious, filthy tease.

"Because if not, I'm going to take you against this goddamn wall."

I flashed him a wry smile, wrapping my fingers in his beard. Yanked, and he hissed.

"Then fucking *do it*," I commanded.

On a low growl, he dragged my panties aside, and Gabe plowed every thick inch of his cock inside of me.

"Holy *fuck*," we both swore, my arms reaching above my head as I took every hard thrust.

Even pushed to the edge, Gabe's long strokes brushed against every nerve ending inside of me perfectly. My hips bruised against the door as I chanted Gabe's name.

He turned, bumping us into the kitchen counter. Shoved pots and pans to the floor. He slapped his hand on the shelves, and I ripped his shirt open, dragging my fingernails through his chest.

"*Christ*, Josie," he groaned. "How do you do this to me every fucking time?"

"I don't know," I sighed, slapping him hard on the ass. "And fuck me faster."

Another slap, and the challenge in his eyes was like white-hot lightning.

Gabe turned again, laying me on my kitchen table, and there was the sound of glass breaking as cups knocked to the floor. The table hit the wall over and over. He propped my legs up on his shoulders and bent me the fuck in half.

"Your cunt feels so good, sweetheart," Gabe gasped, "I've missed this so much." His middle finger slid to my clit, circling roughly.

"You know what would feel even better?" I teased, dragging that finger lower until it met the tight muscle of my ass. "Isn't this what you fantasized about?" Gabe lowered his forehead to mine with a soft curse.

"Every fucking day," he whispered, finger pressing. He slid in to the first knuckle, and I screamed.

"Did I hurt you?" he asked, attempting to still his movements, but I could only kiss him breathlessly.

"No never," I promised. "And please don't stop."

Gabe groaned against my lips, kissing me hungrily, gliding the rest of his finger completely inside my ass and thrusting his cock slowly. I gave him two sharp spanks, and he growled, speeding up. Bent me an inch farther, and I swore I felt him in my throat.

"God yes, *Gabe*," I moaned, so deliciously, deliriously, decadently full that tears sprang to my eyes. "This is everything; *you are everything*." I was panting and knocking utensils to the floor and clutching his face, and then the most intense orgasm of my life screamed through me.

"I need this," Gabe promised, the rhythm of his cock sparking my orgasm into a continual loop of pleasure. "I need this Josie. I need *you*." Another quick snap of his hips, and Gabe came with a roar.

I watched him in absolute awe, muscles straining and sweat on his broad chest.

And then he slowly slid out of me, flipped me onto my stomach, and licked my clit until my hips bucked against the table, another orgasm sliding through my bones like a river.

I was face-down on a plate, hands gripping a chair, legs shaking, and Gabe, sweet Gabe, was licking and kissing and massaging up my spine. Scooped me up and kissed me with such intensity tears spilled from my eyes.

"Don't leave," I begged. "Stay with me."

And he did just that.

## 46

## GABE

Josie's coffee pot hissed and hummed as I stood in her kitchen, bleary-eyed and slightly disoriented. Her kitchen was a wreck, and I was pretty sure we had wrecked it. I also hadn't slept *not* in my bed—and not outside of Big Sur—in a long time.

After our hot kitchen sex, Josie and I had fallen asleep in her giant, sunny bed, the two of us curled tightly around each other. And now all I knew was that it was sometime in the late afternoon. And I was In Los Angeles. In Josie's *home*.

I rubbed my hand down my beard, watching the coffee pot work. And set about cleaning Josie's kitchen.

I'd only ever seen it during our video chats, but up close it was even more spectacularly *Josie*. Pictures of her family members were framed and hung on the wall, shoved into the sides of cabinets and taped to appliances. The refrigerator was a mural of her and Lucia with other friends I didn't recognize; old concert posters and movie tickets and tiny paintings and photos of her clients—a collage of her love and the vibrancy of her life.

I straightened her table and found utensils that we'd flung

across the room. Swept up the pieces of glass and grinned at photos of Josie when she was a teenager: sullen and punky with red streaks in her hair.

Eventually, I grabbed a mug, filled it to the brim, and stepped outside onto Josie's tiny porch. It was already a warm L.A. afternoon, and her streets were filled with people. I perched on one of the chairs and watched as families streamed out of the open doors of the church a block away, bells pealing. Little kids on bikes drove by, speaking Spanish and squealing with delight. Cars blared an endless mash of hip-hop and soul and mariachi music. Across the way, towards Whittier, older women were setting up tamale stands and a small collection of fruit stands.

"*Buenos dias*," Josie said, and I turned to see her leaning against her front door looking sleepy and beautiful, black-and-lavender hair tangled around her face.

"Good morning," I said back. "Or actually, good *afternoon.* I made coffee and cleaned your kitchen."

"I saw that," she said with a smile. "I've also already gotten calls from my neighbors, my brother, *and* my parents. Wondering who the bearded hunk on my porch is."

I laughed. "I'm part of the East L.A. Channel now, huh?"

"Most definitely." She walked over and slid into my lap, hands landing on my beard. I wrapped my arms around her back and pulled her closer. Pressed a kiss to her warm lips. "My whole family... and, well, neighborhood... is intrigued by the hippie lumberjack I've been constantly on the phone with for two months."

"Hippie lumberjack?" I laughed.

Josie kissed my cheek. "You know you've got a certain... *look*."

She reached forward, undid the tie in my hair, and ran her fingers through the length of it. I never, ever wanted this moment to end, but I could already feel the encroachment of our long distance. All around me, Josie's community was enjoying a leisurely Sunday afternoon. The noise, the people, the blend of cultures and languages.

I thought about love and sacrifice. My parents and Isabelle and Maya. About listening because my heart had recognized something in Josie the very first moment we'd met. And I trusted it to know. Like my sister had said, maybe Josie and I were going about this the wrong way.

"If they see us together today, will people talk?"

"That's a fucking sure thing if I ever heard it," she laughed again. "They'll definitely talk. Because it means you're *real.* And this whole neighborhood has been waiting for me to..." she stopped for a second, clearing her throat. "Well, waiting for me to find some happiness."

I brushed her hair off her shoulder. "Can I be that happiness, Josefine?"

"You are," she promised softly. "And wait... you're staying today? I thought you'd have to open The Bar in—" she glanced at her phone, "—right about now."

I chuckled against her collarbone. "My parents are taking over for a few days. I'm all yours, if you'll have me." The mood was light, but the look we exchanged was heavy with meaning. "Why don't you show me your community?"

"An L.A day?" Josie said, clapping her hands together.

"Show me what you love," I said. "Show me everything."

---

I EXPECTED to hate Los Angeles, to be constantly comparing it to Big Sur's magnificence, but with Josie at my side, I felt suffused with wonder and excitement. Especially with Josie at my side, who looked too trendy to be with me. As usual, she was all boots and leather and colorful ink peeking out from the sleeves of her jacket. And she was slightly different here—more confident, more at ease. Lit up with the pride that comes with showing off the place that you love.

We drove down East L.A.'s famous Whittier Boulevard with the windows down and the radio turned up. Low-riders and vintage cars lined the streets. Groups of people were already out, drinking, laughing. Unlike Big Sur, we didn't cruise under a canopy of redwoods but rather old telephone poles and ancient palm trees, strung with twinkle lights. Jacaranda and orange poppies sprung up through cracks in the sidewalk next to massive murals.

We strolled through Mariachi Plaza and watched dancers and artists. Sampled food from Guatemala and El Salvador. Josie bought art at vendors and chatted in Spanish with the older Mexican women selling *aqua fresca*. The sky darkened with stars as we drove towards downtown, which felt alive with lights and sounds. The Hollywood Sign winking in the distance and men and women dressed to the *nines* strolling down the street. The flash of light bulbs when famous people appeared and this almost tangible hum of energy. Like standing on the beach in Big Sur right before a thunderstorm.

On Sunset Boulevard, we sat on bar stools, pressed skin to skin, and drank Old Fashioneds as a Billie Holiday-impersonator crooned into a microphone. Snuck in a late-night Open Mic event and watched burlesque dancers and singer-songwriters grace the stage. Outside, the street had been turned into a makeshift block party with a live brass band, and Josie and I danced for what felt like hours. Breathless with laughter, Josie dragged me to her favorite food truck, and we ate carnitas as grease dripped down our hands, toasting each other with cheap beer and limes.

"How's your taco?" Josie asked, head tilted and eyes bright with amusement.

"Incredible," I groaned happily. "This whole *night* is incredible. And the block party and the music and the dancing and all the *people*. I don't even know what time it is."

"1:30 in the morning," she said, eyebrow arched. "See? You're not that much of an old person."

I laughed, feeling exhilarated, and pulled Josie in for a long, slightly inappropriate kiss as people wolf-whistled behind us.

"What's next?" I said when I finally let her come up for air.

"One more place," she panted, tugging on my beard. "It's my favorite."

## 47

## GABE

We coasted up Mulholland Drive, Etta James on the radio and windows down to let the night sounds in. We passed old Hollywood mansions and rows of palm trees. Climbed up the canyon until we reached a startlingly beautiful viewpoint. All of Los Angeles sprawled naked and glimmering in front of us, still radiating energy even though it was past two in the morning.

Josie parked but left the music on, then slid out and onto the hood of the car. I joined her, pressing my head against hers.

"Something else, huh?" Josie asked, and there was a nervous edge to her voice.

"It's gorgeous," I replied. "I've never seen anything like it."

"It's not Big Sur."

"That's okay," I said, turning to capture her gaze. "It has its own beauty. Thank you for taking me here. For this whole day."

Josie smiled, but there were tears in her eyes.

"I came here the night before my wedding. With Lucia," Josie said. "It was my bachelorette party."

Gabe turned his head towards me. "That's interesting. I would have thought *you* would want something a little wilder than this."

Josie grimaced, shrugging her shoulders.

"Did you suspect something was off that night?" I asked softly.

She shook her head. "I didn't have a clue. We were spending the night apart anyway, so at that point, I hadn't spoken to him since that morning. I thought everything was perfect. But—" she hesitated, biting her lip. "Lucia said something. Told me that if I didn't want to go through with the wedding, she and I could run away. No questions, no judgment. Just get in the car and drive. And briefly… *so* briefly, I considered it."

"Do you wish you had done it?"

"I don't know," she said on a long exhale. "But I'll never doubt my instincts again. They'd been so quiet the entire time I'd known Clarke. Even with the dozens of red flags that would pop up, sometimes *daily*, any hesitancy I felt I squashed. Immediately," I said. "But that night I was really unhappy. I had this surface-level happiness, and if you asked me, I would have told you I was so excited for my wedding. Couldn't wait to marry my soulmate. But that night… that night I was so fucking *anxious*. And nervous and freaked out, and in that moment, the thought of not marrying Clarke felt so right. The most right feeling I'd had in a long time. And I… ignored it. Just like that. Because when someone has spent months gaslighting you, the first thing they destroy is your inner compass."

I cupped her cheek, swiping my thumb along her skin. "I can't tell you how sorry I am. About what happened. What he did."

"It's all in the past now," Josie said. "Truly. He's not in my thoughts anymore."

"And his voice?" I asked.

She smiled. "Nothing. Nothing at all. I'm back in control. And I wanted to bring you here for a reason. To build new memories over the old ones. To... listen again. To my instincts."

"What are they saying, Josie?" I asked because this whole day had been one long moment of my heart screaming *she's the one.*

Josie looked over the view for a moment like she was gathering something. "I don't have a solution. Yet. To how we'd make a... a relationship work."

I swallowed roughly, heart slamming in my chest.

"But I know two things. I want to be in a relationship with you. A real one. And I don't want to do long distance. I want to be with you. Every day."

I pulled Josie in for the softest, sweetest kiss of my entire life, and when I pulled back, I caught a wayward tear sliding down her cheek.

"Actually, I know three things," she said, laughing into the L.A. sky. "The third is I'm so incredibly in love with you, it's ridiculous."

Time stilled in a way that was ancient and beautiful. Because I was filled with the *rightness* of this moment and the winding path we'd taken here. Our week of passion. Our miserable separation. The delicate and deliberate way we'd found ourselves sitting on the hood of a car on Mulholland Drive.

"Oh, Josie," I said, cupping her face in my hands. "Can you say that one more time?"

"I love you, you big sexy Viking," she said, biting her lip

and grinning. I placed her hand on my chest, right over my spinning heart.

"I love you. Probably since the moment you called me *hirsute*."

She laughed again, wrapping her body around mine. There was no tension in her body, only a loose lightness. I could feel what this moment meant to her, so different from two years ago. The way our lives were opening together, like a night-blooming flower.

"You know, my parents almost moved away from Big Sur, right after they graduated from college," I finally said, brushing her hair from her shoulders.

"The high school sweethearts?" she asked.

"The very same. The whole town was swept up in their relationship. But when they first got together, though, they were in love with this idea of moving to Argentina."

"*Argentina?* Why?" Josie's brow furrowed.

"I have no idea. You know, both sides of my family are local to Big Sur, stretching back at least five generations. My dad's family were homesteaders. You remember how The Bar used to be an old school, back in the day? My great-great-grandfather probably went to school there."

"There's a kind of poetry to working and living in the same room where your past relatives sat in small desks and learned," Josie said. "Now, people puke on the floor and sloppily make out with each other."

I laughed. "Smart-ass. The Bar is a beautiful, classy place, and the patrons *never* drink themselves to excess."

"That's a bald-faced lie, and you know it."

I laughed into the stars, tugging on a strand of her hair.

"Also, maybe your parents just wanted to do something different," she said seriously.

"I think that's exactly it," I agreed. "Two newlyweds in love with each other and the world around them. Maybe feeling trapped and claustrophobic by all that small-town intensity. The Big Sur Channel. The gossip. The fact that there is absolutely nothing to do. The fact that *neither* of them had ever stepped foot out of California."

"Did they ever end up going?"

"No," I said. "But they did take a pretty epic road trip in their car all across the country. Slept in the backseat and saw almost every state. It was their honeymoon." I smiled at the memory, recalling the aged photos pinned haphazardly to the walls of my childhood home: my parents at the Grand Canyon and Glacier National Park and pointing at alligators in Florida.

"Then what happened?"

"They made a choice. Saw the entire country and loved it. But realized there was nothing like their home town. Nothing like Big Sur. And they made an *active* decision to move back and commit themselves to that community. Not just because it had always been done. Which, when I was younger, I didn't understand."

"And now?" Josie asked.

"I'm starting to understand more. This," I said, waving to the glittering skyline, "is like nothing I've ever done before. Nothing I've ever *seen* before. I understand their desire to take the entirety of the world in."

Josie's eyes were filled with honesty. "I felt the same way on that drive in Big Sur. The grandiosity of the landscape. Even the fear of the rockslide—it all *touched* something inside of me that L.A. doesn't. Or hasn't in a while. I thought the same thing: what else in this world haven't I seen?"

An idea was forming in my mind, something new and exciting and just the right amount of scary.

"Josie," I said. "What if we did something completely different?"

"Like what?" she laughed.

It was an irresponsible idea. Not even a little bit well thought out. Josie was probably going to toss me over this cliff, then drive away as fast as she could.

"How much vacation time do you have?"

She bit her lip. "I control my schedule. I mean, I'm booked straight through for the next month. I can always cancel, find a colleague to take my clients, but—"

"But what?"

"They won't be happy with me," she grinned. "Although there are much worse things."

I was nodding, mentally doing some calculations. "I think I can get Paige and Austin to run The Bar for a bit. And my parents, too."

Slowly, Josie's head tipped to the side. "What's on your mind, hirsute hunk?"

"Remember when we had an accidental coffee date at the Bakery in Big Sur? I told you I'd take you to my favorite waterfalls?"

"I do," she said. "And you never did. We didn't go to any private beaches either. And I had *plans* for that, if you know what I mean."

Her fingers danced up my thigh, and I kissed her right beneath her ear. She shivered.

"I know a waterfall. It's famous. In fact, it's one of the largest in the whole world." A deep breath, and I kept going. "Let me take you there."

"In Big Sur?" she asked, brow furrowed. "How did I not know this?"

I shook my head with a rumble of laughter. "Not Big Sur. In *Argentina*."

Josie watched me for a minute as recognition flashed across her features. Her eyes narrowed, and then the smile she gave me burned brighter than the city below. She took out her phone, fingers flying across the screen. A minute later she flipped it over, showing me plane tickets: two leaving from LAX to Buenos Aires. Placed her palm against my cheek.

"What else in this world haven't we seen, Gabriel?"

---

AND THAT WAS HOW, not three hours later, Josie and I ended up squeezed into seats on an airplane. Breathless. Exhilarated. Together.

# EPILOGUE

## JOSIE

*Eighteen months later*

Gabe was trying to get me drunk on our wedding night. Or, rather, wedding dawn. We were sitting on the hood of his car overlooking Julia Pfeifer Beach in Big Sur, still in our wedding wear. The ocean swirled and danced in the early light, and you could just hear the faintest bird song.

Behind us, the sun was slowly drifting past the horizon.

It was a new day.

"So," Gabe said, pouring a generous amount of champagne into my glass. "Let's discuss the highlights."

I swooned at the look of the gold band on his left hand. Gabriel Shaw was something to behold in a light gray suit.

"Calvin was the most adorable officiant known to man," I said, smiling into my glass.

He'd laughed and stammered and blushed his way

through our ceremony on the beach as Lucia (loudly) whispered encouragement from behind me. Lucia, and all four of my brothers, were in my wedding party. Gabe had Isabelle, Maya, Austin, and Paige.

Lola, in a hot-pink dress that matched mine, carried the rings.

"And Lucia gave the bawdiest maid-of-honor speech I'd ever heard," Gabe laughed.

"That's why she's the best," I agreed, letting the bubbles slide down my throat. "Also, she was only warming up the crowd for the inevitable perversion of Gloria and Gladys."

"What they gave was not a speech," Gabe said, shaking his head. "That was like... an erotic novella."

I spread my hands over my magenta dress, which Lucia and I had found at a thrift store one sunny Sunday morning in West Hollywood. It was the most *me* dress I'd ever seen, and it only made sense that I'd wear it on the day that I married my soulmate.

I breathed in the scent of the ocean, the stillness of this flawless morning. Remembered the first morning we'd woken up, in Puerta Pirámides, Argentina. Still half-asleep and disoriented, Gabe and I had walked out onto the beach halfway across the world.

And I saw a whale for the first time. Whales, actually, an entire migration.

It was one of the most perfectly beautiful moments of my entire life.

For a month, we hiked mountains in Patagonia. Took a boat from Tierra del Fuego to Antarctica. Drank wine in Bariloche and crossed the border to Chile.

And, just as Gabe promised, found Iguazu Falls, the largest waterfall in the world and watched as hundreds of brightly colored butterflies floated up and through the delicate spray.

It was hard. Harder than we'd thought it would be—to live, for a month, away from our families and our communities. Especially for two people that had never really traveled.

But once we'd pushed past the transition, Gabe and I fell in love with the idea of being nomads. And slowly, over four weeks, as Gabe and I laughed and hiked and fucked our way through Argentina, the solution to our living situation made itself clear.

When we got back, I moved in with Gabe for six months in Big Sur, taking clients in Monterey and Carmel and serving drinks with Gabe at The Bar at night. We hiked every inch of the forest, and I grew into the quiet peace of Big Sur. Started to crave the wilderness.

And then, at the end, Gabe ceded control of The Bar to a rotating blend of family members and friends, and he moved into my tiny house in East Los Angeles for six months. He escorted me to award ceremonies at night and diners at dawn and worked as a bartender at an assortment of trendy, L.A. spots, slowly growing into the frenetic energy of the city.

We weren't different in each location, but we were *expansive*. Allowing our lives to take on the shape of our surroundings.

We'd been back in Big Sur for six months now, culminating in our sweet, glorious wedding, and it was almost time to head back to the city. A bittersweet feeling we were both learning to adjust to. We didn't know how long we'd do the split, and maybe we'd even do it forever, but what we did know was that it worked for us.

And that was all that mattered.

But first: the honeymoon.

"Gorgeous," Gabe said, pulling me onto his lap. "You've been staring at that ocean and *not* celebrating with me for whole minutes now." He kissed up my neck and nuzzled under my ear. My hands tightened around his tie, tugging slightly. "What are you thinking about?"

I swung my legs around his lap, arching an eyebrow when it was obvious he was rock hard against his suit pants.

"I think the question is, dear husband, what have *you* been thinking about?"

With deft fingers, I freed his cock, sighing as I dragged my fingers up and down the length of him. Gabe groaned huskily, big palms cupping my breasts through the fabric of my wedding dress.

"Honeymoon sex," he whispered against my ear.

I shivered. We were due on a plane in just a few hours, heading to Montana. The plan was two weeks in Glacier National Park because Gabe wanted fresh mountain air and crystal lakes. Then, two weeks in Paris because I wanted late-night dinners and famous art in a cultural mecca.

Compromise. Gabe and I had turned it into a fucking art form.

"What did you have in mind?" I teased my bearded Viking, sliding my panties to the side and lowering myself onto his hard cock. We rocked together, kissing and laughing as the sun rose, bathing us in light.

"How much rope are you going to pack?" Gabe growled. He was dragging his thumbs over my nipples, and I was grinding my clit against him, and my orgasm was building just over the horizon.

"So much, Gabriel," I sighed, throwing my head back. His hands landed on my hips, and he lifted me, our rhythm blending together. "And don't worry. I'll have you on your knees and begging in no time."

"*God*, yes, Josie. Please," he said, pulling me down for a feverish kiss.

The kiss of two newlyweds, married for just eight hours. On the precipice of adventure—not a *new* life because we'd already created a beautiful one but a joyous continuation.

I wrapped my arms around my husband and fucked the two of us into spine-tingling orgasms. Gabe squeezed me tight as he shuddered against me, whispering my name over and over. I laid my head against his chest, directly over his heart, and memorized the sound.

"Just so you know, our newlywed sex is going to end up all *over* the Big Sur Channel."

I laughed softly. "They'll be talking about it for weeks."

"Maybe even years."

We were quiet for a moment, and I let all the memories of the wedding flood in.

"Tell me again what you said. During your speech," I said, looking up into his dark eyes.

He grinned, rubbing a hand down his jaw. "I never want to stop discovering new things with you. Never want to be content to do what's easy when we *could* be doing something that's *thrilling*. That I no longer view our life together as linear, a straight line down the same road. But rather a map of continents and stars, glorious and winding, ours to explore without limits. That you—" Gabe cleared his throat, and when his eyes filled with tears, I thought my heart was going to fly from my body. "You are my true soulmate, Josie. In all of this. Forever."

I kissed him for a long time after that.

When I finally pulled back I could only say, "*I love you*," over and over again.

Because Gabe had been right. Love *could* be reckless and passionate and intense and *good* all at the same time.

My inner compass hadn't been broken but merely searching for its true north.

Gabriel.
My Viking.
My home.

# AFTERWORD

## GABE

*Wedding Day*

"So just wait here," Cal said, straightening my tie for the fiftieth time, "and your beautiful bride will....uh, well, she'll surprise you."

"I think I can manage that," I laughed. "And you're sure you're going to make it?"

"Please," he said, with false bravado. "Standing in front of hundreds of people and officiating the marriage of my two best friends in the whole world is like...my *jam*."

I grabbed his shoulders. "Try not to pass out."

He looked serious for a moment, and then his eyes brightened at something he spotted behind me. "I will. And you try not to pass out when you see Josie."

Calvin slipped away, down the path to the beach where I was about to walk Josie down the aisle.

Where we were about to get *married*.

"Ah," I heard Josie say. "A hirsute hunk."

I turned toward her midnight voice, adjusting my cuff links.

And almost fucking passed out.

My soul mate, Josefine Torres, stood in front of me like a vision. Dark hair in a simple bun, high on her head. Just a hint of makeup. Gorgeous, colorful tattoos decorating her dark skin. And a silky, bright magenta dress that draped to her feet, flowing in a long train behind her.

She was bare foot in the sand, beaming up at me like I was her entire world.

"You make a handsome groom," she continued, eyebrow arched.

I had no words. All I could do was slide my arm around her waist, yank her toward me, and capture her lips in a greedy kiss. I gripped one side of her face, holding her in place, plundering her mouth with my tongue.

Josie sighed, sweetly, melting against my chest. And when I pulled back, her eyes were dark with desire.

"I think you're supposed to wait until we're declared husband and wife, Gabriel," she teased.

"Have I told you recently you're the most beautiful thing on this entire planet?" I asked, swiping her cheek with my thumb.

"Only twice today so far," she smiled.

"And have I thanked you for marrying me?"

She leaned up on her tip-toes, kissing my cheek. "I haven't married you yet. And we should probably, you know, get to it."

I chuckled, glancing down the path to where our family and friends were waiting. "I'm actually a little nervous."

Josie smoothed her hands down my chest. "Me too. But really, it's just you and me up there. No one else." All around us, I could hear the waves crashing. The murmur of our friends. Music, laughter. After this, our only plan was to invite people to a buffet on the beach, where Josie and I planned on dancing until dawn with our favorite people.

I let out a long exhale. "You're right. And after this, we can dance."

"And fuck," Josie said, letting her fingers trail up my leg.

"And fuck," I growled, pressing a kiss beneath her ear. "And then four weeks of honeymooning."

Josie sighed. "Sounds like a plan *Vikingo.*"

And with that, Josie tugged on my hand, and we walked together down the sandy path. My heart thudded in my chest, and I was struck by the hundreds of tiny details. The graceful tilt of Josie's head; her bare throat; the sound of Lola's laughter as she dropped flowers down the aisle ahead of us. Gritty sand between my toes. The look of complete love I caught between my parents, when they thought no one was looking.

"Gabe," Josie said, and I turned to look at her. We'd reached the aisle, and hundreds of white chairs stretched down the beach in front of us. Most of Big Sur was here; everyone from Josie's family had flown up from Mexico and Los Angeles. It was going to be a hilariously rowdy, Big-Sur-style party, and *all of it* was because we were loved.

"Hey you," I said, and she gave me a toothy grin. "You ready?"

She nodded, squeezing my hand, and then Josie and I walked each other down the aisle. Ahead of us, both sets of parents stood, holding hands, waiting to welcome us. All four of Josie's brothers, plus Isabelle, Maya, Austin, and Paige stood at the front, smiling.

In the middle, Calvin and Lucia beamed like rays of sunshine.

Lucia was Josie's maid of honor, but she was also Calvin's support to make sure he didn't faint from the pressure.

And I'd been fucking *fine* all day, but when my parents wrapped me in a giant bear hug, I felt my throat tighten and tears sting my eyes.

"I know you're crying right now and it's okay," my mom said, patting my back.

"I've never cried before and you know it," I joked, and she laughed. And then Josie's parents were exclaiming over me, and hugging my parents, and when I caught Josie's eyes, hers were shining. I knew what this second wedding day of her life meant to her—the ugly feelings it could have triggered. And I was prepared to help her through them, make sure she knew I would fucking *be there,* because marrying her was like all of my dreams coming true, all at once.

But surprisingly, all day she'd been calm and happy, and as she tossed me a sassy wink, I understood.

Josie trusted that I'd be here. Trusted *me*.

"Can everyone please take their seats?" Calvin said, voice cracking, and Lucia widened her eyes at me with a goofy smile.

People sat, slowly quieting, and I took in the beautiful scene: the ocean, the sun halfway setting, the feel of Josie's hands in mine.

"Thank you everyone for being here today, at this beautiful location, to celebrate this amazing couple," Calvin said, clearing his throat, and behind him, Lucia stage-whispered "Good job babe."

He laughed nervously, looked at her, then back down at his notes. "I uh...well, I'm sure everyone here knows that Gabe Shaw is my best friend in the entire world. At a time when I needed support, when I needed someone who believed I could do the impossible well...he was there."

My throat tightened again.

"And Josefine, well, we all know how Lucia feels about her," Calvin laughed.

"She's my ride-or-die bitch!" Lucia exclaimed. "And sorry for interrupting. Truly. I'm sorry. But I just wanted to make sure, you know, everyone knew. About me. And Josie. Ride or die, right?"

Josie was laughing, collapsed against my chest.

"You got it," she called out, and Lucia whooped. Behind me, Gladys and Gloria clinked flasks in approval. "Please, Calvin, continue."

Calvin was a shade of bright strawberry, whether from nerves or laughter I couldn't tell.

"So, yes, um.... yeah what I wanted to say was that, I think everyone in this audience feels something similar for Josie and Gabe. They are the kind of people that you hope fall in love. The kind of people you believe deserve that happily ever after – because they're just *good people*." Calvin smiled. "The best, really. Which is why this beach is filled with all of you, here celebrating their love story."

Cal softened his voice. "I know what it took for you two to get here today, and I want to honor your journey. The things you've done – the adventures, the travel. The scary, different things you've embarked on as a couple."

Silent tears streamed down Josie's cheeks.

*I love you*, I mouthed, and she mouthed it back.

"Before we exchange vows and rings, Gabe and Josie have something they'd like to say to each other." Calvin smiled at Josie as Lucia rushed up to give her a piece of paper and a kiss on the cheek.

Josie smiled at me nervously, taking a steadying breath. "When I met you, I told you I didn't believe in love for myself," she began. "I told you that I didn't think I had a soul mate.

Someone had stolen that concept from me, and it took a while for me to get it back." Another steadying breath. "And now, I can't imagine what my life would be like without your big, messy love. I'm pretty sure I fell in love with you the first night we met, Gabriel, and I want you to know that this marriage, this *commitment*, I take seriously. I know it's not always easy, and I know our life together will have challenges and hard times. But..." her voice broke. "You are the most incredible person I've ever met, and I am honored to be your partner in life. To be your love. And to love you for-fucking-ever." She laughed, and I pulled her in for another hug, hand stroking down her bare back. Lucia flashed me a thumbs up as Calvin fanned himself with the program.

"Was that okay?" Josie said against my suit. "Also sorry but I think I'm getting your nice suit all wet with my gross tears."

"That was just perfect," I promised, before sliding out my piece of paper. My fingers trembled more than I realized, and a wall of emotion rose up in my throat. Josie stayed close, wrapped around my body, head tilted up to meet my gaze.

"Thank you for choosing me," I began. "It is a privilege to love you every day, Josie. We've discovered so much together, and I never want to stop discovering things with you. Never want to be content to do what's easy when we *could* be doing something that's *thrilling*. I don't view our life together as linear, a straight line down the same road. But instead," I said, stroking her hair, "a map of continents and stars, glorious and winding, ours to explore without limits. *You* are my true soul mate. In all of this. Forever."

Josie didn't say anything, but she didn't have to, staring up at me with so much love and so much beauty it took my breath way. After that, Calvin said some more words, and we said our vows—enthusiastically—as we slipped rings on our fingers. It was a blur, but in a good way, because Josie captivated my every thought. And when Calvin declared us to be husband and wife, all I could do was kiss her with every ounce of passion that I had. There were wolf whistles, and laughter, and Lucia *definitely* made a sex joke. But when I pulled back, there was Josie, my wife, flushed and happy.

"We did it," she grinned. And then the dancing began.

## A NOTE FROM THE AUTHOR

I started writing LANDSLIDE in a tiny hotel in Ocean Shores, Washington, in August 2017. My husband and I were in the first month of a six-month road trip across the country, living in a van we'd named Van Morrison. We'd had sudden engine trouble in Olympic National Park, and a kind-hearted tow-truck driver had taken us to the only mechanic around for miles. I'd first introduced readers to Gabe and Josie in BOHEMIAN and wanted to write a sexy, insta-love novella for them that would come out in November.

But Gabe and Josie had other ideas. For a hundred different reasons that you're about to discover, neither insta-love, nor the hard limit of 40,000 words, was going to work. In draft after draft, I struggled to force Gabe and Josie into a plot that just didn't fit them. So I took to the woods, literally. My husband and I are big hikers, and during this road trip, we sometimes spent four or five days a week on some kind of dirt trail: lakes, mountains, streams, rivers, canyons and miles of verdant forest. In the quiet and the stillness of nature, Gabe and Josie revealed themselves over time: their motivations, their fears, their joys and sorrows. And five months after I first started their story in Ocean Shores, I was driving home after a lovely weekend with Lucy Score (#TacoTwin), and their perfect ending came to me in a blinding flash—so strongly I had to call my best friend and have her write it down over the phone so I wouldn't forget.

All of this is to say I've never had two characters make me work harder to tell their story truthfully. For lovers of BOHEMIAN, thank you for your patience. I hope I made you proud. And for new readers, enjoy your first trip to Big Sur!

# ACKNOWLEDGMENTS

Big Sur, California, is a very real place. And it will change you. The Big Sur Bakery (which makes a small cameo in this book) is where I began my first outline for BOHEMIAN. It's also where my husband and I came up with the idea to travel across the country in a van. If you're lucky enough to go, enjoy the gorgeous trails in the Ventana Wilderness of the Los Padres National Forest. Visit Nepenthe (the inspiration for Fenix) and the Henry Miller Library (the inspiration for The Mad Ones).

For my fearless beta readers, Faith, Jodi, and Julia: thank you for your perfect notes, support, and ideas. LANDSLIDE wouldn't be the book it is without your exquisite feedback.

Thank you so much to Maria Blalock for reading and offering feedback on Josie's Mexican-American heritage. And to Michelle Rodriguez for double-checking my Spanish. In both areas, any mistakes made in this book are my own.

For Joyce, Jodi, and Julia, my Wonder Women: you make this journey worth it. I literally cannot thank you enough for the thousands of amazing things you do for me each and every day. You have created a community of loving affirmation—and that comes from your big, beautiful hearts.

For the Hippie Chicks, the grooviest ladies around! Thank you for bringing such passion and bravery to our little group. Your endless support and cheerleading means more than I can say.

For Faith, my best friend and *my* favorite author: I can't wait until the world gets to read your words.

And always, always, always for Rob, who is not only the World's Best Husband but who very enthusiastically brainstormed LANDSLIDE with me on every hike. Let's never stop adventuring together.

## HANG OUT WITH KATHRYN!

Sign up for my newsletter and receive exclusive content, bonus scenes and more!

I've got a reader group on Facebook called **Kathryn Nolan's Hippie Chicks**. We're all about motivation, girl power, sexy short stories and empowerment! Come join us.

Let's be friends on
Website: authorkathrynnolan.com
Instagram at: kathrynnolanromance
Facebook at: KatNolanRomance
Follow me on BookBub
Follow me on Amazon

## ABOUT KATHRYN

I'm an adventurous hippie chick that loves to write steamy romance. My specialty is slow-burn sexual tension with plenty of witty dialogue and tons of heart.

I started my writing career in elementary school, writing about *Star Wars* and *Harry Potter* and inventing love stories in my journals. And I blame my obsession with slow-burn on my similar obsession for The *X-Files*.

I'm a born-and-raised Philly girl, but left for Northern California right after college, where I met my adorably-bearded husband. After living there for eight years, we decided to embark on an epic, six-month road trip, traveling across the country with our little van, Van Morrison. Eighteen states and 17,000 miles later, we're back in my hometown of Philadelphia for a bit... but I know the next adventure is just around the corner.

When I'm not spending the (early) mornings writing steamy love scenes with a strong cup of coffee, you can find me outdoors -- hiking, camping, traveling, yoga-ing.

## BOOKS BY KATHRYN

BOHEMIAN

LANDSLIDE

RIPTIDE

STRICTLY PROFESSIONAL

NOT THE MARRYING KIND

SEXY SHORTS

BEHIND THE VEIL

UNDER THE ROSE

IN THE CLEAR

WILD OPEN HEARTS

Made in United States
Orlando, FL
15 June 2022

18836844R00211